broken promises

THE SHATTERED HALO SERIES BOOK 3

PATRICE ASHLEY

Blood is thicker than water, but sometimes water is there when blood isn't. For everyone who created the family they weren't given, this is for you.

WILLA

7 YEARS AGO

I'M NOT AN OUTDOOR GIRL. I hate the leaves and mud sticking to my shoes. I don't enjoy the smell of the forest or whatever Belle is going on about. I'd much rather be reading a book or binge watching a period drama on Netflix.

"How long do we have to stay?" Kai asks. Our band just played in front of my high school graduating class and a few alumni. Shattered Halo is going to be big, according to Callahan. That man is a dreamer, though. Kai is more realistic and is as big of a fan of these parties in the woods as I am.

"I have no idea. I lost Cal immediately. You pissed Belle off, and she wandered away an hour ago, and I don't know where your reflection is."

Kai snorts. He and Ezra are identical twins, but they're easy to tell apart by how they wear their hair. Kai likes messy where Ezra prefers a close and neat cut. Their personalities are opposite too. "I'll go look for Ez, and we can give you a ride home. Cal knows he's responsible for his sister."

I shrug as he walks away, completely ignoring my comment about pissing Belle off earlier. I take out my phone to check the time and smile at the missed call. I hit the name to call them back immediately.

"Hey Princess. How did the show go?" Declan's soothing voice makes me smile even wider.

"It was great. Totally won over a bunch of slightly drunk high school kids."

Declan laughs, and I can picture the way his green eyes flash in amusement. "Don't undersell yourself. A female drummer is badass."

Declan and I have been friends since our parents picked spots next to each other at the campground when I was six and he was eight. We spent two weeks together every summer, and they're still my most cherished memories.

"Cal sang 'Fortunate Son'," I tell him.

"Was it better than the video you sent me last week?"

"I think it was worse," I admit, earning me another laugh. Cal is a great singer, but he keeps trying to put his own spin on that song and it just isn't working out for him. "How's being a big hockey star?" Declan signed with the San Diego Barracudas right out of high school. He's currently on the second line as the right wingman. Which means this is the second summer in a row I won't see him.

"I'll miss you, you know," he says, hearing the words I didn't want to speak. He's always been good at that.

"You'll be too busy with all your model girlfriends and insane parties," I say, deflecting so I don't have to deal with my feelings.

"I'm never too busy for you, Princess. I'll always take your call."

"I know," I say and sigh. "Everything is changing, and I still don't even know what I want to major in. How am I supposed to know what I want to do for the rest of forever?"

"Figure it out as you go. Whatever you choose to do, you're going to be amazing."

"Says the guy that's been a hockey golden boy since the moment he put skates on," I mutter, but Declan hears me and laughs.

"I fell a lot. I just got back up."

"You make it sound so easy."

"It is," he says. He pauses for a moment before speaking again. "So, what are you going to do?"

"Get back up."

"That's my girl." That comment has me smiling like an idiot, but I can't stop. No one believes in me like Declan does.

"Willa. I can't find Ezra," Kai says. I turn to him and frown. He looks worried.

"I have to go," I tell Declan.

"I'll call you soon, Princess." He hangs up and usually I would pout alone for a few minutes, but Kai grabs my hand and pulls me back to where most of the party is happening.

"I'm sure he's around, Kai," I say, searching the crowd. It's not easy considering I'm all of five foot two.

"No one has seen him in a while." His voice is starting to shake. Kai is hardly ever concerned about anything, so now I'm worried.

"Have you seen Belle? They're probably together."

Kai stiffens for a moment. "You're right. I'll find her. Can you keep looking?"

"Of course," I tell him.

It only takes a few minutes and a couple of questions to figure out that no one has seen Ezra since we finished our set. Kai found Belle and Cal, who were also no help. Now we're searching the woods and yelling Ezra's name.

We spend the entire night searching. The police eventually took over, but that didn't stop us. We looked under every log and behind every boulder. I'm pretty sure Kai was about to try to jump in the river at one point and look, but Cal stopped him.

He's gone. There isn't a single trace of him. No one saw him leave. One of my best friends just vanished into thin air.

If I didn't like the woods before, I fucking hate them now.

"For someone who just signed a major record deal, you don't seem excited."

"I am," I say, mustering up as much enthusiasm as I can. The loud sigh from the other end of the phone tells me Declan isn't buying it.

"When did we start lying to each other?"

"I'm not lying, Dec. I'm just confused." I throw myself dramatically onto my bed in my very purple bedroom. My mom decorated it when I was five, so it's covered in unicorns and rainbows. The walls are light purple with unicorns running on rainbows painted on them. The carpet is dark purple with polka dots that used to be white but are now more of a light gray. Even my comforter is purple. Not really my style, but I haven't been able to bring myself to change it since she died when I was eight.

"Alright. Let's talk it out. Pros and cons, Princess. You want me to start?" I smile despite myself. Declan is one of the least organized people I know, but he knows how much I love a good pros and cons list.

"Go for it, hockey boy."

"The pros are easy. Rich, famous, you get to travel like you always talked about. Men and women will want to be you and be with you." There's a pause that causes me to pinch my lips between my teeth to stop myself from laughing. "On second thought, that last one is on the con list."

I laugh this time, not bothering to smother it. "Are the rules different for me? I was going to follow yours. No kissing. Never sleep with the same person twice. Make sure they know what this is upfront so feelings aren't hurt. Always use a condom."

"I hate this conversation," Declan mumbles.

"I'm not a virgin, Dec."

"No one is good enough for you, Willa." I sigh at his words. Declan has always been overprotective, which is really a feat considering we lived six hours apart. And that was before he moved to the other side of the country.

"It doesn't matter if people don't like us."

"People are going to love you."

I bite my lip and stare at the ceiling, trying to figure out how to put my fears into words.

"Whatever it is, you know you can tell me," Declan says, his voice soft.

"Sometimes I feel like I make decisions too fast and one

of these days, it's going to catch up to me," I admit. "What if it's the worst thing I could do, and I won't know it for another twenty years?"

Declan chuckles. "Princess, what if it's the best? Even if it backfires, you'll still have a really cool experience."

I look at my purple walls and try to remember the face of the woman who painted them. I have so few memories of her, but I remember how much she loved to live in the moment. If it started to rain while we were outside, we would dance in it, our matching blonde manes plastered to our faces. If the store was out of oranges, it was a great time to try dragon fruit. When the radio died in her old beat-up station wagon, we would sing at the top of our lungs.

I'm on to my next adventure, my darling. I'll see you again when you join me and oh, what fun we'll have. Those were her last words to me, and I think I've been unconsciously living by them. I didn't realize it until hours after I signed my name on the line next to Kai's. There was no hesitation in my decision. Because it was the next adventure.

"Do you want to do this?" Declan asks, interrupting my thoughts.

"I do," I admit.

"Then give it everything. If you fail, you won't be able to say you didn't try to make it work."

I get up from my bed and move to my mostly packed suitcase. On top of all the clothes is a picture of me with my parents at my kindergarten graduation. I'm in a dark blue graduation gown, the cap slightly skewed on my head, standing in front of my parents. My dad's arm is slung around my mom's slight shoulders. We're all grinning at the camera. My dad was dark where my mom was light. Dark hair to her blonde. Brown eyes to her green. He was also twenty-four years older than her, so he looks more like a grandparent. Tears start to form in my eyes as I look at the happy family I barely remember.

"What if I get sick?" I whisper into my phone.

"Don't say that!" Declan shouts. "You're not getting sick, Willa. You're going to become the most famous and badass lady drummer. You're going to live a long and happy life. Probably marry some bastard I'll hate and have a truckload of children."

"It could happen, Dec." My mom had what my dad would simply call a weak immune system. It wasn't until later, after he passed, that I found her death certificate. She died from complications of type 1 diabetes. That's all it said. A quick Google search let me know it could be hereditary.

"Yeah, and I could take a skate to the carotid or end up in a plane crash or choke on a fry while eating alone in my apartment."

"Don't say things like that!" I yell at him. He just hums in response, and I sigh. "I get it. Don't mention dying and leaving you."

"Best friends forever and ever and ever, remember?" he says, and I can hear the smile in his voice.

"I was ten when I phrased it like that," I grumble.

"Still stands. You're my best friend, and I will not let you die."

I roll my eyes. Not even the great Declan Monroe can stop death. I'm about to tell him as much, but there's suddenly a lot of commotion coming from his end.

"I'll be right there," he says to whoever is in the room with him. "I have to go, Princess. It's Finn's turn to drive to practice, and he might have a stroke if we're not at least ten minutes earlier than everyone else." Declan's roommate, Finn, is an anxious guy from what I've been told. So I'm not surprised being late gets to him.

"Maybe you can use that extra time to get your ass off the second line," I say.

He barks out a laugh of surprise. "You should've been a coach."

"I do love making grown men cry."

He laughs and grumbles something to Finn. "Talk to you soon, Princess."

"Thanks for talking me off a ledge," I say quietly.

"Anything for my best friend forever and ever and ever."

I snort and hang up on him before he's in even more trouble with his roommate.

***

"Hurry up, Willa!"

I flip Cal off as I stand in the doorway of my childhood home. It's not like I won't be back. We're flying to LA for a month to record our first album. We all refused to move out there in case something developed with Ezra here.

I own this home now, with its worn hardwood floors and flowery wallpaper. The large black sectional taking up most of the room that I spent a lot of my time watching movies with Belle on. My dad died a month after I turned eighteen. I graduated from high school as an eighteen-year-old orphan. Kind of a depressing start to the rest of my life. As I play with the ends of my newly purple hair, I take a deep breath and shut the door.

I take out my phone to text Declan as I walk to the limo taking us to the airport.

Is it weird that leaving my house right now feels a lot more final than it should?

HOCKEY BOY

One door closes, another one opens, right?

Yes? But I'm still going to live here.

Don't remind me.

Declan was hoping we'd be on the same coast once we signed the recording contract. We haven't seen each other in two years. He would've come home for my dad's funeral, if I had told him. I didn't because I didn't want him to do anything to risk his career. He's still a little mad about that one.

I'm nervous.

You're going to kill it. I'm proud of you no matter what, Princess.

I have to go. Media day. Have a safe flight and text me when you land.

I will.

BFFEE!

I shake my head and shove my phone into my pocket as I slide into the seat next to Mav. I have no idea how Kai talked him into joining us, but he really doesn't look like he wants to be here.

"Nervous flyer?" I ask him.

His honey brown eyes meet mine, and he looks devastated. "No. I've flown a lot. Leaving here without Ezra . . . I guess I didn't realize it would be this hard."

"I didn't realize how close you guys were." I honestly didn't even know they knew each other until Kai told us they were friends.

"He's my best friend," Mav says before taking a deep breath like he's trying to force calm into his body. A lump forms in my throat and all I can do is nod. Ezra is one of my best friends and what happened to him is hurting us all. No one is convinced he's dead, but we don't know what else to do at this point.

So we're all trying to move on with our lives as much as we can. Life doesn't seem to care when you need it to stop or slow down. I learned that too young, and it sucks to watch everyone I care about learning it now.

"I like the new hair," he says, giving me a small smile.

"Thanks. It was my mom's favorite color. I wanted to take her with me somehow," I explain, even though he didn't ask.

"I can tell," he says, nodding towards my house. I laugh at where he's gesturing to. The purple lilac bushes surround the small white house.

Kai and Cal pile into the limo. Kai's expression is blank like it has been for weeks, but Cal is vibrating with excitement. I tune out his excited ramblings and stare out the window as our homes become smaller and smaller. I hear my mom's voice in my head.

On to the next adventure, my darling.

ONE

willa

2 MONTHS AGO

NORMALLY, the swaying of the bus as we drive to the next city for our next show lulls me to sleep. Tonight seems to be the exception. Jo is asleep in the bunk above me, while Mav's quiet snores are coming from across the aisle. We gave Kai and Belle the small bedroom in the back, so we didn't have to hear them.

Instead of sleeping, I'm doom scrolling through a different social media app every three minutes. I'm about to give up and try to get some sleep again when an alert pings, the notification freezing my fingers in their tracks.

San Diego Barracudas Star Declan Monroe Involved in Car Crash

I sit up so quickly I make myself dizzy.

"No, no, no, no," I mutter as I jump out of my bunk and race to the front of the bus as quietly as I can. Cal and Harlow have their own bus, so at least I don't have to worry about waking up Cora. I'm hitting Declan's number over and over, but it keeps going to voicemail. "Come on, Dec," I growl, my grip on the phone turning painful. I take a deep breath and try to steady my shaking limbs before pulling up the article. Dec's red super car is wrapped around a tree. It's hard to tell from the fuzzy image and all the first responders and their vehicles blocking the picture, but it looks totaled.

My hands shake so badly that I drop my phone. It immediately starts vibrating, and I scramble to pick it up. Declan's name and the picture I took of him a few years ago after one of his games, his brown hair plastered to his forehead from sweat, green eyes shining, and his smile bright as always, flashes across the screen. It takes a few tries of shaky swiping to answer the call.

"Dec," I breathe, throat tight with barely withheld tears.

"I'm okay, Princess," his soothing voice comes through. I let out the breath I was holding and with it comes the tears. "I'm so sorry, Willa. I swear I'm okay."

"You need to stop this, Declan!" I whisper-shout into my phone. I need him to understand how serious I am, but I don't want to wake everyone else up. I angrily swipe the tears away while wishing I could reach through the phone and strangle him.

"No one was hurt. I was just trying to figure out how to do something. I swear I made sure no one was around first."

"This is the third accident, Dec! The third!"

"Hey, the other two were —"

"Stop! Please stop all this Declan. You need to grow up. It's not funny anymore," I beg him. He sighs loudly, and I can hear his footsteps. I bet he's pacing right now.

"Princess —"

"Don't even try to soften this with nicknames, Declan," I say, interrupting him again. "Do you understand how hard it is to constantly see your best friend ripped apart in the media? Then, to make it worse, you give them more fodder for their bullshit fire."

"I'm sorry," he whispers. The pacing has stopped.

"You're the best person I know. Why are you trying so hard to be someone else?" I ask as calmly as I can.

"I've been like this for years, Willa. Maybe it is who I am." I can hear the defeat in his voice. I stare at the gray floor of the bus, watching the lights come and go as we pass by street lamps. Declan is lost, but can someone who feels just as lost as he does help him?

"I know who you are, Dec. Even if you don't. I'll remind you every damn day if I need to."

"You're my best friend forever and ever and ever."

I laugh and shake my head. "You're mine too, hockey boy."

"Thanks for the kick in the ass, Princess."

"Just do better, Dec. If I get another notification in the middle of the night that gives me a heart attack, I'm going to kill you myself."

"I'll work on it. I promise," he says. It's the best I'm going to get right now, so I let it go.

"I'm going back to bed. I'll text you tomorrow."

"Sweet dreams, Princess."

"Good night, hockey boy."

I slowly shuffle back to my bunk, my heart rate finally back to normal. Glancing over at Mav's bunk, I see him leaning out of the curtain and staring at me. He raises an eyebrow in question, and I shrug. He holds my gaze for a moment before shutting his curtain. The good thing about Maverick is he never asks questions.

Sleep is fitful at best. My dreams are filled with images of my best friend going up in a fiery blaze.

declan

EVERY INCH of me is covered in sweat as I continue to push myself to the limit on the treadmill. After the call with Willa last night, I've been feeling like more of an asshole than usual. Willa doesn't cry, yet she did last night. I made her cry. I haven't been able to stop myself from hearing the sound of her sobs.

A tanned forearm reaches over and slams on the red stop button before I can stop it.

"What the hell, man? I wasn't done!" I shout at Hank. Well, I try to shout. I can barely catch my breath. He just rolls his eyes and points to a bench on the wall. I follow him and take a seat.

"What's going on? You ran over ten miles," he says, his eyes assessing my every move. Hank is our captain and the best defenseman in the league. I tip my head back and rest it on the wall behind me. We're the only two in the team's gym right now. Which means I'm not getting out of this interrogation.

"I was sore. I came to stretch out my muscles and felt

good enough for a long run," I say and peek at him. The scowl on his face tells me he doesn't buy it.

"So the accident yesterday didn't injure you enough to prevent running?"

"You heard about that, huh?" I ask with a half-hearted laugh. Hank is still scowling. I sigh and sit forward, resting my elbows on my thighs and clenching my hands together. "Willa chewed me out for that last night. I know I fucked up. I'm going to do better. I don't need to hear it from you too."

I chance a look at him to see surprise briefly flash across his face before he schools his features back into a scowl. "It's not the first time she hasn't been happy with you."

He's not wrong. Willa has been less than impressed with some of my antics over the years. Hank has even overheard her yelling at me over the phone more than once. But I hear the question he's asking. What makes this time any different?

"She cried, man. Willa doesn't cry," I admit, shame flooding my body. He nods in understanding.

"Any word on that contract?" he asks. I shake my head. My contract expires before the next season starts in two months. Usually they expire at the end of a season, but mine was different. I'm usually contracted for camps or media appearances for the team in the off-season. They hadn't wanted me for those much in the past few years.

"I've been with this team for nine seasons. Are they really going to make me sweat like this?" I ask him. I don't like the look of pity he gives me.

"After what happened with Bethany, I'm surprised you're not out on your ass already."

I roll my eyes. "Going into this, I told her that it would be one night. It's not my fault she didn't understand what that meant," I argue. Sleep with one wrong person one time and apparently you can tank your whole career.

"What am I going to do? No other team seems to be trying to get me and the one I've given everything to is fine throwing me away," I ask, desperately hoping he has an answer.

"Retire," he says.

"Thanks, but I'd rather do it on my terms," I grumble, standing and walking away from the unhelpful bastard.

"Then figure out a way to do it on your own terms," he calls after me.

Great. Super easy.

willa

NOW

"ARE you sure you don't want to come with us?" Harlow asks. She's following some lead in New Hampshire that might help us with Ezra's case. Cal and Cora are going with her as well as Belle and Kai. I look behind me at Maverick's door. With every new revelation, it feels like he's been beaten down further and further.

"I'm going to stay," I say, and she nods. She glances over her shoulder at Mav's house, concern etched in her features. Harlow has one of the biggest hearts, and I know she's struggling with looking into Ezra because of how it's affecting Maverick. "I've got him. Just try to bring home good news this time," I joke.

Harlow laughs. "I'll try my best."

I watch them drive away. I make my way up the path to Maverick's house. Jo is still staying with me, and she's immersed in all her work for the band right now. So I try to give her space. She's tried to move out several times, but after what happened to Harlow, she was kind of forced to continue living in my guest room. It's nice to have someone else in the house. I've lived alone for a long time and sometimes the silence can be suffocating.

"What do you want to do today?" I ask, stepping into the house and shutting the door behind me.

"I already have plans, Willa," Maverick says, looking slightly annoyed.

"You're ditching me?" I feign hurt.

"I don't need a babysitter."

"Not babysitting. Jo is busy at my house, and Belle is on her way to prance in the woods like a fairy."

Maverick chuckles. "Feel free to hang out here then." He walks around me and opens the front door.

"Wait. You're really leaving?" I ask. I assumed he made up plans because he hates how he feels like a burden to us. I've been trying to be better about making him feel like that. It's hard not to worry about him, though.

"Yeah, I'm meeting with Millie. I want to see how I can help with her charity stuff. My mom might not want to admit my dad hit her, but I saw the proof of it growing up. Plus, after what Brad did to Belle," he shrugs. "I just want to do something."

I nod in understanding. Millie is Belle and Cal's cousin, and she runs a charity that focuses on getting more shelters up and running for women and children fleeing from bad situations. "Do you want me to come with you?" He shakes his head. I sigh dramatically, which makes him laugh.

"I'm sure you can entertain yourself for a few hours," he says before leaving me alone in his house.

I look around and realize that I don't know when the last

time I was alone was. "I actually don't think I know what to do with myself right now," I tell the empty house.

My phone rings in my pocket. "Perfect timing," I say to the walls.

"Hey hockey boy."

"Hey, Princess. How's the tour going?" I smile at the sound of Declan's voice.

This is exactly what I needed.

declan

"I REALLY DON'T KNOW what you were expecting," Finn says, hands on his hips as he looks down at me like a disappointed mother.

"I'm twenty-seven, not forty!" I argue, throwing my hands up and leaping off the chair I've been occupying outside of our coach's office.

"You're a twenty-seven-year-old playboy that drinks too much and crashed three cars this year while he was under contract with a team that is notoriously strict with their image."

"I win them games! Who cares if I like to have fun and appreciate women?" I huff and cross my arms over my chest.

"And the cars?" he asks, his judgmental face still firmly in place.

"Only one of those was my fault, and you know it." I somehow managed to be rear ended twice in the same month. The third accident was me thinking I knew how to drift. Which I guess I did. Once. Into a tree. At least it was in a closed parking lot, so no one was hurt. A fact everyone seems to ignore when they bring it up.

Finn sighs and pushes his hand through his shoulder-length hair. We've been on the same NHL team since we were both drafted at eighteen. He's become my closest friend here by default, and I think he might be reaching his limit with me.

"Monroe," Coach barks. I wince before following him into his office. My agent, Diego, is sitting in one of the two chairs in front of his desk. Shit. This isn't good.

"You wanted to see me, Coach?" I ask as I take the open seat in front of his desk. I nod at Diego, who doesn't look happy with me.

"We're not renewing your contract, son," Coach says, skipping right to the point as usual.

"What?" I shout, leaping from my seat. "I'm the top scorer on the team!"

Coach nods calmly. "Management has decided you're not worth the risk to their image anymore. You're one of the oldest players on the team. You probably have two or three years left at most."

"Why does everyone keep acting like twenty-seven is old?" I say, pulling at my hair. I know it's practically nursing home worthy in hockey years, but I've been playing just as good now as I did at eighteen. Better, actually.

"I tried to get them to change their minds, but it's final. Clear out your locker by the end of the week," Coach says, rapping his knuckles on his desk. "It's been an honor to coach you, kid. But take my advice and get your shit together if you want to keep playing. I'll let you two talk." He leaves me in his office with Diego.

"Sit down, Declan."

I plop back in my seat dramatically. "What the fuck am I going to do now?"

"I have two offers," Diego says, not sounding overly excited about either of them.

I sigh and a nod for him to keep going.

"Texas —"

"They suck," I groan, interrupting him.

"Or Boston," he continues like I haven't spoken. I perk up at that.

"Boston?" I'd love to go home.

"There's a catch."

"Of course there's a fucking catch. What is it?"

"You need to clean up your image. No more partying. No being photographed with a different woman every night. They want zero bullshit in the press from you."

"Fine. What else?" I say.

"You need to prove it before they'll let you sign."

"How the fuck do I do that? I'm the top scorer on this team and fourth in the league! Teams should be rushing to sign me," I say. I don't mean to sound as cocky as I do, but it's true. My stats speak for themselves. "I swear if you say it's my age, Diego," I point at him.

"It's part of it, but not all. You messed up, Declan. You slept with the daughter of the owner of the team you play for and expected no repercussions."

"I told her what to expect from the start. It's not my fault she thought she was the one that could lock me down." Okay, I hear how that sounds, but I'm sticking with it.

"It doesn't matter. Owners speak to each other. And unfortunately for you, most of them have daughters."

"Great. You're making me sound like a predator," I say, my mood turning angrier by the second. "I still don't understand what you want me to do. They waited until the last minute to decide. Practice is starting for all teams this week. I missed the mini camps that would've been beneficial to getting to know my new team. How the hell do I prove I'm not the irresponsible playboy they think I am by tomorrow?"

"Stay out of the press and maybe get an actual girlfriend. A committed relationship and no bad press could get you signed and playing by mid-season. Unless you want to hear the Texas deal, but you're right, they suck, and they would pay you less than a rookie."

Staying out of the press is the easy part. There hasn't been a single picture or article written about me since I crashed my car. I've kept my head down and stayed out of the public eye. There was no way I was going to do something to hurt Willa any more than I already had. Where the hell am I going to find a girlfriend on such short notice? Do I even want a girlfriend? Honestly, with my reputation, I'm not sure just having a girlfriend would be enough for Boston to believe I've settled down.

Unless...

"I'm engaged!" I blurt. I can't sit out the beginning of the season. I won't admit it out loud, but my body can't take that kind of break and be able to get back to where I need to be in the middle of a season anymore.

Diego's eyebrows shoot up. "Engaged?" he says, not at all believing me.

"Yes. Engaged, Diego. You know, where I got down on one knee and begged my woman to stay with my dumb ass forever?" I'm covering my idiot-panic with sarcasm.

"This seems unlikely, Declan."

"When was the last time I was actually photographed with someone?" I ask, knowing it's been over six months. It might be longer for all I know. I've been getting sick of this lifestyle for a while now. Meaningless hookups were great for a long time, but as I get older, they hold less appeal.

Diego studies me, and I know he knows the answer. "You're going to need to be seen with her. I advise you to push up the wedding as soon as you can. The sooner you're a boring married man, the quicker and easier we can get you that contract."

"Uh. I'll talk to her, but she's kind of on tour right now, so I don't know how soon I can push things," I say, scratching the back of my head.

"She's well known?" Diego asks, suddenly very interested. "That might work in our favor depending on how she's seen in the media."

"Squeaky clean," I say immediately.

"Who is she?"

"I need to talk to her about all this," I say, rushing to the door. "We've kept our relationship quiet, and I'm not going to put the spotlight on it if she doesn't want to." Or if I can't get her to agree to this. *Fuck*. I'm so stupid.

"Okay, but Declan . . ."

"I know," I say, rushing from the office.

"Fuck, fuck, fuck," I mutter to myself as I rush into the bathroom and fumble with the lock on the door.

Willa is going to kill me.

I take a deep breath and make the call.

"Hey hockey boy."

"Hey, Princess. How's the tour going?" I ask, mentally trying to figure out how to ask her what I need to.

"It's on hold. You don't pay much attention to social media, do you?" she asks with a laugh.

"Not if I can avoid it," I admit. "What happened with the tour? The last time we talked, you were really excited. I listen to the album all the time. It's fucking amazing." And it is. They're really talented.

Willa catches me up on everything that happened to Harlow, and my jaw is on the floor by the time she's done.

"Why the hell didn't you call me?" I ask, a little more anger behind it than there really should be. But she keeps trying to keep things from me to protect my career. Which is stupid and clearly pointless since I'm doing a great job of ruining it myself.

Willa sighs. "It's hard. The distance, I mean. There's been some progress in Ezra's case. Cal is a dad now. Maverick is either doing well or hitting rock bottom, depending on what news we get that day." I know what she means about the distance. Not being able to hang out with your best friend when you need to vent or just want to watch a new show together sucks. I've only managed to go to a handful of Shattered Halo concerts over the years and wasn't even able to stay to the end because of early morning practices or needing to catch a flight to the next game. Willa has been to more of my games, but I only got to see her for maybe an hour after before she was back on a tour bus.

"What about you? It's you I care about. How are you?"

"I don't really know. Sometimes I'm angry. Sometimes I'm fine. Today I'm good."

"I'm sorry I haven't called," I say softly. We used to call

each other every day. For years we spoke daily. The shirt storm I got myself into the past few months had me hiding, even from her.

"I miss you, Dec. I wish you were here," she says, her voice sounding small.

"About that. You remember a couple of years ago when you said you'd trade a kidney to get me traded to Boston?" She doesn't say anything for so long that I have to check to make sure the call didn't disconnect.

"Did you sell my kidney to Boston? I'm not even sure I'm mad if you did. Are you moving here?" She sounds excited now, and I smile. Then I remember what I need her to do, and my smile drops.

"No kidneys, but I need you to do something else for me," I say.

"Anything," Willa says immediately.

"I need you to become Mrs. Monroe." I hold my breath and wait for her response. The hysterical laughter that nearly blows out my eardrums isn't what I was expecting.

"Willa," I yell into the phone, holding it away from my ear so I can continue to hear.

"That was funny. You got me," she says, still laughing, but at a more manageable decibel.

"Princess, I'm serious." I explain the meeting I just had and admit to what I told Diego.

"Declan!" she says, sounding both shocked and angry. "You could've at least called me first!"

"I know! I'm sorry. I panicked." I rub my hand over my face, frustrated with myself for putting her in this situation. "You know what? Never mind. I won't do this to you. If my career ends here, it was still one hell of a career."

"Will you hold your dang horses and give me a flipping second?" Willa says, and I laugh. "Shush. I'm trying not to swear. Cora keeps repeating everything, and I'm babysitting her right now."

"It's really alright, Princess."

"It's really not, but that's more on the controlling angle these teams are playing with than your dumb penis and it's even dumber choices."

I laugh because I can't disagree.

"I'll do it. When will you be home?"

I smile even though she can't see me. "I'll move as soon as I can." I pause, giving her time to change her mind. "Thank you, Willa. I promise I'll be the best husband you've ever had." She snorts, and I know she's shaking her head right now.

"We'll figure all this out when you get here."

"See you soon, wifey."

I hear her mutter *Jesus Christ* under her breath before she hangs up.

"What did you do?"

I jump and turn to see Finn standing in front of the door I thought I locked. His blond hair is loose around his ears, which would trick anyone just meeting him into thinking he was a relaxed guy. That's if they didn't register how tall and wide the man is. Or how grumpy his face usually is.

"I asked my best friend to marry me," I say, a little smugly.

"You're an idiot."

"Why? People do it all the time. How many weddings have we been to? They all say they're marrying their best friend," I point out.

Finn shakes his head and looks disappointed in me again. "They were also in love with their best friend."

"It'll be fine. We'll make great roommates until I retire." I should probably talk to Willa about the actual length she's willing to tie herself to me before bragging about my genius plan to my back-up best friend.

Finn is just glaring at me. Sometimes it feels like those icy blue eyes are looking directly into my soul. It's unnerving, and if I didn't know how much of a marshmallow that stone exterior was hiding, I would probably be scared of him.

"We both know I only have until I'm thirty at most. My knees aren't going to hang on much longer. Willa has been my best friend for most of my life. This isn't going to change anything."

"Sure it's not," he says. He turns and leaves without saying anything else.

"Nothing can ruin our friendship!" I call after him.

Because nothing has and nothing ever will.

willa

"SORRY!" I yell over my shoulder to the person I just practically shoved out of the way. The yellow strands of the itchy wig I'm wearing slap me in the face as I run. The wig is the easiest way for me to be out in public with no one recognizing me.

Declan's plane landed half an hour ago, but I was stuck in traffic. He texted to say he's waiting for me by baggage claim. I slow down my pace when I see him surrounded by women. I can't blame them. The man is six foot two and all muscle. His light brown hair does that perfectly disheveled thing that people pay a lot of money in hair products to get. His green eyes sparkle as he signs autographs for anyone who asks. Declan is sex wrapped up in a sweet package. I've always known that but have done a pretty good job avoiding it so far. Rolling my eyes, I elbow my way through the crowd and throw myself in Dec's arms. He startles and drops the sharpie he was using to sign something so he can catch me.

"Uh. I appreciate the enthusiasm, but I'm happily

engaged," he says, trying to remove me from the koala hold I have on him.

"Are you sure about that hockey boy?" I ask teasingly, pulling back so he can see my face.

It takes him a moment before I see the recognition in his eyes. A heart-stopping smile breaks out on his face. "Hey Princess," he says, hugging me tightly. I squeeze him as tightly as I can with both my arms and legs, but he's so broad and muscular, I doubt he feels it.

"You're engaged? *To her?*" someone says from behind me. I lift my head from Declan's shoulder to see who's speaking. A curvy brunette with an angry scowl on her face zeroed in on me. I get the jealousy. I know Declan is attractive. I'm not blind. We've just never had any sort of romantic feelings between us. At least not any that I would let go anywhere.

"I don't see a ring," someone else says.

"It's such a big diamond I was afraid it would get stolen if I wore it to the airport," I say, ignoring the rest of the angry stares. "Can we go now? This is weird," I whisper in Dec's ear.

He lowers me to the floor, an amused expression on his face. "Sorry everyone. I need to take my future wife home and get her boulder back on her finger." His hand finds my waist as he leads me away from the angry estrogen mob and towards the parking lot. "What's with the wig?"

"I was trying to go unnoticed, but then someone had a harem of women trying to get in his pants in the middle of baggage claim."

"It's more likely they wanted in my wallet, which is

going to be significantly lighter after I buy you a diamond that can be seen from space," he teases.

I shrug. "I'm worth it."

Declan laughs and kisses my temple. "That you are, Princess." I don't have this with any of my other friends, the easy affection I have with Dec. Not even Belle.

"What's the plan?" I ask when we get to my car. Declan tosses his bag in the trunk and shuts it before turning to me.

"Can we talk about it over a burger? I'm starving."

"You're literally always starving. I meant, where am I taking you?" He looks confused, apparently thinking asking for burgers was enough direction. "Your apartment or do you have to report right to the Bruisers? We can get burgers on the way."

"My apartment, which we also need to add to the list of things to talk about. I report to the Bruisers in the morning," he says, giving me a knowing look. We can't be married and live separately if we want people to buy the ruse. I made him get his own apartment for now. He wasn't thrilled but did as I asked. "Diego suggested you come with me to that," he adds.

"To your hockey meeting?"

"I think he wants me to prove to him and the Bruisers' management that I didn't make you up," he says, rubbing the back of his neck and getting in my car.

I roll my eyes before getting in the driver's seat. "Burgers and planning it is."

"I think it would be easiest to just stick to the truth as much as we can," Declan says around a mouthful of cheeseburger. We're sitting on his uncomfortable gray couch in his barely furnished apartment. The plan is for him to move in with me when we get married, since I already have a house here. So he didn't bother to get more than he needed for the short term.

"Says the man who is going to fake marry his best friend," I mutter.

"Hey! It's going to be real! At least in the legal sense," he argues.

"Fine. We met as kids, became best friends, and fell in love." I pause. "When did we decide we were more?"

"Let's go with the night you called me and yelled at me," he says, smiling around a mouthful of fries.

"Which one?" I counter with a laugh.

"The most recent one, obviously."

"I'm not sure anything about this is obvious, hockey boy."

He looks sheepish. "We can scratch this," he says, but I know we can't. His career would be over if we did. I won't do that to him when I can easily help.

"I'm with you, Dec. Quit giving me an out," I stare at him so he knows I'm serious. He nods and goes back to shoveling food into his face like a starved man. "How long do we have to be married for?"

"Until I retire?" he asks in a small voice, not even looking at me.

"When is that? I'm not going to be fake married to you for a decade. No offense, but I'd like to find an actual husband one day."

He laughs. "I love that you think I have another ten years left in the tank, Princess. I have three years at most. If I'm really being honest with myself, this will probably be my last season." I can see how sad that makes him, so I scoot closer and throw my arms around his waist, hugging him.

"So what now? We know each other better than most married couples, so we don't need to go over personal facts or anything."

"Pick a date?" We both pull up our calendars. It's the middle of September, and we don't go back on tour until after the new year, but Dec starts practice tomorrow and his first preseason game is in two weeks. He also has a ton of media commitments and physical therapy for his knees.

"Um, we have today," I joke. But the more I look between our calendars, it becomes less of a joke.

"I'll call city hall and see if they can get us in. Maybe see about getting us some rings," he says, pulling up the number for city hall on his phone. "I'll have to special order your engagement ring, so just bands."

I watch Declan as he's suddenly all business. It takes a moment to snap out of my stupor from how fast this is moving, but once I do, I find the closest jeweler. The call is quick and easy. It always amazes me what you can get done when you throw money around.

"We're getting hitched in two hours," Declan says with a smile.

"Perfect. We need to get to the jeweler now. He's willing to size whatever bands we pick right away for a fee you so graciously agreed to," I tell him, grabbing his hand and pulling him to the door.

Once we're in the car, I turn towards Declan. "I know

we'll be legally married, but can we wait a little to announce it? I still have to figure out how to break this to my friends in a way that they'll believe."

"You don't trust them with the truth?" he asks, looking worried.

"It's not about trust. It's about the number of people that are always around us. One slip backstage where we think we're alone, but someone is hiding in the shadows and the media knows we tricked your new team into signing you. Then what happens? You get sued and your entire career ends in a scandal?"

His eyes widen like he hadn't thought of that. "Shit. You're right. How long do we keep it secret?"

"Let's just figure it out as we go. Your schedule is about to get crazy," I say, feeling a little guilty. "Your team will know, but I don't want your name connected with mine until it has to be."

Declan looks angry, but I hold up my hands before he can say anything.

"Someone is after us, Dec. You know that. I refuse to be the reason someone attacks you in a parking lot or tries to take out your knees Tanya Harding style."

I thought that would get a laugh out of him, but instead he's intently studying me. "I hate you being in danger. Maybe you should stay with me. Or I can figure out how to take you with us on away games, so I'm never far from you. Wives usually have to travel separately, but maybe I can get an exception for you. Or you can get a random job with the team that lets you travel with us?"

"I'm safer here with my friends. Cal hired an absurd amount of security. Plus, as much as I would enjoy traveling with you, I'd just end up alone most of the time. Which would make me vulnerable."

Declan sighs and slams his head back into the headrest. "Fine, but I want you with me at my apartment when I'm home. I'll sleep better knowing you're with me. My building has security too." I frown at his demand. "I want to spend time with you. I miss you, Princess."

I hold my argument. I already hate feeling like I'm being trapped at home, and now Declan wants to smother me some more. But I don't say any of that because the truth is, I really missed him too. So instead I say, "Deal."

declan

"QUIT FIDGETING," Willa says. We're sitting in the stiff plastic seats outside my new coach's office. I've been playing with the platinum band on my finger, spinning it around and around. She grabs my hand and holds it in her small one when I fail to comply.

I look over at my wife. Her lilac hair is down in soft waves that frame her sweet face. Although, she keeps pointing out that I'm the only one that thinks she's sweet. It's probably because of the scowl she usually wears around other people.

"What?" she asks when she catches me staring at her. Her blue eyes have small specks of gold in them. I haven't noticed that before. "You okay, hockey boy?"

"Sorry," I mumble and shake my head. "I think it just hit me, what you're doing for me."

She smiles and nudges my arm with her shoulder. "We would do anything for each other. That's just how it is."

She says it so simply. I guess it is that simple because she's right. We would do absolutely anything for each other.

The fact that she's possibly in real danger makes my chest constrict and my pulse race every time I think about it. When she left my apartment last night after our quick wedding, I stayed up most of the night wondering if I should just retire now so I can stay by her side to protect her. I shot myself down pretty fast because I know she would hate that. It would also have made getting married pointless.

I kiss the back of her hand. "Thank you, Princess."

Her smile brightens, and she leans her head on my arm. "You're welcome, hockey boy."

"Holy shit. You didn't lie." Willa's head snaps up at Diego's voice. She immediately scowls at him, and I laugh loudly. "You have an actual fiancée."

"I'm his wife," Willa says, now fully glaring, which just makes me laugh harder.

"I meant no insult, Mrs. Monroe," Diego says, smiling and thinking he's going to charm her. I lean back in my chair to watch the show.

"You may not mean to insult me, but you are insulting my husband by implying he isn't worthy of a committed, loving relationship. Either that or you're implying I'm stupid or a gold digger," Willa says, flames in her eyes. "So, which is it? Who are you insulting?"

Diego's eyes are wide, and his hands are raised like he's asking her not to shoot him. I'm grinning like a fool as I pull my wife to my side. I'm six foot two, and Willa is a full foot shorter than me, but I wouldn't want to go toe to toe with her. Diego seems to be learning that the hard way. His eyes keep darting to me, but I just shrug.

"I really meant no offense. I was just joking with Declan," Diego says, still looking at me to help him.

"You meant offense. I'm the only one that gets to insult him. Remember that," Willa says, turning her gaze to me and smiling in a clear dismissal.

"Who says you get to insult me?" I ask playfully. She holds up the copy of our marriage certificate. "Yeah. That's fair."

"You married Willa Prince," Diego says, because the man has no self-preservation skills.

"Do you have something to say about that?" Willa challenges.

"No!" Diego says quickly. "Shattered Halo is my favorite band." Willa eyes him suspiciously but stays quiet. "You didn't tell me you knew Willa Prince," he says to me.

I frown. "You knew about Willa."

"But I didn't know she was Willa Prince!" he says, his voice squeaks on her name.

"Are you fangirling right now?" I ask and start laughing again. I look at Willa to see the corners of her mouth twitching. "I'm sure she would've autographed your shiny bald spot if you hadn't started off this entire conversation by insulting her handsome, talented, perfect hockey god of a husband."

Willa snorts and hits my chest with the back of her hand.

"The woman you were photographed with at the airport was blonde and witnesses said you claimed you were engaged to her," Diego says because he really wants to die today.

Willa turns to me. "Did you fuck her?" she asks, a fake frown on her face. Diego looks like he's suddenly about to pee himself. Probably just realizing he caused an issue.

"No. She stuffed me with burgers and left me alone in my bed," I say. Willa smiles and shakes her head.

"I wear a wig in public. I don't like being photographed without my permission," she tells Diego. She's being marginally nicer, but I can tell she hasn't decided if she likes him or not.

"Oh. It was you," he says, releasing a breath.

"Who are you?" she asks him.

"Oh! I'm so sorry. My name is Diego. I'm Declan's agent." He holds out his hand to shake hers. She does, but her gaze narrows.

"Are you sure he's right for the job?" she asks me.

"I did until right now," I say, earning me a glare from Diego.

"Are you going to be alright for the meeting, Diego?" We all turn to see a man standing in the doorway. Coach Jones is older than my last coach. His hair is fully white, but he's in shape and has that look in his eyes that tells you he takes no shit. I already like him.

"I'm fine," he says, adjusting his tie and clearing his throat. His cheeks are red, and he is avoiding looking at me.

I stand and offer my hand. "It's great to meet you, Coach. This is my wife, Willa." Willa smiles and shakes his hand.

"It's lovely to meet you, Mrs. Monroe."

We follow him into his office. Diego, being the idiot he is, takes one of the two available seats. So I take the other and pull Willa into my lap. She comes willingly and wraps her arm around my neck. I kiss her cheek. I really missed the comfort of having her close after all the years we spent apart. Even before I signed with the NHL, we only saw each other over the summer, but for whatever reason, we've always been comfortable with each other.

Coach Jones stares at the casual display and smiles. "Do you know why you were asked to attend this meeting, Mrs. Monroe?"

"Please call me Willa," she says, still smiling. I think I like it more when she scowls at other men. "Can I speak candidly?"

"I'd rather you did," Coach says, returning her smile. Okay, I don't like that either. Who knew getting married, even if it is a farce, would make me possessive?

"Declan has spent a lot of his life thinking with his dick," she says casually. I make a sound of surprise, but that doesn't stop her. "We've known each other since we were kids. I know more about his antics than anyone else." She's not wrong. "But he's been working on himself, and I promise that part of his life is over."

"What made you decide to make a change?" Coach asks me.

I look at Willa and see pain in her eyes. I know she's thinking of the same night I am. "I made her cry." Willa lowers her gaze, not wanting me to see whatever emotions are on her face.

"That's it?" Coach asks skeptically.

"Willa doesn't cry. Making her cry cut my heart to shreds. I knew I would do everything in my power to make sure it wouldn't happen again." My words are for her as much as they are for my new coach. I hug her tightly to my chest.

"You married her to get her to stop crying? Please tell me

you got a prenup," Diego says. Willa shoots up from my lap before I can stop her.

"I've had about enough of you. All you do is insult my husband and now you're insulting me. You're supposed to be his advocate, not his bully," she says in that eerily calm way she does that's scary as fuck.

Coach clears his throat and pushes a paper in my direction. "Sign this and then I suggest you find someone else to represent you that will have your best interests in mind." I sign the paper quickly and stand, pulling Willa back to my side.

I shake Coach's offered hand and thank him. "You're not fired, Diego. Because contrary to what happened in here, I do think you have my best interest in mind. You just really need to get your shit together around my wife."

I pull Willa out of the office and away from Diego before he can protest. Once we're away from everyone, I pull her into my arms and spin. She laughs while holding me tightly. "We did it," she whispers in my ear.

"You did it, Princess. I said nothing in there." I put her down and check my watch. "I only have a few minutes until I need to be in the locker room."

"That's fine. I need to go meet with Jon."

I frown. "Who the fuck is Jon?" Willa just laughs at me.

"My manager. The rest of the band will be there too. We've had a lot of brand deals coming in and requests for interviews. Then there's the whole tour rescheduling thing."

"Right. I knew that."

"I'll see you tonight. We can eat your boring healthy food since you'll officially be in season and maybe watch

Where the Heart is?" She smiles up at me in a way she knows I won't say no to. I groan and act put out, anyway.

"Again?" It's her favorite movie. She's made me watch it with her over FaceTime a bunch over the years. We'd always talk about which snack foods we'd name future children. My favorite so far is Cheese Puff. Willa's is Pizza Roll. "Fine," I relent, just like she knew I would.

Her phone vibrates in her hand, and she glances at it. "Shoot. I'm going to be late." She hugs me quickly and runs for the parking lot. I watch her go, noticing, not for the first time, how great of an ass she has.

"She's a fuckable little thing." I turn, grabbing the collar of the man who just spoke and shoving him into the wall.

"What the fuck did you just say about my wife?" I growl in his face. He lifts his hands in a placating gesture and laughs.

"Just calling as I see it, new guy."

"Stop hitting on people's wives, Cameron." I turn to see Gideon Banks, Captain of the Bruisers, center, and my line mate, assuming I make first line. "I apologize. Martinez likes to test out the new guys."

"I like your aggression. We can be friends," the guy I'm still holding against the wall says. I let him go and back up. Cameron Martinez is smiling at me a little psychotically. He's on the defensive line and one of the best there ever was. And I just had him pinned to the wall like an asshole. Great first day so far.

"I didn't ask to be friends," I say, questioning his sanity.

"It's decided," he says and then just walks away.

"It's easier just to accept it," Banks says, coming to stand next to me. "You're married to the drummer from Shattered Halo?"

I tense and look at him. He's about my height, but with a slimmer build. He has blond hair and brown eyes that seem kind enough. But I should have asked Willa to wear her wig to the meeting. I didn't realize how many people would see her, and she wanted to keep this out of the press until they figure out for certain who tried to kidnap Harlow.

"I really need that to stay a secret. She's not exactly safe right now," I admit, hoping a guy that's good enough of a person to be chosen as captain can understand.

He nods. "I heard about Callahan's wife."

"You're a fan too?" I ask. I mean, I knew they were famous, but I didn't realize how hard it would be to be married to someone so recognizable and keep it quiet. It's been one day, and I'm already failing miserably.

"Sure. I'm from Bangor, which makes Shattered Halo basically hometown royalty. People still talk about what happened to Ezra Irons. I don't blame you for wanting to keep her close."

I nod, my eyes still on the spot where I last saw Willa even though she's probably halfway to her meeting by now.

"Did Martinez recognize her?"

"He may have. I'll have a chat with him."

"I appreciate it."

"Come on. Let's get you introduced to the rest of the team, and then you can show us what you've got." I smile and follow him to the locker rooms.

"You're one fast motherfucker," Banks jokes, taking the spot next to me on the locker room bench. Practice went great. I gelled really well with Banks and Anatoly Ivanov, who make up the offensive first line. Boston's right winger retired last season, so the spot is wide open for me to grab. There are a few guys on the second line and farm team that are less than happy with how quickly I claimed that spot. Unfortunately for them, I'm really fucking good at hockey. Coach hasn't made it official, but after that practice, I'm not worried.

"It's why they pay me so much," I joke back.

"You're getting us the cup this year, new friend," Martinez says in a way that makes it sound like a threat.

"I'll do my best," I say and laugh.

"You will get us the cup," Martinez repeats as he unlaces his skates.

"Uh. Sure thing," I say. He nods, seeming satisfied.

I quickly get undressed and showered so I can get back to my apartment. Banks laughs while watching me struggle to get my wet legs into jeans.

"I remember the honeymoon phase."

"You're married?" I ask. Willa and I might not be in the honeymoon phase, but she's still my best friend. I missed her like crazy, and I'm about to miss her again when official games start. So I want to get in as much time as I can.

"I am. Have been for six years now," he says proudly. "Is Willa going to be able to come to any of our games?"

"I'm not sure. We were going over schedules last night. It would've been easier for her if," I stop and look around at the other guys in the room with us. One of them is married to an actress and another to a model. It's not like they don't get the need for privacy, but I also won't risk letting them know about Willa yet. "If that *thing* didn't happen to reschedule everything."

Banks nods. "If she decides to and she wants to hide with the fans, that's where my wife usually sits. She likes being close to the action instead of with the other WAGs."

"That's probably where she'd want to be, so I'll take you up on that once I figure out everything. She used to tell me to get my ass in gear when I was still on the second line. Once she called me after a playoff game loss and laid into me about hogging the puck."

Banks laughs. "You've got a keeper."

I smile. "That I do."

He pats my shoulder. "Great first day. I'll see you in the morning."

I grab my stuff and dig my phone out of my bag as I make my way out of the locker room.

PRINCESS

How was your first practice? Was everyone wowed by your stick skills?

I'm running a little late. The meeting is still going on. I don't know how.

Actually, I do.

Practice was great. I made a friend against my will. That's a new one for me.

What's keeping you from me?

I'm going to need you to explain that one later. We're finishing up rescheduling the last leg of the tour, and I may have fought for weird dates so that I could go to some of your games. But I couldn't tell anyone why.

I'm smiling at my phone like an idiot. I forgot how great it feels to have Willa in my corner. Not that she hasn't always been there, but it's the first time in years she's fighting to come cheer me on. My parents retired early thanks to my paychecks. Now they're traveling all over the world and rarely come to see me play anymore. It'll be nice to have someone there for me again.

> You could just tell them.

I slide into my car and wait for her reply.

> Not yet. I need to figure out how to tell them without blowing everything up.

I frown.

> You think they won't like me?

> Honestly, I think you and Cal will be best friends, but everything is fragile right now, and I'm scared of rocking the boat.

> I get it.

I don't. It's not like I'm some random guy. I've been in her life for most of it. I doubt they'd even be that surprised. But considering she's doing this for me so I can retire how I want to, I keep my thoughts to myself.

> Soon. I promise.

> I think Jon is either ready to wrap up or the vein in his head exploded. Either way, I should be out of here soon.

See you soon, Princess.

I think about her the whole drive back to my apartment. I never meant to add more stress to her life. I honestly thought I'd just move into her house and be around her friends all the time. But I need to accept her caution because she knows them better than I do.

I've never really met them. I was there for her mom's funeral, but I was ten, and I don't remember much other than how sad Willa was. I probably met the others, but maybe I didn't.

Fake marriage is hard when you actually care about your wife.

willa

"I HAVE good news and bad news," I tell Declan around a mouthful of the Pad Thai he ordered for me.

"Give me the good stuff first to cushion the blow," he says, clutching a green throw pillow to his chest dramatically. I ignore the way his forearms flex and the tattoos covering his arms. They do weird things to my stomach.

I roll my eyes. "We finalized the rest of the tour schedule. I can make a lot of your home games. Not all of them, but more than I was expecting." I wanted to see Declan play anyway, but we realized it would be smart to have me at as many as I could get to, so our marriage looks more real.

"Fuck yeah!" Declan yells, pumping his fist in the air. I throw my head back and laugh. I forgot how easy it is to laugh around him.

"Do you want the bad news now?" I ask, sobering a little.

"Nothing is going to stop the high from hearing my girl is going to my games."

Ignoring the strange feeling in my chest when he claims me as his, I say, "I have to leave Thursday."

He stops smiling. "But that's my first preseason game."

"I know. I can go, but I'll need to leave right when it ends," I assure him. "But it's also the only preseason game I can make."

Declan flops sideways with a huge sigh, his head landing in my lap. "Can we do that thing where I'm walking to the locker room, and you run to me yelling my name? Then when I turn, you jump into my arms and kiss me in front of all my teammates and coaches?"

"I'm not going to kiss you," I say, digging my fingers into his side, making him squirm and slap my hands away.

"Hate to break it to you, Princess. We're married. We're going to kiss. And I would like the cinematic one. You can pick what kind you want."

"So we kiss twice and that's it?" I'm weirdly nervous about this. I'm completely comfortable with the intimacy we have now, but adding kissing feels like crossing a line. He's, unfortunately, right though.

Declan rolls off my lap and kneels in front of me, grabbing my hands and suddenly looking serious. "I won't ever do anything to make you uncomfortable, Princess. You know that. I just don't see how anyone is going to believe I'll be able to keep my lips to myself with you as my wife."

I shake my head and look down at my lap, trying to hide my blush behind my hair. "You don't kiss, Dec. It's in your rules."

"Meaningless hookups, absolutely not. Kissing isn't how you keep feelings separate. But my wife?" he shrugs. "I'm obviously going to be kissing my wife all the damn time."

"We've been married for two days, and it feels like we're already blurring lines."

"I disagree. We both have jobs where we put on a show for an audience, right? It's no different from that."

Looking at it from that perspective makes sense. I don't need to kiss him behind closed doors and start questioning things. "Okay. I can handle it if I think of it like that."

Declan laughs and stands. "Glad to know you think kissing me is repulsive." His tone is joking, but his eyes look hurt.

"I don't, but I won't do anything to ruin our friendship, and I think kissing you without a set boundary would really blur lines and hurt our relationship once this marriage ends."

I can't read the look in Declan's eyes, but he nods anyway. "So, what's your kiss of choice?"

"I'll think about it and get back to you," I tell him, still trying to decipher the look in his eyes. But it suddenly vanishes, and he's grinning again.

"Does that mean I get my movie kiss?"

"Yes, hockey boy. You can get your movie kiss."

He points at me as he walks backwards into the kitchen. "I'm going to rock your fucking world, Willa Prince."

Yeah, that's what I'm worried about.

declan

"WHAT ARE YOU DOING?"

"There's only one bed in this apartment," Willa says. She's standing at the foot of it, staring with wide eyes.

"It's a California king. We can easily sleep together and not even know." I crawl into my side and set my phone on the charger. I'm fully clothed in my black pajama pants and a white t-shirt. It's not like she has to crawl into bed next to a naked guy.

"How did I not realize I'd have to sleep next to your smelly ass?" she mutters, snapping out of whatever stupor she was in.

"We've shared a tent before. I don't see how this giant comfortable bed that has zero rocks or sticks in it is a problem," I playfully grumble.

"I know. That's how I became acquainted with your farting and snoring." She walks into the bathroom and shuts the door.

"I do not snore!" I yell. Do I? She's the only person I've ever slept next to.

"You didn't deny the farting!" she calls back, and I laugh.

"I'll work on clenching my cheeks while I snooze," I promise.

"See that you do," she says as she steps back into the room. Any smart ass reply I have dies on my lips as I take her in. She's just in sleep shorts and a tank top, but it's the way it all hugs her body. Willa is fucking beautiful, and her body is killer. I seem to be just now realizing I have a wet dream for a best friend. And I asked her to sleep in my bed until I move into her house. *Fuck me.*

"Hey, Princess?"

"Yeah, hockey boy?" she says, getting comfortable on her side of the bed and turning to face me.

"Thank you. For everything."

Willa smiles. "Stop thanking me and go to sleep."

Turning the light off, I snuggle down into my bed. It's a really expensive mattress to help with all the aches in my body after a long skate or a rough game. It's the only piece of furniture I took with me from San Diego. It also usually puts me to sleep within minutes, but instead I'm staring at the ceiling, hyperaware of the woman in my bed with me.

"You don't really snore. Stop thinking so loud so I can get some sleep."

I laugh in surprise. "I knew it!"

"Good night, hockey boy," she says. Her breathing evens out soon after.

"Good night, Princess," I whisper and follow her into oblivion.

willa

I NEED to either get rid of the purple hair or get a less itchy wig. The hair has become part of my whole image, so it looks like the wig is getting an upgrade after this game.

"I look ridiculous," I mutter as I shimmy sideways into the row and find my seat. The woman in the seat next to me laughs. She's cute and looks about my age.

"Are you Willa? I'm Maggie Banks." She points at one of the players. "That one is mine." I look at who she's pointing at.

"Your husband is Gideon Banks?" I ask, surprised. Dec said I would be sitting with one of the other wives, but I kind of assumed it would be one of the guys that don't see a lot of ice time. Not the captain of the team. I thought she would be up in the WAGs box.

Maggie is around my height with curly brown hair in a bob around her chin. Her brown eyes are big and round on her small face, making her look sweet.

"He sure is. I have to wear the giant jersey too," she laughs, gesturing to the Boston Bruisers jersey she's wearing that matches mine. Declan insisted I couldn't wear the type available in a store. I had to wear one he's actually worn. It seems Maggie is in the same boat. Except hers is number 27 with Banks on the back, and I'm wearing Monroe with a 14.

"Possessive hockey players," I say and shake my head.

"I know who you are," she whispers, causing my whole body to stiffen. "Gideon saw you at the training center last week. Don't worry. Your hubby swore him to secrecy."

"That obviously didn't work," I say, but I'm laughing because she's just so sweet.

"Gideon told me so that I could help you steer clear of any press. Your secret is safe with me." She winks and then turns to watch the warm up.

Maggie asks a few more questions about the band and what's going on with Ezra. She's apparently a huge fan and is excited for the first episode of Harlow and Jo's podcast, *Melt the Ice*, to drop. She even introduces me to the people around us. They're all-season ticket holders that Maggie knows by name. I guess the seats we're in belong to her parents, but they're on a cruise. They have four tickets, and we're only using two of them.

"You're my security, aren't you?" I ask the large and bored looking man sitting next to me.

"Yes, Mrs. Monroe," he says, eyes scanning the area continuously.

"That one too?" I ask, pointing to the large man next to Maggie.

"Yes, Mrs. Monroe."

I roll my eyes. "Sorry," I say to Maggie. She just laughs and offers the guy on her side some of her popcorn.

"I can get you and Gideon tickets and backstage passes if

you want. Declan is going to one of the New York shows because they'll be there for a game. He'll also be in Boston for the last show in March." It seems like the least I can do for her since she let me sit with her and apparently bring security with me.

Maggie squeals so loud the guys hear her on the ice. Gideon turns and sees how excited she is and smiles. You can tell from the way he's looking at her that he absolutely adores her. Declan, on the other hand, is looking very confused. I realize it's probably my face. I tend to either scowl or show every emotion. Nothing neutral. And Maggie's squeal was alarming.

I catch Declan's eye and smile. He returns it, all the worry and confusion fading quickly, and he starts waving with a little too much excitement. I laugh at him.

"That man is obsessed with you. I can tell. I have an eye for these things," Maggie says, bumping my shoulder with hers.

"He's something alright," I reply, not acknowledging her words.

We watch the rest of warm-ups in companionable silence. The sounds and smells of the arena are familiar. We're in the front row so I can smell the cold of the ice and the rubber of the pucks. There's always an underlying scent of sweat and fried food in ice rinks. I only made a few of Declan's college games, but my dad was a huge hockey fan. So I went to a lot of the local college games growing up.

Before I know it, both teams are getting into position for the puck drop. "Who is that man and why is he waving at us?" I ask Maggie. She looks at the large, dark-eyed defensemen and laughs before waving back.

"That's just Martinez. It's easier just to wave and get it over with or he'll keep doing it."

I do as she says, and he immediately sets his stick down to wait for the play. Weird.

"He does it every game. Says waving to the other player's wives gets them riled up, and they need the aggression to win."

I laugh so hard I snort when I realize where I heard his name. "Cameron, right? Dec said he was his friend against his will. I thought he was joking."

Maggie laughs along with me. "I'm not surprised."

The sound of a whistle has my head turning back to the game. Declan skates in front of me with a frown. "You're not watching," he mouths.

"Sorry!" I yell and make a show of facing forward and paying attention.

"Men need so much attention," Maggie jokes, but I notice her focus is on Gideon.

"I can't make another game until right before Thanksgiving. So I better pay attention, or I won't hear the end of it for weeks."

Maggie and I watch the Bruisers dominate the first period. Dec is playing with his line like he has been with them for years and not two weeks. It's really impressive. They're only up by one, but they've kept the puck on Tampa's side for most of it.

"I'm sorry you have to sit down here with me," I say to Maggie while we wait for the next period to start.

"I always sit here. I like watching the game up close," she says, waving off my apology.

"I'd like to sit with you at all the games, if that's okay

with you. I'm not sure my screaming would be appreciated up there," I say, gesturing to the WAG box with my chin.

"I would love another wife to sit with!" She's practically bouncing in her seat. Her joy is contagious and soon I'm smiling so hard it hurts. "Oh, they're playing!"

I turn just in time to see a player from Tampa taking a cheap shot at Declan's knees. I'm out of my seat and screaming while gesturing wildly at the dirty player. His knee injuries aren't a secret. He's been out for part of a season more than once to have surgery on one or both.

A ref turns to look at me since I'm making so much noise. "Don't look at me! Pay attention to that dirty shithead!" I'm pointing at the asshole who tried to hurt Dec. "Do your fucking job, ref!"

Maggie is cackling next to me. "I like you, Willa. You can sit with me anytime."

I take my seat, crossing my arms and scowling at the back of the Tampa player's head. "I'm watching you 39!" I yell.

Gideon wins the face-off, passing it directly to Declan, who skates like his ass is on fire, easily maneuvering around Tampa's defense. He lines up the shot and slaps it. I watch the puck fly from his stick directly into the top left corner of Tampa's net. The lights flash and the horn sounds.

"Let's fucking go, hockey boy!" I'm screaming and jumping. You'd think it was a game that mattered and not just preseason. Between the excitement that is hockey and watching Declan, I'm having a great time.

Declan raises his stick and points it right at me. "That one's for you, Princess!" he shouts over the crowd. I smile and touch my heart. He returns the gesture before getting back in position. It's something we started doing when I had to leave immediately after his games without being able to see him.

Boston is up by two going into the third period. Tampa is struggling to keep up. Their team is young, a lot of rookies where Boston is mostly veterans. Their inexperience is showing, but so is their frustration. Cheap hits and shitty calls make up the rest of the game. Declan has been thrown into the boards twice when the ref's backs have been turned. Gideon took a nasty slash to the shoulder. The left wing on the second line, Mikhail Slava, left the game with a broken finger. But through all of it, Boston kept their composure and fought them off without resorting to their dirty games.

"The guys are going to be sore tonight," Maggie says as we stand and make our way to the locker room. "I hope you have good massage oil at home. If not, I can send you the one I get."

"I have to get on the tour bus and head to New Jersey right after I see Dec," I say.

Maggie frowns. "It must be hard when you're apart so much."

"We've talked almost every night since my dad got me my first phone when I was thirteen. The distance sucks, but we're used to it." Maggie nods, but not in a way that makes me believe she understands.

"There they are," she says. We took our time getting to the locker rooms. The game ended earlier than I planned for, so I didn't need to rush. Our guys are already waiting for us in their game day suits. I don't know who made the rule that hockey players need to wear suits on game day, but I could kiss them for it.

Speaking of kisses.

"Declan," I shout when I see him. I turn to Maggie and quickly rip my wig off. "Can you hold this?" I toss it to her before she has time to respond. Shaking out my hair quickly, I run.

Declan's smile lights up his whole face when he sees me coming for him. He crouches down slightly and opens his arms. I jump into them, wrapping my legs around his waist and my arms around his neck like I've done a million times before. Except this time, I lean down and press my lips to his. I meant for it to be soft and quick, but he grabs the back of my neck and takes over. His lips move against mine, his tongue flicking the seam, asking for entrance, and I let him in. I get lost in the feel of his body against mine, the softness of his lips and the teasing of his tongue.

He pulls back and looks at me. He's breathing just as heavily as I am. "Hey, Princess," he whispers in a husky voice. I look into his eyes, pupils blown so wide the green is barely visible.

"That was some kiss, hockey boy."

"I wanted my movie kiss," he says, kissing the tip of my nose. Then he rears back, eyes widening in horror. "Willa, your hair is out." He looks around him in a panic, like he's looking for somewhere to hide me.

"Dec, it's okay," I try to tell him, but he's already moving towards the exit. "Declan," I say louder and try to wiggle out of his hold. "They got him, Dec."

He freezes a foot from the door that leads directly into the players' parking lot. "Got who?"

"Senator Wolfe. He's been arrested for a ton of stuff, but Harrison, Harlow's dad and the private investigator Kai hired, found evidence connecting him to Harlow's kidnapping."

"You're safe?" The relief in Declan's voice hits me right in the chest.

"I'm safe," I say softly.

"Can I move out of my shitty apartment now?" he asks, breaking the tension. I laugh. His apartment costs more per month than most people make in a year, but I don't think this is the time to point that out.

"Can we figure that out when we're both here at the same time again?"

Declan stares at me. His eyes showing his disappointment.

"I know, but I'm on the road for the next seven weeks. And then the week I'm back, you're away for three days."

He sighs and lays his forehead against mine. "I'm going to miss you."

"I'm going to miss you too, hockey boy." He lets me down but takes my hand as he leads me into the parking lot.

"Did you enjoy the game?" he asks as he leads me to my car.

"Tampa is a bunch of dirty fuckers. You're going to have to watch out for them during the season. If they play like that in the preseason, they're going to be causing serious injuries when the games actually count." Declan laughs so loud he gets the attention of his teammates who are making their way to their own cars. "Everyone is staring at us," I say, looking around.

"Good," he says and then leans in kissing me again. This

one is different. It's softer, less urgent. "Drive safe Mrs. Monroe. Call me when you can." He opens my door and waits until I'm buckled and the engine is started before he shuts my door and blows me a kiss. I watch him walk to his own car, a little stunned.

We agreed to kiss for show. Which both kisses were, but they weren't supposed to make me tingle.

Fucking hell.

declan

I TOSS and turn for over an hour before I give up and grab my phone. He answers on the third ring.

"What?"

"I miss you too, buddy," I say.

"What do you want, Dec? It's late," Finn complains.

"It's ten pm where you are. Stop being such an old man."

Finn sighs loudly. "What do you want?"

"I can't sleep without Willa in my bed. What does that mean?"

"That this was a terrible idea and now you have feelings for your wife," Finn says. He's so monotone all the time I can't tell if he's joking or not.

"She's my best friend. If I was going to develop feelings, it would have happened a long time ago. Is it possible I just got used to the sound of her little snores and now I can't sleep without them? Like white noise or something?"

"When was the last time you were able to be together for a long stretch of time?"

"Probably the last time we went camping together. I

moved to San Diego right after that trip," I say. Any time we spent together since then felt like stolen moments in between chasing our dreams.

"That was nine years ago, Declan."

"Yeah, but we talked every night. We even watched movies or binged TV shows together over FaceTime at least once a week. It's not like she's been absent from my life since then."

Finn sighs even louder this time.

"What?"

"You want to know what I think?" he asks.

"That's why I called you," I say, laying back down and staring at the streaks of light that broke through my curtains and are painting lines on the ceiling.

"I think something was always there. I think you were too young and focused on hockey to realize it, but it was there, simmering under the surface. There's a reason she's the only person to ever be that close to you. There wasn't room to let another woman in when Willa was already taking up all the space."

"I've been with loads of women in a way I've never been with Willa," I point out, even though his words are rattling around in my brain.

"Women you refused to kiss in case there could be feelings."

"For them, not me."

"That's exactly my point," he says smugly.

"I kissed Willa today. Twice," I admit. "Well, technically, she kissed me the first time, but I asked her to." I omit the painful erection I had the entire ride home or that I kind of wanted to keep kissing her. Which is weird for me. I'm not a kisser. Maybe I should have been this whole time.

I can hear Finn muttering distantly, like he moved the phone away from his face.

"How long are two going to be apart?" he asks.

"Seven weeks," I groan dramatically.

"I suggest you use that time to figure out your feelings for her before you cross a line you can't come back from." The line goes dead. Apparently, he was done with me for the night.

I reach over and grab Willa's pillow, hugging it to me and inhaling the smell of her sugary apple shampoo. My eyelids are soon too heavy to keep open. I replay the way she looked watching me play tonight. The passion on her face every time she screamed at the ref for a shitty call, or the way it lit up like a Christmas tree whenever I skated past her. The kiss. . .

My eyes fly open. Oh shit.

I think I might have feelings for my wife.

willa

"FAMILY MEETING!"

"Jesus Christ, Callahan," I complain, rubbing my right ear. "Look around you before you start screaming. We're all sitting right here."

"I'm standing. Not sitting," Maverick says, grinning at me from where he is, in fact, standing next to the hotel window. Ever since Harlow found the pictures of Ezra in New Hampshire alive and well after he was assumed dead for years, Mav has been in a great mood.

"Dada," Cora says in a tone that sounds disappointed. I laugh, hard. I love that little girl.

"What are we meeting about?" Harlow asks, passing me a paper plate that's already soaked in grease from the pepperoni pizza on it.

"Harlow and I are hosting Thanksgiving. You're all invited," he says and looks around the room, waiting for some sort of reaction.

"This could've been a text," Jo says, not having lifted her eyes from her phone since we checked in over an hour ago.

"Don't make me take away your invite, Demon Barbie," Cal says, shaking his finger at Jo, who acts like she hadn't even heard him.

"Was that it?" Belle asks.

"Well, we need to figure out who is bringing what," Cal says, a little defensively.

"We've been sleeping on the bus for a week. Everyone needs time to relax and sleep in a real bed. We can figure out what needs to be done later," Kai says, patting Cal on the shoulder as he stands. "You coming?" he asks Belle.

"I want to hang out with Willa. I feel like I've barely seen her, and we live on the same street."

I tense for a moment before forcing myself to smile. I had planned to go back to my room and call Declan. Something feels off between us, but I don't know what it is. It's like the week we spent together made the distance so much harder. I thought we were used to the distance, but maybe it was the closeness that we weren't ready for.

"Willa?"

"Sorry," I say to Belle. "I'd love to hang out. We can go back to my room and watch a movie. You can help me touch up my roots. The blonde is coming in."

Belle smiles, but it doesn't reach her eyes. I don't like the way she's examining me right now.

"Anyone else want to join us?" I ask, hopping up from the couch and throwing the rest of my pizza in the trash.

"I'm in," Mav says, pushing off the wall and following me to the door. Belle walks closely behind him, still giving me a weird look.

I pull out my phone and quickly text Declan while we walk to my room.

I can't call you tonight. Belle wants to
hang out.

HOCKEY BOY

You could both call. I'll be nice to her. I
won't even flirt.

I bite the inside of my lip and peek at my friends over my shoulder. They're quietly chatting about our manager, Jon. He's been acting weird lately too. Fucking men.

I'm sorry, hockey boy. Not tonight.

Did I do something wrong? I'm sorry if I haven't been as awake on our calls as I used to be. Coach Jones is running me ragged, and Boston plays differently than San Diego, so I've had a lot more to learn than you'd think. I've been really tired.

I'm really sorry, Princess.

I don't think I've ever felt more like an asshole than I do in this moment. I'm not trying to blow him off, but I don't want to answer the questions Belle is going to have.

I swipe my card against the reader and swing the door open. "You guys go pick a movie. I'm going to run downstairs and get some snacks."

I turn towards the elevator without waiting for them to answer. The moment I'm behind the elevator doors, I hit call.

"Princess," Declan answers, and I hate how unsure his voice sounds.

"I'm sorry, Dec. I didn't mean to make you feel like you

upset me somehow. You haven't," I rush to tell him. "I'm just stressed."

"You're my best friend, Willa. I miss you," he says softly.

"I miss you too, hockey boy."

"I'm sorry I interrupted your night."

"You didn't. If anything, they interrupted our night," I say, trying to force a laugh.

"How come you never call me when any of them are around?" he asks, surprising me so much it takes me a moment to answer.

"I wouldn't be able to hear a word you said. There's five or more people with me at any given time. I'm only alone when I get into bed at night and call you."

"Promise that's it? Because I was starting to feel like you were embarrassed by me," he says, laughing half-heartedly.

"I promise. I could never be embarrassed by you," I tell him truthfully.

Dec yawns loudly. "How much longer until you're home?"

"Six weeks," I say. "Actually, hold on." I look at the calendar on my phone and count the days. "Thirty-eight days until I'm home, but you won't be. So, forty-one until we're in the same place."

He sighs. "How is it we've gone years at a time without seeing each other and it wasn't a huge issue, but now it sucks so hard?"

I snort. "Probably because you can't sleep with everyone anymore."

"I don't want to. Haven't in a while."

I don't know what to say to that, so I just stare at my reflection in the shiny elevator door.

"You want to know what I think it is?" he says.

"Tell me," I say quietly.

"I think it's because now I know what it's like to have you in my life permanently. Is our friendship lifelong anyway? Sure as fuck is. But now we live together, and I get to hang out with my best friend every night. When we're in the same city, anyway. Now that I've had that, I don't want to go back."

"I think you might be right, hockey boy."

"When aren't I?" he says. I laugh but can still hear him yawn.

"Get some sleep. You have a tough game tomorrow." They're playing Seattle, who came out of preseason as the favorites.

"You're going to watch, right?" he asks, yawning again.

"I'll be onstage while you're playing, but Nate is recording it for me."

"Who the fuck is Nate?" he asks, suddenly more awake.

I laugh and shake my head. "Our tour manager. He's married and also like fifty. Relax."

"You work with too many men, wife."

I laugh so hard I start wheezing. "You're nuts. Get some sleep, husband. I'll text you with my notes on your game tomorrow."

He laughs lightly. "Oh, I'm sure you will. Good night, Princess."

"Good night, hockey boy."

The door pings and opens, revealing Jo eyeing me suspiciously. "What are you doing?"

"Uh, going to my room," I say, stepping around her. I never hit a button for a floor, so I'm still on mine.

"Right," she says, hitting the lobby button. Her eyes stay on mine as the door shuts.

"Perfect," I grumble to myself and head back to my room. I walk in to see Belle and Mav on my bed watching ESPN. "What are you doing?" I ask, my voice shaking. Do they know about me marrying Declan? I have an alert set, but the news is quiet so far.

"Mav wanted to watch the interview with Jasper. That baseball player that knew Ezra. He threw no balls or something," Belle says.

"A no hitter?" I ask, instantly relaxing. Belle knows nothing about sports. Mav might know even less. Kai and Cal are huge sports fans. I've worried about them figuring something out before I can tell them. "He threw a perfect game?" I ask Mav after Belle shrugs.

"That's what her dad said." He gestures to Belle. "Hey, where are the snacks?" he asks when he looks at me.

"There wasn't anything good," I say, crawling in bed next to Belle. She turns to face me, examining my face like she can find all my secrets written there.

"Are you seeing someone?"

"Who?" Mav asks. "Her options are Jon or your dad. Actually, I think Harrison is single too." He looks around Belle so he can see me. "Do you have a thing for older men?"

I roll my eyes. "No, I don't have a thing for my friends' dads."

"But you're seeing someone?" Belle asks.

"No, I'm not."

"Promise? You'd tell me, right? I know I wasn't around for a few years, but I thought we were close again."

Well, that hurt my heart. "I promise I'll tell you if I'm

seeing someone." I lean my head on her shoulder. "We're good, Belle. It's like those missing years never happened."

"There he is!" Mav says, pointing at the TV where Jasper is speaking with an ESPN analyst.

"Why are we watching this?" I whisper to Belle.

"He thinks he can get some clues from Jasper about Ezra," she whispers.

I lean up so I can see her face. She shrugs and turns a worried look towards Mav. Jasper may have known Ezra, but he told us he doesn't know where he is now. So I'm not sure what Maverick thinks he's going to get out of this.

My eyes feel heavy, so I let them close, letting sleep take me while snuggling up to my best friend. But in the moment between awake and asleep, I can't help feeling like it's the wrong best friend.

declan

"HOW MUCH LONGER?"

"Twenty-four days," I answer Gideon.

"I don't know how you guys do it. Away games are bad enough for me and Maggie."

"Her tour was supposed to be over by the time the season started," I say, sulking. Gideon nods in understanding.

"Listen up," Coach says. "We have a new team photographer." A man steps out from behind Coach. He's tall, maybe an inch or two shorter than me, but he's muscular. His build plus the burly beard and long dark, curly hair make him look like he lives in the mountains and chops a lot of wood. "This is Ben Miller. We poached him from New York."

"Are you the guy that takes those shots from crazy angles? Your work kicks ass," Davis says. He's a d-man on my line and usually pretty quiet.

Ben smirks and nods.

"Unlike the other photographers, Ben is going to be

around as much as possible. He's going to be getting pictures of practice, games, travel, you idiots dicking around in the locker room, you name it. Management wants to make this team all anyone can talk about."

"I don't think Monroe's ugly mug is going to help with that," Slava says. I throw the wadded-up ball of stick tape at him.

"That ugly mug pulled a smoking hot wife," Martinez says.

"Dude, quit hitting on my wife!" I complain.

"It's got him to stop hitting on my wife, so I'm all for it," Oliver Bouchard, our goalie, says as he shrugs on his practice jersey.

"Get your asses on the ice and try to look impressive," Coach says, leaving us with Ben.

"Do you have a wife?" I ask Ben.

"No. Never will."

"Husband?" I ask.

"Not yet," he says, but his brown eyes are pinned to me, waiting for my reaction.

"Can you get one so my wife isn't Martinez's target?" I ask, smiling.

Ben smirks and looks over at Martinez, who shrugs. "I'm an equal opportunity instigator."

"What's the plan?" Gideon asks, nodding to the camera slung across Ben's chest.

"I'm going to get some shots of you guys getting ready. Some close-ups of you tying your laces, strapping on pads, things like that. Keep your compression shirts on and the bottom half of your gear, and I'll get some candids of you talking and laughing."

"You don't want shots of our abs?" Martinez asks, seeming genuinely shocked.

Ben shakes his head. "This isn't about thirst traps. We're going for teamwork, friendship, family friendly, that type of angle."

"Can you send me some good ones to send to my wife?" Gideon asks.

"Me too," I say. "But mostly me. My wife isn't able to go to as many games as his wife."

"Wait. My wife is filming a movie in Greece right now. I want pictures to send her," Bouchard complains.

Ben raises his hands. "All photos that aren't being used by the team are going into a drive that you will all have access to. I'm sure you can find something there."

"Alright. Get dressed and let Ben work his magic," Gideon says.

The mood in the locker room lightens significantly with the promise of action shots for our wives. Most of the guys are either married or have girlfriends they want to show off to. We're coming off of a tough loss to Dallas last night, and we have to go straight from this practice to the bus to travel to Pittsburg, so the break in moping to take pictures was really needed.

I've done what Finn asked and thought about how I feel about Willa. I can't keep denying that there's something there. Something more than the deep friendship we've always had. But I'm not getting that same feeling from her. I want to ask her on a date when we're both back home, but I'm starting to doubt she'd accept.

I pour all my frustration into practice. I shoot on the net like we're down by one and the clock has seconds left. I go through the drills like I'm trying out for the team and trying to impress Coach. Sweat pours down my body, and I'm breathing heavily by the time Coach calls an end to practice.

"You didn't need to go that hard for the camera," Ben says from behind the lens as he snaps pictures of us filing back into the locker room.

"I was just working through some stuff, so I didn't take it with me to the game tomorrow."

"Did it help?" he asks, aiming the lens at Slava, who is taking his shoulder pads off.

I sigh. "Not really."

"Monroe!"

"Yeah, Coach," I say. I just walked into the hotel with the rest of the guys, so I can't imagine what I could've done wrong already.

"You're rooming with Ben for the rest of the season," he says, handing me my room key.

I turn around and look for Ben. "Sweet. I got an upgrade."

"Oh, fuck off," Marcus Wells says. He's a rookie and the alternate goalie. I got stuck rooming with him because I was the new guy. The dude snores so loud it's like trying to sleep with a weed whacker right next to your head.

"Let's go, Benny boy. I need to call my wife before I pass out for the night." I start walking and I feel him follow me.

"What's that like?" he asks.

"Having a wife?"

"No. Just the distance part. How do you make it work?"

I shrug. I don't want to give him bad advice since my marriage isn't exactly conventional, and I'm really not sure I'm making it work. "We met when we were kids. We've been friends all these years with an entire country between us. There's always been distance. We make sure to call each other as often as we can. And I plan to keep her to myself the moment she's home."

Ben nods and swipes the key card on our door. I follow him in and claim the bed next to the window.

"What about your guy? You dealing with the distance?"

Ben sits on his bed and sighs. "We've been apart for a while. I don't think the distance would matter. I just haven't been honest about some things, and I don't know what that will do to our relationship. If we even have one."

I nod in understanding. I have no idea what my relationship status is. Other than married to my best friend that I may or may not have more than friendly feelings for and who may not return those feelings. I can't tell Ben that, though.

"Honesty's the best policy."

Ben throws his head back and laughs. "You sound like my mom."

I laugh with him. "I sound like my mom too."

"Here, give me your number. I'll text you a picture I think your wife might like," he says, handing me his phone. I quickly type my number in and hand it back. My phone pings moments later with a picture message.

"Fuck yeah. Thanks man," I say.

"You got it. I'm going to shower while you call your wife." He heads to the bathroom while I look at the picture he sent. It's from right after practice ended. He got a closeup with a lens that must be crazy expensive with the amount of detail I can make out in it. My hair is wet from sweat and sticking up in every direction after taking my helmet off. You can even see the steam coming off me from the temperature difference between the ice and my body. I'm smiling at something Gideon said and looking just past where the camera must have been. It's a fucking great candid. I send it off to Willa immediately.

You have time to talk to this sexy beast?

PRINCESS

How could I not? Look at him. He's smoking. Literally.

I call her, and she answers immediately.

"Hey, hockey boy. That's a great picture of you. Who took it?"

"We got a new photographer. His name's Ben. He's also my new roommate."

"Does that mean you'll actually get some sleep?" she asks. I've been complaining about how hard it is sleeping on the road with Wells.

"I fucking hope so."

We chat about our day, which has become the norm these past few weeks. I feel like Willa is pulling away, but I have no evidence of that other than just a feeling. So I never bring it up or mention that I can't sleep when I'm home either because thoughts of losing her keep me awake all night.

Ben gets out of the shower and climbs into his bed, keeping his back to me like he's still trying to give me privacy.

"I have to get some sleep. I'll call you tomorrow."

"Good night, hockey boy. Kick Pittsburg's ass tomorrow," she says, her voice insanely cute when she's sleepy.

"I will. Good night, Princess."

willa

"WHERE ARE YOU GOING?"

I freeze in my tracks. Turning around, I see Belle and Jo heading in my direction. We just finished our last San Diego show, and I'm rushing to get to Declan's game. He doesn't know I'm coming since I wasn't supposed to make a game until New York next week. Our show was supposed to be last night, but we had to move it to tonight due to some electricity issue the venue was having.

"I told you I have plans." I shrug.

"Anything fun?" Belle asks, and I can tell she wants to tag along. Which means Kai would want to tag along. Then Cal would hear about it and tell Maverick who would also want to come. Then Cal would feel left out but wouldn't go unless Harlow could come too. And Harlow would insist Jo be invited. It would be a disaster I don't want to deal with while watching my fake husband play hockey.

"I'm going to a hockey game, remember?" Belle knows I love hockey, and the rest of the band knew I went to games during our tours in the past. So it was easy to be honest with them. About where I'm going, at least. The why is something I still haven't figured out how to tell them. I need to figure it out before Thanksgiving, which is the deadline I gave myself. That's two weeks from tomorrow.

"I'll never get your obsession with that sport," Belle says. "It's cold and everything moves too fast. There's no way to tell what's happening."

I laugh and give her a quick hug. "There is, if you pay attention." Belle scrunches her nose. I look at the time on my phone. "I have to go. Warm-ups are almost over."

"Are you staying out? The bus is leaving at eight tomorrow morning." Jo raises an eyebrow, like my answer is going to determine something for her.

"I wasn't planning on it. Should I text you if I'm going to be out past midnight, Mom?"

She rolls her eyes and starts walking away. "Eight on the dot or we leave without you," she calls over her shoulder.

"Have fun tonight. Take one of the players home. Let loose. You've been just as stressed as the rest of us," Belle says, winking at me.

"Did you just tell me I need to get laid?" I laugh. Belle shrugs as she walks past me into the dressing room to get her things. I follow her and grab my bag that has a better-quality wig and Declan's jersey in it.

"Yup!"

"I'll work on that. Don't let the bus leave without me!" I yell as I run out the door.

"No promises," she calls back.

"Your car is waiting at the back entrance, Willa."

"Thanks, Nate!" I say, running past him.

I text Maggie the moment I'm in the car.

I'm on my way! I might be a little late!

MAGGIE

Don't worry about it. I'll wait out front for you. I got us front row seats! Don't ask how. The guys are going to be so surprised!

I could kiss you.

That would REALLY surprise them.

I let out a surprise laugh. I've been texting Maggie a lot since we exchanged numbers at the first game. She's really sweet and has a funny side that I wasn't expecting.

I dig through my bag and quickly throw on my wig and jersey. "Shit. Where is it?" I mutter to myself as I blindly search for my wedding band. "Ah huh!" I yell, startling the driver.

"Are you okay, ma'am?" he asks.

"Yes. Sorry. I thought I had lost my wedding ring. Just found it," I tell him, sliding the sparkly, diamond encrusted ring on my finger. He just nods and continues driving. I relax into my seat and smile.

"I'm so sorry!" I pant, running up to Maggie, where she's standing at the entrance of the arena. "We hit traffic. I made my driver let me out and ran here." I double over and grab my knees, sucking in air.

"Let's go. We missed the first period and . . ." she pauses and bites her lip while dragging me through the arena and to our seats. She barely stopped long enough for someone to scan the tickets on her phone.

"What? What's happening?" I ask, having mostly caught my breath. My hand is still in hers, and I'm letting her lead because she seems to know where to go.

"Your husband is kind of playing like complete garbage. He's missing passes and skating like someone filled his skates with cement. They're down two to zero already."

My eyes widen in alarm. "Is he injured? He didn't mention an injury. I talked to him right before I went on stage tonight." I know his knees have been bothering him. He has ice on them more often than not.

"I'm not sure. I was watching the game on my phone while I waited. I wasn't close enough to tell."

We find our seats just in time for the start of the second period. I watch for all of a few seconds before I see what's she's talking about. Declan manages to miss an easy pass from Ivanov and get checked pretty hard into the boards in the first minute of play.

"What the hell is going on with him?" I mutter.

"He's overhyped, that's what." I turn to the man next to me. The asshole is in a San Diego jersey.

"Oh, is he? Is that what you were saying last year when he was the one leading the team in goals? Or maybe it was when he secured the playoff spot? No thanks to the rest of your shit team."

"I. . . Well, he, uh — you see the thing is," the man stutters, cheeks turning red.

"The thing is, he gave nine years to San Diego and suddenly he's the villain because he's now with Boston.

Grow the fuck up." I turn back to the game in time to watch Declan shoot and miss wildly.

"Maybe there's something going on with his eyes," Maggie says, watching him with genuine concern.

I stand and bang on the glass when Declan skates by. It could get me kicked out of the game, but the refs are on the other side of the ice trying to prevent Ivanov from punching one of the San Diego guys. Dec turns to the noise, his face pained, probably from how badly he's playing. I watch as he sees me without seeing me, but then does a double take. The way his face lights up when he realizes it's me will be imprinted in my memory for the rest of my life.

"Princess!" he yells, ripping his glove off and pressing his hand to the glass in front of me. I put my hand against the glass on the other side and smile.

"Get it together! This asshole wants you to lose," I say and point with my thumb at the man next to me. Declan eyes him, and I can feel the man shrink under his stare.

"You got it, wife!" he yells just as the whistle blows. He skates back, quickly alerting Gideon that Maggie is here. Gideon beams at his wife before schooling his face back into game mode. They take their positions, and Gideon wins the face off. He passes it to Declan, who doesn't miss it this time.

"Looks like he just needed you," Maggie says with a small laugh. I watch Dec power his way past San Diego's defense like they're not even there and sink the puck right between their goalie's knees. The goalie also happens to be Finn. And he does not look happy with his old roomie right now.

"That's how you do it, hockey boy!" I scream. Maggie and I are jumping and hugging like they just won the Stanley Cup, her brown curls slapping me in the face. Not bringing the game to two to one. They're not even winning.

Declan skates in front of me again and taps his heart. I tap mine and smile. Gideon is right next to him, smiling and making a heart with his gloved hands at Maggie.

I swear you can feel the mood in the entire arena change. Where it was light and happy before, the air is suddenly heavy with stress. San Diego was winning on their home ice against their old superstar player. Now they're tied thanks to a goal by Ivanov with an assist by Gideon.

By the third period, the tension between Finn and Dec is at its peak. Declan has taken all the shots on goal since the period started. Which is a mistake because Finn knows how Declan plays better than anyone. The shot through his knees was lucky. I wish I could text him and tell him to let someone else try.

"Will I get kicked out if I go over to the bench and try to talk to the players?" I ask Maggie.

"Definitely," she says and laughs at me like I was making a joke.

Our seats are close to San Diego's goal. So the next time Finn covers the puck and the whistle blows, I wave my arms to get Declan's attention. He sees me and quickly skates over. There's no way he'll hear me now with how loud the crowd has become. So I make a line across my throat with my fingers in a *stop* gesture and then point at Gideon and Ivanov and nod. Declan frowns, and I quickly do it again. He nods like he understands, and I point at Finn, make an x with my arms and point back at him. I watch Dec's eyes light up with understanding, and then he quickly frowns. He knows what I'm saying, but he wants to score. There's no time for anything else because he has to get back in line.

"Do you think that worked?" Maggie asks. I shrug because I have no idea if he's going to listen to me.

San Diego wins the face off, but it's quickly recovered by Adam Rogers, a recent trade from Montreal and Martinez's defensive partner. Rogers gets the puck to Dec, and I sigh, ready to watch Finn predict exactly what Declan is about to do. Again.

"He passed!" Maggie shouts. I sit up straight. Gideon has the puck, but San Diego is on him. He's able to make a quick pass to Ivanov before being slammed into the boards. Maggie grabs my arm and gasps. I'm too invested in the play to comfort her. Plus, I can see Gideon skating back into the play, so I know he isn't injured.

Ivanov is trying to line up a shot, but he can't get an opening. He passes to Dec. "Dammit," I mutter. Declan skates around the large man blocking him and lifts his stick for a slapshot. I sigh, knowing Finn could block that shot from Dec in his sleep.

But the puck doesn't speed towards Finn's waiting glove. It's slipped back to Gideon, who shoots for the top right of the net. The buzzer on the goal sounds moments before the one ending the last period and the game.

"They did it!" I scream, leaping up and hugging Maggie. Our guys both point at us with their sticks moments before they're surrounded by their team. "He listened," I say, surprised. He always takes my critiques after a game, but I've never seen him actually listen to what I'm saying.

"Let's go get to them before the press wants to talk to them," Maggie says, grabbing my hand. I follow her, feeling happier than I have in weeks.

87

declan

"WHAT DID Willa do to get your head on straight?" Martinez asks.

"She showed up," I shrug. I'm smiling. I have been since I saw her face in the stands. Gideon catches up to me as we make our way down the tunnel and back to the locker rooms.

"Dec!"

"Giddy!"

We both turn and see our wives holding hands and running towards us. Willa has her wig in her other hand, letting her lilac locks fly freely behind her. I drop my stick and gloves and run for Willa. Well, run as much as you can in skates on a rubber floor. She leaps into my arms like she always does, but I hold her extra tight this time.

"I missed you so fucking much," I say into her hair, breathing in that candy apple scent that's become an addiction. "How are you here?" I don't give her time to answer before I crash my lips into hers. She hesitates for a moment before she lets me in. I kiss her like I'm trying to memorize the feel of her lips, the tiny noises she makes, just her. She feels right in my arms, even with all my gear in the way. Kissing her makes my chest constrict and my heart beat faster than it was while I was just skating. And I know in that moment how absolutely fucked I am.

"Monroe. Banks. Get moving. You have press in five minutes. Bus leaves for the airport in thirty," Coach barks.

"Fuck," I mutter, pulling back from Willa, but then going in for a quick kiss before I put her down.

"That was some kiss, hockey boy." Willa's voice is playful, but there's a small crease in her brow that tells me she's confused. I grab her face and kiss her again, slowly and with a softness I hope she understands. From the look on her face when I pull away, she's not feeling the same things I am. That's okay, though. I have plenty of time for her to catch up.

"I'll call you when we land. Thank you for coming." I kiss her temple. "You're the best surprise."

I turn from her and jog to the locker room, Gideon on my heels. "Let's go, Giddy!"

I hear him curse under his breath. I just laugh him off. This was one of the best nights of my entire fucking life.

Now I just have to figure out how to ask my wife to date me.

***

The reporters were brutal. All they wanted to know was who the blonde woman was and how she got me to pass the puck instead of shooting. No matter how many times Gideon and Coach tried to help me divert the questions, they wouldn't give up. I got up and left, not willing to give them anything until Willa is ready.

"You would've lost if she didn't show," Finn says. He's walking towards me, probably having watched that nightmare.

"Probably," I admit.

"Definitely. You were playing worse than I've ever seen you."

"I scored on you." I cross my arms and frown.

"Once and it was a fluke. If I had known you suddenly remembered how to play hockey, I would have seen you as more of a threat," he says with a small smile. "You didn't get another chance."

I curse him out under my breath and then hug him. Finn hates hugs, so he's stiff at first before patting me on the back. "I miss you too, buddy."

"Monroe!" Coach barks.

"I gotta go. I'll call you soon." Finn shakes his head and leaves me to my verbal beating.

"Sorry, Coach. I couldn't handle all their questions about Willa."

He sighs, looking exhausted. "I get it, son. I understand why you two want privacy, but you're going to need to go public. And soon. I'm already getting emails from PR wanting information. The team wants your image clean and even though you've stayed out of the press like you promised, it won't be good enough. They want the wife and the story."

"I can't force her to do that just to protect myself," I argue, even though everyone on the planet knowing Willa's mine is becoming more appealing by the minute.

"No, but you can ask her. She's your wife. She comes to your games. It's not going to stay a secret, Declan. Figure it out."

"Yes, Coach," I say to his back. He's walking away, already having dismissed me.

I rush to the locker room to grab my bag and then head onto the bus. I take my now usual seat next to Ben. He's already uploaded tonight's photos onto a tablet and is going through them. He pulls back his hair when he's editing like this, which reveals a thick, jagged, white scar on his forehead. I want to ask him about it, but Gideon said it was rude.

"You didn't get any pictures of my wife, did you?" I ask.

"Your wife was there?" He looks up at me in confusion. I may have spent a lot of time last night complaining that I wasn't going to be seeing Willa for another week. He fell asleep in the middle of my rant.

"Yeah. She surprised me." A smile breaks out on my face just thinking about the way I felt when I saw her. The heaviness in my heart that I've been carrying around all these weeks instantly lifted with her little frown. I love when she gets angry and puts me in my place. She's fucking adorable.

Ben releases a breath and his shoulders relax. "Thank fuck."

I laugh a little too loudly. There's a lot of grumbling and "shut ups" thrown my way from the guys trying to nap. Which is honestly stupid since we're heading for the airport, not another city.

"I didn't get a shot of her. I wasn't at the right angle for that, and San Diego's security were being dicks about where they would let me go to get a shot."

"I'm sure they didn't want you to get a shot of me and make them look bad. It was their choice not to resign me, and I just made them look dumb."

Ben chuckles. "I thought you were cheating on your wife," he says with a sigh. "Then I was annoyed with myself because I got some really good shots of you interacting with her." He tips the tablet so that I can see the screen too and shows me the shots he took.

"I would never cheat on my wife," I say, not looking at what he's showing me because I'm still hung up on what he just said. "I would never risk losing her."

"I thought that too, but then you spent over an hour complaining that you wouldn't be seeing her. Add that to what these pictures are telling me, and you can see where I would get confused."

I look down at the pictures. There's one of me touching my heart, a huge smile on my face. The next one is of me and Gideon, our arms around each other and our sticks pointing towards the stands. You can tell from our faces we're pointing at people we care about. The last one is of me with my hand on the glass, a look of complete awe on my face. Willa's hand is visible, but that's it.

"You didn't take pictures of her on purpose, but you still took them of me when you thought I was cheating?" I ask.

"I could've probably taken a picture of her, but I would have had to change angles, and I was there to shoot the team, not the crowd," he says. "And I took them because of how you look. Like you were in love."

"You thought I was in love with a mistress?"

"No." Ben pinches the bridge of his nose. "I was praying

it was your wife. But I didn't know for sure. If I was certain, I wouldn't even be sitting next to you."

"Ouch."

"I've had enough of morally shitty people in my life," he shrugs. "I won't choose to have a friend like that."

"Does that mean you'll send me those?" I ask.

He laughs quietly. "Yeah, I'll send them to you and then delete them. I caught the tail end of that press conference."

"You're a really good friend, Benny boy."

"Just send them to your secret wife like you know you want to."

"Hey! You have a secret boyfriend," I point out.

"He's not a secret. It's just complicated," Ben argues.

"I like that. I'm stealing it. My wife isn't a secret, it's just complicated. Sounds way better than what I've been saying."

"What have you been saying?"

"That she's so hot she'll melt brains. So I'm basically saving lives."

Ben sighs loudly and turns back to his tablet.

I smile and grab my phone. There's already a text waiting for me.

PRINCESS

You want to tell me what was going on with you before I got there?

No.

I was having an off night. Being on my old home ice was weird. Having to shoot against Finn was even weirder.

That was part of my problem, so I'm not lying. I just think telling her the real reason was how much my heart hurt from missing her should be an in-person conversation.

I didn't even think of that.

It's okay, Princess. Seeing you was the perfect distraction.

I still can't believe you were there. Top five best nights of my life.

What's number one?

Hasn't happened yet.

You're going to get the cup this year. I can feel it.

I smirk. I agree with her, but that's not what would take the number one spot.

Don't jinx it!

The bus comes to a stop at the private airstrip. Our team plane is waiting.

I have to board now. Call me after tomorrow's show?

I will. Good night, hockey boy.

Good night, Princess.

"Did she like them?" Ben asks. He's standing in the aisle waiting for me.

"I didn't send them. She's not ready to see them yet."

Ben's brows furrow as he tries to make sense of what I'm saying. "I don't understand women," he grumbles.

"Me either, my man," Martinez says, holding out his fist for Ben to bump. He does before shaking his head and leaving the bus.

"How many more days?" Gideon asks, following me off the bus and straight onto the plane.

"Ten. She'll be at the New York game next week, but then she goes straight home from there, and we're on the road for three more days."

"Maggie wants to get together for dinner whenever you're both free. She said to invite you to our place. Apparently, Willa was telling her all about how the two of you almost burned down a forest more than once trying to cook hot dogs."

I bark out a laugh. "Yeah, neither of us should be responsible for cooking if you want to be able to eat it."

"So, you'll ask her?" he asks, stopping in front of his usual seat next to Ivanov, who is somehow already asleep.

"Sure. Just tell us when."

He pats my shoulder and takes his seat. I find mine next to Ben. He's back to editing on his tablet. I put my headphones in and close my eyes.

Ten more days until I tell Willa how I feel.

willa

"GO AWAY," I grumble to whoever is knocking on my door before the sun is even up.

"Open the door, Willa." Jo's voice is low and stern. Like she's trying not to wake anyone else. I look at the red numbers on the hotel alarm clock. It's six in the morning. At least I'm not late for the bus.

I stumble my way to the door and open it, cringing when the light from the hallway hits my eyes. "Why are you waking me up this early?"

She grabs my hand and pulls me back into the room and onto the small couch. I yelp when she flips the lights on before sitting next to me.

"This better be an emergency," I hiss, still trying to get my eyes to adjust to the light, and my brain to wake up.

"There's a rumor going around small parts of the internet that you're the side piece of some big shot hockey player."

"What?" I screech. How the fuck did anyone find out?

Maybe I've been more careless than I realize. Wait. "Side piece?"

"You're not denying you're with a hockey player?" Jo asks, locking onto me like a shark to blood in the water. It doesn't help that I've been sleeping in a man's shirt this whole tour. I stole a few of Declan's when I was packing. They're more comfortable than women's pajamas.

I sigh and slump onto the couch. "Jo, it's early, and you woke me out of a sound sleep. Can you please spell this out for me?"

"This picture is circulating. None of the big news outlets have picked it up yet. Probably because the rumors you were even there don't have any photographic evidence to back it up." She hands me her phone. It's a picture of Gideon pointing his stick at the crowd after his last goal. Whoever took it was on the opposite side of the ice and cropped out Declan. It's on some weird forum I've never seen and loads of people are claiming to have seen me at the game and then later climbing into a limo with Gideon.

I snort. "Jo, they don't leave in limos."

"That's the problem with this?" she says, giving me a look that makes me feel like an idiot.

"I'm not with Gideon! I'm friends with his wife. She was sitting right next to me. Neither of us are even in that picture." It's not like Jo to believe these rumors. "Why are you asking me this? You had to have known this was fake."

Jo doesn't say anything. Instead, she turns on the TV and puts ESPN on. They're reporting about last night's game. Or more specifically, the press conference that happened after. Where both Gideon and Declan walked out.

"Okay?" I ask. "They weren't asking about the game, so the players left. Is that my fault too?" I'm getting defensive.

"I think you're involved with one of those men."

"So?"

"Willa. Come on. If you are and your friends find out through ESPN, they're going to be hurt. If they're hurt, the music suffers. The music suffers, my job gets harder." She's glaring at me now, but I'm angry.

"So that's what this is? Not concern from a friend to another friend. You just don't want me to make more work for you. Got it. You can leave now."

"Willa . . ."

"No. My relationship status is none of your concern. No one will be reporting anything."

"I'm sorry, I just —" Jo starts, her eyes downcast like she may actually be sorry, but I don't care.

"You just knew I was in a relationship. You knew I wasn't spending nights at my house since you also live there. You knew I was dodging questions about where I was going. You know what else you knew?" Jo doesn't answer. She sits still, face impassive as she lets me speak. "You knew I was happier than I've been in a long time."

"With a married man, Willa?" Jo says, not keeping the judgement from her voice.

"Yes. With a married man." I leave it at that. She doesn't need to know I'm the one he's married to. She doesn't need to know he's been my best friend for most of my life. Hell, she doesn't get to know any of that. "I'll see you on the bus."

I go into the bathroom and slam the door. I'm angry. I'm angry she jumped to conclusions before even asking me. I'm angry she thinks so little of me that she would assume what she did. But I'm even more angry with myself. I should've been honest with everyone this whole time, but I don't know how.

I wasn't lying when I told Declan I was afraid someone would slip, and he would get in trouble. Thanksgiving is creeping up quickly, and I thought I would have a solution by then. I promised myself I would have a solution by then.

"Fuck," I mutter under my breath. The only way this is going to work without hurting everyone is if Declan and I continue to do what we're doing.

Put on a really convincing show.

SIXTEEN

declan

"IT'S A SUNDAY NIGHT GAME," Diego says.

"Are you talking to yourself?" I ask him, unsure why he's telling me that the game we're playing against New York tonight is on a Sunday. Like I don't know what day it is or that I get to see Willa tonight.

"It means you're competing with Sunday Night Football."

"So? What do you want me to do about it? Land a perfect triple axel in the middle of a breakaway?"

Ben snickers from where he's sitting on his bed and pretending not to listen. Diego is leaning against the hotel desk and glaring at me. He's the one speaking in riddles, so I don't know how I'm the one to be mad at right now.

"Your coach has been holding everyone back. Insisting you need time to figure it out," Diego says, pulling at his usually perfectly styled hair. "So they're on my ass instead. I'm getting calls and emails from the team's PR and social media departments. Hell, I even got an email from one of the owners this morning."

"Why is everyone so interested in my wife? None of the other guys have to parade their wives around for the media." As far as I can tell, no one knows I'm married. People are just speculating about who the woman was at the San Diego game. Even then, that's died down because Willa hasn't been to a game since that one.

"The media know who their wives are. They never kept them a secret. You two wanting privacy has inadvertently caused a clusterfuck for your team," Diego says and Ben snorts.

"Dude, what do I do?" I ask Ben.

"Make the Bruisers' media team earn their money."

I laugh and point at Ben while staring at Diego. "I like that answer."

Diego lets out a frustrated sigh. "Don't you want people to know who you're married to? She's. . . *her*," he says, his eyes doing the far-off thing it does whenever he gets all starstruck about Willa.

"I really hate when you get weird like that. She's my wife. Not yours."

"And yet, no one knows that."

"Can we circle back to this after the holidays? I haven't slept in the same bed as my wife in seven fucking weeks, Diego. I refuse to have the first thing I say to her be about strangers wanting a look into our lives. It's honestly frustrating that I even have to have this conversation."

"I agree with that," Ben adds. "Privacy isn't a crime."

"Thank you." I gesture to Ben with a *see* motion.

"Declan not keeping his private life private was the problem in the first place," Ben adds.

"Hey!" I complain.

"Speaking of that," Diego says. "Bethany was at the San Diego game."

"So?"

"Rumor is she wasn't happy about your actions and cried to daddy. I guess she thought you two would have some romantic reunion."

I groan into my hands.

"Coming forward as a married man with happy pictures of you and your wife would be the easiest way to get her to back off."

"I hate you," I mutter to my dick.

"I'll do a photoshoot for you once you figure it out," Ben offers.

"Thanks, Benny boy."

"So you'll go public?" Diego asks, his face annoyingly hopeful.

Do I want to claim Willa publicly? Hell yes I do. But I want to do it when she's really mine.

"Go away, Diego. I'm not talking about this until I'm ready."

Diego curses under his breath but leaves like I asked.

"Is Bethany going to be a problem?" Ben asks me once the door shuts behind Diego.

"She might try, but I'm married. The owners of the Bruisers are aware of that. So even if her dad tries to complain to them, they know I'm not with her."

"Let me know when you want that photoshoot. I have a feeling you're going to need it," Ben says, getting up and gathering his equipment.

"Can you get a shot of her watching me play tonight?" I ask as I follow him out.

"Where is she sitting?"

"The wrong side again, probably. Maggie is in some season ticket exchange group. So the seats she gets for the two of them are in the home team section." Neither of the girls liked the tickets Gideon and I could get for them. They weren't close enough.

"I'll try, but that's the side of the ice I'll be on too. It'll likely be the back of her head."

"She'll be the one in the middle of a bunch of New York fans wearing my jersey."

Ben laughs. "Hard to miss."

"See you on the bus," I call to him. He waves as he heads for the ice to scope out his angles, and I go in the opposite direction to the locker room.

I'll see her tonight and then in three days, I'll ask her to be mine.

New York is out for blood. They're playing like we're on game seven of the Stanley Cup finals. Not a regular season game in November. A normal season goes well into April. June if you make it all the way. There's no reason for them to be playing like this so early in the season.

Willa has been screaming at the refs and players both. Even Maggie, who usually watches happily, is angrily shaking her fists. The crowd seems split. We're on their home ice so the cheers for them should be louder, but even their fans seem confused.

"There's a target on your back," Bouchard says to me.

We're in the locker room between the second and third period while they flood the ice.

"I don't know what the fuck for."

"Maybe they saw the San Diego game and knew because your wife is here, you're going to play better," Gideon says. His blond hair is sticking up in all directions from the sweat and his helmet. He looks almost wild.

"That's crazy. Like actually crazy. I wasn't even the one who scored the winning goal for that game. They should be after you," I point out.

They are after me, for whatever reason. I've been thrown into the boards more times tonight than my entire high school career combined. And that was a lot because I liked to instigate back then.

I groan when I lean over to retie my skates. My whole body hurts. My knees want to give up. Part of me wants to let them win so the beating can be over.

"We just need to hold them off. We're up one nothing. Normally that kind of lead wouldn't be good enough, but I don't want you boys hurt and that's what will happen," Coach says. He turns to me. "Monroe, I think you need to be pulled."

I flinch, even though I know it's not because of how I'm playing. No one wants to hear they're being benched.

"I want to stay dressed and on the bench in case I need to go back in."

Coach looks at my knees where a trainer has taped bags of ice to each one. "We have a real chance of taking the cup this year, Declan. But not if you're out on injury for half the season."

I sigh and drop my head into my hands. "Yes. Coach," I

mumble between my fingers. It's not worth fighting him on tonight.

"Text Willa and have her come back and sit with you," Gideon says once Coach is out of earshot. "You'll get to spend more time with her," he says, and winks.

I wish my team good luck as they file out of the locker room. I hit the showers quickly and then text Willa.

> I'm benched. Come back to the locker room?

PRINCESS

> What the hell did you do to get benched?

> Come talk to me.

"I was already on my way back here when you didn't come out of the tunnel."

I look up at her. Her cheeks are red either from the cold of the rink or how angry she was watching the game, but her eyes sparkle when they meet mine. She's fucking beautiful.

"Hi, Princess."

She walks over to me and kneels in front of where I'm sitting, taking over taping the ice back on my knees. I shift a little to hide how hard the sight of her on her knees for me instantly made me.

"What happened, hockey boy?" she asks, taking a seat next to me on the bench.

"Coach didn't want to risk New York successfully taking me out."

"Why are they after you? You barely played them when you were with San Diego."

"I don't know. I wish I did."

Willa wraps her arms around my waist. The game is playing on a TV across from us. There's no sound, but we can still watch the third period play out from here.

"You look a little silly wearing a suit with ice taped to your knees," she says, breaking the silence.

"I would tape ice to my whole body right now if I could," I admit.

She tries to pull away, but I hold her tight. "I don't want to hurt you."

"You're not. You're making me feel better," I say, dropping a kiss to the top of her head.

"They're not doing it anymore," she says, pointing to the TV.

I watch a few plays. She's right. I'm not there to target anymore and now they're playing a much less dirty game.

"I really was the target. I don't understand."

"Does Bethany have any connections here?" Willa asks.

I shrug. "Probably, but she would have connections with other teams, too, and this is the first time it's happened."

"You need to be careful."

"You worried about me, Princess?" I smile at her, but she frowns.

"Yes, Declan. I would die if anything happened to you." She looks so distraught that I pull her into my lap and hold her as tightly as I can without hurting her.

"Nothing is going to happen to me. I promise I'll be careful."

"Good," she mumbles against my chest.

"The game is almost over, and the guys are going to be back in here," I sigh.

"I'll see you in three days, hockey boy." She gets up from my lap, kisses my cheek and leaves me alone in the locker room.

I hate this part, being separated from her. I was hoping this wouldn't be my last season, but I know it is. My knees are hurting worse after each game and are so stiff in the mornings it makes getting out of bed miserable. If this was a year ago and I had to retire, I would have been lost and angry.

But now I have Willa. In whatever way she'll have me. I'll travel the world while she sells out stadiums, if that's what she wants. I don't care as long as I'm with her.

willa

I WANTED to be at Declan's apartment when he got home, but Belle reminded me I'm supposed to be bringing mac and cheese to Thanksgiving tomorrow. She actually asked me if she should have the fire department on standby when I attempt to cook it, but it reminded me nonetheless.

"I'm sorry I'm late!" I yell, barreling my way into Declan's apartment. "Trying to find a pre-made mac and cheese that looks like it's homemade was harder than I thought." I frown when I get no response. "Dec?"

His duffle bag is on the sofa, but he's not there. The kitchen is empty except for some takeout containers on the counter and a burned smell that's still overpowering the peach scented candle he's lit. If Declan tried to cook, it's a miracle this building is still standing.

I make my way to the other side of the apartment to where the bedroom is. The door is wide open, and I can hear Declan singing in the shower. I laugh to myself and throw my overnight bag onto the bed. The man can play hockey like no other, but singing is definitely not in his skill list.

I turn to tell him as much when my jaw drops. I didn't realize the door to the en suite was open. There in all his wet, naked glory is Declan. I watch the water run down his broad shoulders to the firm muscles of his back, straight to his perfectly round ass and down his muscular thighs. Jesus, it's like someone sculpted him from marble.

"You like what you see, Princess?" My eyes fly up to meet his. He's looking over his shoulder at me with a smug grin on his face. The green in them is sparkling in that way it always does when he's being a little shit. My face heats, and I slap my hands over my eyes way too late.

"Your tan line is blinding!" I complain before turning and running out of the room.

"You should see it from the front!" he yells before laughing at his own joke.

I curl up in a ball on the couch with my face in my hands. The heat of embarrassment refuses to leave my cheeks. I feel Declan sit next to me before his warm arms wrap around my shoulders.

"I know you're still reeling from seeing my magnificent ass, but can we eat? I'm starving."

"Why were you in the shower?" I mumble into my hands. "Did you suck so bad at practice that they didn't let you use the shower?" Declan and his team got back to Boston late this morning, but they had to head straight to the training facility for practice and strength training. Dec also had physical therapy for his knees, so he's just getting home.

Declan laughs. "I may have tried to cook, and the smell may have clung to me."

I peek through my fingers and look at him. His hair is still wet with water droplets clinging to the tips. His smile is warm, no hint of awkwardness. At least on his end. I'm still feeling weird about seeing him naked. He gently pries my hands away from my face and pulls me up to stand with him.

"Come on, Princess. Let's dance," he says, pulling me into him. One of my hands lands on the center of his chest while the other is still firmly in his grasp.

"There's no music," I say, swaying with him anyway.

"Remember, you asked for this," he says before belting out the most off-key version of "Young and Beautiful" by Lana Del Ray. I sway in his arms and laugh at his singing. The embarrassment slowly seeping from my body and replacing it with joy.

"Those are my favorite memories, you know. Summer nights with you." Declan pulls me completely into him, my cheek against his chest and his arms wrapped around me. He's still swaying, but luckily he's switched to humming.

Memories of nights just like this flash behind my closed eyes. Declan singing while we watch fireworks over a lake. Me faking a twisted ankle anytime our parents made us go on hikes so he would carry me on his back. Both of us dancing around the campfire, trying to summon whatever spirit could make the summer last longer.

"Mine too," I admit. I have tons of great memories with Belle and Cal. Kai and Ezra, too, just a little later. Even Mav, but his tend to be tainted with the loss of Ezra. But the memories I have with Declan will always hold a special place in my heart.

Declan's hand gently cups my chin. I look up at him. The way he's looking at me makes my stomach clench and my heart race. There are so many emotions in his eyes, but the adoration is the most prominent.

"Dec," I start to say, but he leans in and captures my mouth before any more words can escape. His kiss is soft, gentle, but it sends electricity through my body. I shudder, and he pulls me against him, wrapping me in his arms. I kiss him back with more urgency and desperation. Every kiss we've shared before has been public. The little voice in the back of my mind is telling me this isn't supposed to be happening. I ignore it and sink into the way he's making me feel. My heart feels like it's about to burst, and my underwear is soaked through. There is no part of me that doesn't want to be kissing Declan right now.

Too soon, he pulls away. "Date me," he says between ragged breaths.

"What?"

"Date me," he repeats.

"We're married. I think we skipped that part." I laugh, but it sounds strange in my ears.

"I don't care. I want to be with you, Willa. I want a real relationship with you." His eyes are so earnest and hopeful that I want to agree, but I can't get the words out.

"What?" is all I can manage.

"Say yes. Let me take you on a date. Let me show you how good we are together." He leans down and kisses me sweetly. "Let me kiss you whenever I want, not just for other people."

I'm still wrapped in his arms, my brain switching between total shut down and complete overload.

"Say yes," he whispers in my ear.

"Yes," I say so quietly I'm not sure he heard me. The smile that breaks out on his face tells me he did.

He swings me up into his arms. "Let's go to bed. It's late."

I look at the clock as he carries me to the bedroom. "It's only nine."

He ignores me.

"Dec," I say and laugh when he tosses me on the bed.

"Get ready for bed, Princess."

I head to the bathroom and quickly change and brush my teeth.

"Are we really going to bed?" I ask, making my way to my side even though I'm protesting. I'm actually exhausted and an early bedtime sounds wonderful. "Dec?" I look up to find him staring at me. The look in his eyes sets my body on fire.

"You look fucking perfect in my shirt, Princess." His voice is low and sexy as hell. He gets in on his side, never taking his eyes off me. "Come here." He lifts the covers, and I quickly scramble under them.

"Good night." My voice is wobbly either from the nerves or how turned on I am.

Declan pulls me into him. My head is on his shoulder and my hand lands on his chest. He pulls my leg over his thigh before nuzzling the top of my head. "I missed you so much. I just need to hold you."

His hold tightens around me, like he's scared I'll say no and leave. "I missed you too." His body relaxes with my words, and he's sound asleep within seconds.

I watch the rise and fall of his chest while I come to terms with what just happened. I agreed to date my best friend. To date Declan. And I'm not absolutely terrified like I thought I would be anytime I dared to imagine this situation over the years. Instead, I feel content, happy. I smile and snuggle deeper into Declan's chest, his arm tightening around me automatically, even in sleep.

I don't overthink it. I just let myself fall asleep to the sound of Declan's breathing and the memories of nights dancing under the stars.

declan

I GROAN and roll over to silence my alarm, then snuggle back into Willa.

"Why," she grumbles, her voice thick with sleep.

"I have a morning skate and then PT." I kiss her neck and then her shoulder.

"It's Thanksgiving," she mumbles into her pillow.

"That's why I only have one practice." I unwillingly get out of bed. "Where are we going today, anyway?"

"Cal's?"

"Are you asking me?" I laugh as I get dressed. She's still so sleepy.

"No. Pretty sure it's Cal's. Stop asking me questions this early in the morning."

"It's almost nine." Practice is at ten this morning. Coach wanted to let the guys with kids have the morning with them.

Willa's eyes fly open. "Shit. I told Harlow I'd be there early to help."

"You're cooking?" I ask, not even trying to keep the

shock from my voice. I dodge the pillow she chucks at my head and laugh.

"No. I'm hanging out with Cora and probably setting the table. That's all I'm allowed to do."

"I thought you got mac and cheese duty." I sit on the edge of the bed and tie my sneakers, trying to ignore the pull of my bed and my woman. I'd stay wrapped up in them all day if I could.

"I did. I never found any by the way. But Cal definitely has a back-up. He knows I burn empty pans."

"I'm excited to finally meet them in person."

Willa smiles, but it doesn't reach her eyes. She gets out of bed and quickly dresses in jeans and a cream sweater.

Dammit. I wish I had turned the lights on so I could watch her dress. I couldn't even tell what she was wearing until she got closer to me. That's what I get for getting the expensive blackout curtains.

"I already packed my clothes. What's your bed like? We can take mine. I can have someone move it this weekend."

I turn to find her staring up at me with a strange expression on her face.

"What? I like my mattress, but I'm sure yours is fine too."

She bites her lip, which would be sexy if her eyes weren't starting to look a little panicked.

"I'm going to have a shitty practice if you don't tell me what that's all about," I say, making a circle around her face with my hand.

She sighs and takes my hand, pulling me into the living room.

I have a feeling I'm not going to like this.

willa

"WE'RE MOVING IN TOGETHER today, right?" Declan asks. "We talked about it, and I thought we agreed."

I bite the inside of my lip as I look into his playful green eyes. "I have something to confess."

His eyes narrow. "You better not have a secret boyfriend living in your house. You promised Jo was a girl."

I throw my head back and laugh. "Zero boyfriends, secret or otherwise. Jo is definitely a girl." Jo and I haven't spoken much since she confronted me in my hotel room a few weeks ago. The three of us living together might get awkward.

He reaches over and grabs my hand, intertwining our fingers. "What is it, Princess? You know you can tell me anything."

I look at his sincere face and really hope I'm not about to hurt his feelings. "They don't know about you," I confess.

His forehead crinkles with his confusion. "You didn't tell them we're married?"

"I haven't told them anything, Dec. They don't know

you exist at all. Well, they might know of you because of hockey, but they don't know that we're friends."

Declan pulls back like I just slapped him. The hurt on his face is unmistakable. "What the fuck, Willa?" he shouts before standing and pacing in front of me. "Are you that embarrassed by me? I know I haven't exactly been an angel, but I never guessed I was so horrible you had to hide me."

"It's not like that!" I swear, the burn of tears starting to sting my eyes.

"What is it like? Because it fucking hurts," he says, anger flashing in his eyes.

"I didn't want to share you! If they knew about you, if they met you, then you would be theirs too. You were the only thing I've been selfish with. I share my friends, I share Belle with Kai, I even share my damn house."

Declan stays quiet and just watches me, his face impassive.

I jump up from my seat and grab his hand. He pulls it back immediately, causing the first tear to fall. "I just wanted to keep you," I whisper. "You've always been the one thing that was only mine. I just wanted you to stay mine for as long as I could."

Declan's face softens, but the hurt is still in his eyes. He closes the distance between us, cupping my face in his large hands. The rough pads of his thumbs brush against my skin as he wipes away my tears. "I've always been only yours, Willa. I probably always will be." He brushes a soft kiss on my temple before leaving and slamming the door behind him.

"What's going on with you?"

Belle is sitting next to me on the floor, stacking blocks for Cora to knock over.

"Nothing," I say and try to smile. Belle looks at me with a face that lets me know she doesn't believe me for a moment. Cora knocks over my tower and laughs. I smile genuinely at her. She's the sweetest little girl, and I still can't believe she came from Cal.

"Wanna try again?" Belle asks. I should tell her about Declan, but the words get caught in my throat. I don't know if he's going to show up for dinner. He isn't responding to my texts. He told me last night that he wanted a relationship with me, and I couldn't even make it past the morning before I ruined it.

"Things are awkward between Jo and I." It's part of the truth. Jo isn't the friendliest person, but we got along really well until recently.

"What happened?" Belle asks.

"She accused me of sleeping with a married man."

Belle's eyes go wide, and her mouth hangs open. "Why would she do that?"

I shrug. "I'm not, by the way. I haven't slept with anyone in almost a year at this point." I sound whiney. But it's hard to get laid when you're concerned about your well-being. Or that you might get kidnapped for trying to find your missing friend.

"I'd never accuse you of being a home wrecker, Willa. But why would Jo?"

I tell her about the random rumors Jo found and how she connected them to Gideon Banks. Belle knew I was at that game, just like the rest of our group. So she wasn't surprised that someone may have spotted me.

"I told you the wig wasn't a good disguise," she says.

"That's all you have to say?"

"Are you sleeping with Gideon Banks?"

"No!" I scoff. Cora thinks that's funny and giggles while clapping for me.

"Then yeah, that's all I have to say."

"Willa! Can you set the table?" Cal calls from the kitchen. Belle breaks out into a fit of laughter.

"Shut up," I mutter, rising from the floor and sulking all the way to the dining room. I pause in front of the plates. There's nine of us here right now, not including Cora.

I grab ten.

declan

I STAND in front of Callahan Griffin's house. Willa has been texting me all day, but I haven't responded. I was angry with her at first, but that quickly changed to hurt. I know all about the people in that house. We've talked about them in detail since we were kids. I feel like I know them, and yet they don't even know I exist.

I understand Willa's reason. I really do, but I wish she had told me from that start, instead of making me feel like a fool that's been living on the outside of her life all these years.

"Fuck it."

I make my way to the front door before I can change my mind. My finger pressing on the doorbell before I tell it to. I can hear the bell echo through the house and the sound of voices instantly quiets. Seconds later, the door flies open.

"Happy Thanksgiving, Princess."

"You came." Her eyes are wide, and her lip wobbles.

"Of course I came." I lean down and kiss the corner of her mouth. "Introduce me to everyone." I throw my arm around her shoulders and lead her inside. I follow the sound of soft voices until I find the dining room.

The moment we enter the room, we're greeted by silence. Cal is at the head of the table with Harlow to his right. Their daughter Cora is at the corner between them in her highchair. Jo is next to Harlow with a man who I'm guessing is Harlow's dad from the red hair. There's another man next to him and an older looking one at the other head of the table. I'm not sure how they fit in with this group. Maverick, Belle, and Kai are all to Cal's left and have turned around in their seats to stare at me.

Willa clears her throat. "Everyone, this is Declan. My husband."

Forks clang on plates, but everyone is still staring. Except Cora, who is shoving mashed potatoes into her mouth with her small fists. I look around at all the different expressions. Mostly, it's shock. But Belle looks as hurt as I felt this morning, and Jo looks horrified. I catch the moment Cal realizes who I am.

"Holy shit. Declan Monroe is in my house!" he shouts and then immediately stands to shake my hand.

"Callahan," Belle says. "Did you not hear what Willa just said?"

"That wasn't a joke?" he asks Willa.

"Nope," she says, holding up her left hand, wedding ring glittering in the light. Cal's eyes widen so large, it would be comical if this wasn't such an awkward situation.

"That reminds me," I say, digging in the pocket of my jeans. "You forgot your engagement ring, Princess." I pull out the six-karat oval diamond I bought for her. It came in while she was still on tour. It's obnoxious and the most expensive thing I've ever purchased, but she was right when she said she was worth it. Willa gasps as I slide it onto her finger.

She throws her arms around my neck like she's giving me a hug. "This thing is huge," she whispers into my ear.

"It's a skating rink. So you never forget who you're married to," I growl low in her ear before kissing her temple and standing back up. She pulls me to the two open seats next to Kai. She takes the one next to him as I sit on her other side.

"I can do that, Princess." She's loading up my plate with everything on the table. "Willa," I say, grabbing her hand to stop her from trying to put even more turkey on my plate than the massive pile she already put there.

"You're married to Declan Monroe," Jo says to Willa.

"Yes. I am," Willa responds. There's a tension between the two women that must be pretty new. Willa always told me she likes Jo.

"The married man you're with is Declan Monroe and not Gideon Banks," Jo states.

I bark out a laugh. "Why would Willa be with Gideon? He's married and so obsessed with his wife that I'm not sure he's aware that other women exist."

"Can someone please tell me what the fuck is going on right now?" Kai says, leaning around Willa to glare at me.

"Yeah, Princess. What's going on right now?" I'm not going to help her with this. I want to say something that would out all her lies, to hurt her the way I'm hurting. But no matter how upset with her I am, I will never do anything to cause her pain.

TWENTY-ONE

DECLAN'S HAND finds mine under the table. He laces our fingers together and squeezes, letting me know that even though he's angry, he's still here for me. I don't deserve him.

I take a deep breath. "Declan has been my best friend since I was four years old."

I watch the hurt in Belle's eyes deepen and it bruises my heart. "Four?" she says with disbelief.

I explain how we spent every summer together. How we spoke every single day once we had the ability to do so. I even tell them about all the games I went to so that I could watch him play and the shows of ours he came to, but I didn't bring him backstage for.

"Why wouldn't you tell us about him? Why keep him a secret?" Kai asks, still eyeing me suspiciously.

"I wanted him for myself. I know how it sounds out loud. But he has always meant so much to me that I didn't want to share him. As a kid, it didn't matter because we lived six hours apart, and you guys weren't going to meet, anyway."

"And as an adult?" Kai asks.

"As an adult, I had nothing that was just mine. So I clung to the one person that had always been just mine."

"How did that lead to marriage? How could you possibly keep a whole ass husband secret?" Cal asks. "A famous hockey player husband who could really pass more often."

Declan laughs next to me. The sound alone calming some of my nerves. "Eight months ago, I had a serious wake up call. My life was going downhill pretty fast and the only consistently good thing I had was Willa. When I had the opportunity to sign with Boston and be with her, I took it immediately."

"I did tell him I'd give a kidney to get him back here," I admit, smiling at the way Declan is looking at me. He's speaking to everyone else in the room, but his attention hasn't let me.

"We dated long distance until I moved here in September. I proposed immediately, and she accepted. We got married the same day," he laughs, almost to himself. He kisses me quickly on my temple before continuing. "It was the best day of my life."

I pull on his shirt collar and kiss his lips. Not for show. Just for me, for us.

"Where do you live?" Jo asks him, apparently over the guilt from accusing me of being a home wrecker.

"I'll be moving into Willa's as of tonight. I was renting an apartment in the city. She wanted me to stay there while you were on tour. I didn't understand why until this morning."

I flinch, but he just pulls my chair closer and wraps an arm around my shoulder.

"What happened this morning?" Harlow asks. I see the way her eyes are flying between me and Declan. She's worse than Jo when she senses something. She's going to start digging if she thinks something is off. And knowing Harlow, she'll find the truth.

"I feel like I know you guys," Declan says. "Willa talks about you all the time and always has. She called me and woke me up in the middle of the night to tell me Cal had a little girl. The night Ezra went missing, I was on the phone with her when Kai came to ask her where he was. We talked for hours the night Belle showed up covered in bruises. She was at one of my games when she had to leave early because Maverick drank too much and was causing a scene in a bar."

"We had no idea who you were," Maverick says, his cheeks flush with embarrassment.

"Yeah. Found that one out before leaving for practice this morning," Declan says. I know he's trying to hide how hurt he is, but I can hear it in his voice.

"I'm sorry," I whisper to him, sure my voice is going to break if I speak any louder.

"Shit," Kai says, leaning back in his seat and blowing out a breath.

"But why, Willa?" Belle asks, tears in her eyes. "You can tell me anything. Why lie about someone who means that much to you?"

I roll my lips between my teeth, trying to figure out how else to explain this.

"I'm not asking why you lied to everyone. I get it. But why did you lie to me?"

"I don't know, Belle. I really don't," I admit. Out of all of this, that has been the biggest question I had for myself. Belle would have understood and kept Declan quiet from the rest of them if I asked her to. But I never gave her the chance.

Silence falls around the table. I don't think anyone knows what to do or say right now.

"Well, it's nice to meet you, Declan. I'm Harrison, Harlow's father," Harrison says, doing that head nod thing guys do when they meet each other.

"I figured that one out," Dec says, gesturing to Harrison's red hair that matches his daughter's. Harrison laughs and nods.

"I'm Jason, Belle and Cal's dad." Declan shakes Jason's hand since he's sitting next to him.

"Jon," Jon mutters from across from Declan. He never stopped eating during all the drama and is on his third plate. I think something is going on with his home life because he's around a lot lately and grumpy nine times out of ten.

Harrison, Jason, and Cal get into a conversation with Declan about hockey. The rest of us eat in silence. Declan keeps his arm around me for the rest of dinner and it's the only hope I have that I haven't destroyed everything.

declan

"WHAT'S HER FAVORITE COLOR?"

I'm in the kitchen washing dishes while Harlow dries them. I offered to help and now I'm thinking I've been left in here alone with her on purpose. Willa warned me to watch what I say in front of her. And if Willa wasn't somewhere with Belle right now, I don't think she'd let us be alone.

"She'd tell you lilac like her hair if you asked, but it's a cop-out, so she doesn't have to keep telling people it was her mother's favorite color. Because then they ask about her and Willa still gets pretty broken up talking about her." Harlow watches me, her face not giving away what she's thinking. "Her real favorite color is green."

"Like your eyes?" she asks. My brows raise at the question.

"Is that why? She hasn't told me if it is." I grin. "Man, I hope that's why."

Harlow laughs at that. "I don't know, but it wouldn't surprise me with what she just told us in there."

"Why did she keep her parents' house? She could've sold it. No one else still has a house in Maine."

I take a deep breath and hand her the plate I just washed. "That one is complicated. Some days I think it's just because of sentimentality. She doesn't have a lot of memories of her mom, but she painted the inside of that house. Her mom hand-painted the unicorns on her bedroom walls.. There are other areas like daisies on a green wall in the kitchen, or the bathroom painted to look like a forest." I've never stepped foot in that house, but I spent many hours on FaceTime with her while she lived there and could describe it from memory.

"And other days?"

I shrug. "Other days, I'm afraid she's lost and is holding onto it, expecting to need somewhere to crash land."

Harlow nods as if she expected that answer. I know they're pretty close, so I'm not too surprised. I am a little worried I shouldn't have said anything, but I'm so over secrets tonight.

"Why do you call her Princess?"

"Because when I first met him, I said 'Hi, I'm Willa Prince, but I'm not a prince. I'm a princess.'" Willa walks into the room, a tired and sad smile on her face when she looks at me.

I hand Harlow the last dish, dry my hands and walk straight up to my wife. Grabbing her face in my hands, I kiss her like I've wanted to all night. I try to show her how much she means to me and that we're going to be okay.

"And I said, 'yes, Princess.'"

"So, does this mean we can go to his games?" I turn to

see Cal coming into the kitchen with Cora in his arms. He goes straight to Harlow, pulling her into him too.

"Of course. You let me know when and how many tickets you want. You won't be able to sit with Willa, though. She sits with Gideon's wife in her season ticket seats." Unless Maggie's parents don't go. I don't want to give Cal false hope, though.

Cal smiles. "That's even better. I went to a few University of Maine games with her and her dad. She's terrifying to watch with. And a little dangerous. I got an elbow to the nose once because I was too close when the player from the other team tripped our center."

I laugh and squeeze Willa to me. "That sounds like my girl. You should see the long texts I get after every game."

"You do realize that I've been sending you those texts after every game for nine years, and you've still barely listened to me." Willa smiles up at me, and I would have to be blind to miss the affection there.

"I'll do better," I promise her.

"Ready to go home?" she asks.

"Thank you for tonight. Even though you had no idea I was coming. I still had a lot of fun," I tell Cal and Harlow.

"It was nice to meet you, Declan," Harlow says.

Willa takes my hand and pulls me towards the door. "Where's the fire?"

"I want to take you home," she says. I swear my heart skips a beat at that.

"What about Jo?" I ask. Not that I'm expecting too much, but even if we're just talking through what happened tonight, I'd like privacy.

"She's staying here tonight."

I sweep her up into my arms the moment we step outside. Willa's house is right next to Cal's, so I'm at her door within a minute.

"Code, Princess."

"Zero eight one four." Her mother's birthday.

As soon as I have her over the threshold, my mouth is on hers. I let her slide down my body so she can stand, but she pushes away.

"Dec, wait. I wanted to apologize. I swear I never intended to hurt you."

I grab her chin and force her eyes to meet mine. "There's something you need to understand, Willa. You're mine. You can rip my heart out and run it over for all I care because it's yours. There is nothing you can do that will stop me from wanting you."

She gasps and the sound goes straight to my dick. I take her lips again, trying to swallow all her sounds. I kiss her again quickly before pulling away.

"Where are we sleeping?"

She takes me upstairs and leads me to the first bedroom. "We're definitely going to need your bed."

Willa's bedroom is large with white birch floors and dark wood furniture. The walls are the same emerald green as my eyes. That makes me smile. Maybe Harlow was right.

"I'll get it moved here as soon as I can, but I'll enjoy having you snuggled against me until then."

"Just snuggling?" she asks, biting her bottom lip. I pull her to me and kiss her softly at first, then deeper.

"Just snuggling," I say against her lips. "When I take you, Willa, it will be to make love to you. Not just sex. But you're not ready for that yet. I'll wait for you to catch up to me. I'll wait an entire lifetime for you, Princess." I kiss her forehead, quickly strip down to my boxer briefs and climb into her queen size bed. "Let's get some sleep."

She stares at me for a moment, the frustration and confusion warring in her features. Finally, she quickly strips down to just her black lacy panties, but her back is turned so all I can see is her perfectly round ass. I stifle a groan, reminding myself that I want to do this right and not just pounce on her like a horny idiot. Willa knows what she's doing though, because she throws a smirk over her shoulder before grabbing one of my shirts out of her dresser and pulling it on.

"How many of my shirts did you steal?" I laugh when she shrugs innocently. "Come here."

Willa gets in and snuggles next to me. I pull her as close to me as possible. Her bed would be the perfect size for most people, but I'm a hockey player. I'm tall and broad naturally but add in all the work I put into my body, and I'm taking up most of the bed by myself. Luckily, Willa is small enough to fit right against me, otherwise she might have to sleep on top of me.

Wait.

Maybe I should get a smaller bed.

willa

"CAN WE TALK?" Declan's eyes go wide, and I see the panic flash across his face. "It's not bad," I add, trying to hide my laughter when he relaxes so quickly it makes him look like a balloon that sprung a leak.

"No one ever asks that question for a good reason, Princess," he points out, frown showing his disapproval.

I walk up to him where he's standing by the front door and wrap my arms around his waist. He was about to leave for practice before I decided I couldn't wait to talk to him. "I was thinking it's probably time to go public."

"Yeah?" His smile is so bright it's blinding.

"I've been thinking about it, and I think it's a good idea. Bethany was at the San Diego game waiting to sink her claws into you. The New York game was dangerous for you. Then Jo tells me the internet thinks I'm sleeping with Gideon." I bite my lip and look into his eyes. He's smiling down at me, like he's just happy to be here. "I also kind of hate all the articles trying to guess who you're making heart eyes at during your games."

Declan chuckles. When he dips his head and kisses me, I melt into him. "You're cute when you're jealous." I scowl, but he just chuckles again and kisses my scrunched forehead. "Fucking beautiful."

"I need to get to practice, but we can go over the plan to announce to the world you're mine," he says, giving me a chaste kiss before letting me go.

"No need. I have a plan."

He raises his eyebrows. "Do I get to be in on it?"

"Nope. But you'll love it."

Declan shakes his head, but he's smiling. "I'll be back for lunch."

I watch him walk out the door and to his car; his jeans hugging his ass perfectly while they stretch tightly around his thick thighs. Ever since we decided to be more than just friends, I've been noticing how attractive he is. Not that I wasn't aware before, but I wouldn't let myself look or even think about it. Between his tattoos and all the muscles, my underwear is never dry.

I'm still terrified of us not working out and losing him. But I'm hoping that he's my next adventure. The kind that lasts a lifetime.

***

"Where's Declan?"

"Hi, Callahan. Please come in," I say sarcastically as he lets himself into my house.

"Is he here?" Cal looks around, his face eager like an excited puppy.

"He has practice. He'll be back soon, but he has a game tonight, so he can't play with you today."

Cal and Declan met two days ago, and they're already inseparable. It's something I knew would happen, but I'm not as upset about it as I thought I would be. It's actually been kind of nice to have the two parts of my life come together.

"I know he has a game. I wish I was going," he says, plopping himself down next to me and crossing his arms with a pout.

I roll my eyes. "You're over here trying to get tickets, aren't you?"

"No, but if you have some you'd like to give me, I'm sure Kai and I would find good use for them."

"I'll see what I can do." I laugh. Cal is as subtle as an explosion.

"I came over because Jon and Harrison are both on their way for a family meeting. Feels a little wrong to leave Declan out, though."

I smile at how quickly Cal accepted Declan as one of us. Maverick and Kai have, too, mostly. It's Belle who hasn't. I don't think, anyway. She hasn't spoken to me much in the past two days. Whatever Declan said to Harlow the other night got her on his side as well. I don't know where Jo stands with me, never mind Declan. She's still staying at Harlow and Cal's.

"Jon and Harrison? What does one have to do with the other?" I ask.

"Oh, nothing. Jon wanted a meeting and then Harrison called Harlow about some concerns related to Senator

Wolfe, so she told him to just come over so she didn't have to repeat everything he was saying to all of us."

I hold in my sigh. If Jon wants a meeting, it means we need to get back to work already, even though we've been off the road for less than a week. Harrison needing to talk is likely going to throw Mav back into a depression. There's no way there's good news about his criminal father. I just wanted some time without being worried about everyone I care about.

"Come on," Cal says, standing and holding out his hand to help me up. I let him, suddenly feeling defeated. "Harlow is making quesadillas for lunch."

"Why didn't you mention that sooner?" I ask, perking up. Cal laughs and throws his arm around my shoulder. Declan picks that moment to walk through our front door.

"You making a move on my wife, Callahan?" Dec asks, chuckling, but the way he's looking at where Cal is touching me is anything but funny.

"Fuck no," Cal says, quickly dropping his arm and stepping away. "Even if I wasn't madly in love with my own wife, yours is terrifying." I scowl at him, a little offended. Cal points at my face. "See what I mean?"

Dec laughs and pulls me into his chest. "I find it sexy as fuck."

Cal looks horrified. "You're serious."

"As a heart attack," Dec says, leaning down and kissing me in a way that is inappropriate for company.

"Gross," Cal mutters. "Lunch is getting cold."

"Lunch?" Dec pulls away and perks up so fast that I laugh. "Why didn't you say that sooner?"

"Same fucking person," Cal grumbles under his breath, stomping out of my house on the way to his.

"Come on." I grab Declan's hand and tug him out of the house. "Harlow is making quesadillas."

He scoops me up into his arms, causing me to let out a surprised scream, and runs right past Cal and into his house. "What are you doing?" I ask, laughing as he sets me down on a stool in front of the island in Cal and Harlow's kitchen.

"I love quesadillas," he says, like the answer is obvious.

Harlow laughs from where she's standing behind the stove. "I made double the amount I normally would for this amount of people, plus a few extra."

"Are you allowed to eat that amount of cheese before a game?" Kai asks, snagging the quesadilla Cal was about to put in his mouth and taking a giant bite.

"Hey!" Cal complains, but Harlow is right there with another one. He smiles and kisses her. "Thanks, Firecracker."

"I don't stick to the super clean eating thing like some players do," Dec says, shrugging. I snort, which earns me a wink. He eats healthy. He just refuses to give up cheese. Not that I can blame him.

Everyone stacks their plates with quesadillas, salsa, sour cream, and the Mexican rice Harlow also made. We decide to eat at the dining room table even though normally we would be in the living room. With the way our family is growing, Cal is going to need a bigger table.

"Alright, who wants to go first?" Jo asks after we've finished eating.

Jon clears his throat. "I had a meeting with Isla from the

label this morning. They want to add more tour dates. Local this time. They want to advertise it as a hometown tour type of thing. Only New England venues and only for a two-month period."

I look at Declan. He's already looking at me, a small smile on his face, but it's not making his eyes twinkle in the way his real smiles do. He's happy that Shattered Halo is doing well but hates the distance.

Jo hands out a mock schedule she printed for us, but before I can look at mine, she slides a second schedule next to mine. I look up and she gives me a small smile before going back to her seat. Comparing the two, I realize one is a proposed tour schedule with dates and locations and the other is Declan's game schedule.

I gasp when I realize what she did. "Jo." It's all I can manage. She worked the tour around Dec's games. He has twenty-eight in the two months we'd be touring. Thirteen of them are home games, and Jo made sure I'd be here for all of them.

"I couldn't work in any of his away games since they're not really close to where we'll be. The only one that I think would be possible is Buffalo. We're home for a week around that one," she says. I smile at her, and she smiles back. All the hurt feelings between us disappear with her thoughtful gesture. "He can even make both Boston shows."

"Thank you," I tell her.

"This is awesome, Jo," Declan says, looking close to tears. "You have no idea what this means to me."

"Don't cry! If you cry, I'll cry and then Mav will cry. It'll be a whole thing," Cal says, sniffling.

Declan chuckles and turns to me. He's smiling again, and it's not forced to make me feel better this time.

"So, can I approve this and get the venues booked?" Jon asks, looking confused at why everyone is being emotional right now. We all give our agreement.

"Your turn, Dad," Harlow says to Harrison.

"I've been trying to figure out where all of Wolfe's money is coming from." Harrison glances at Maverick. "Since you told me that your dad claimed he was using old money to fund his campaigns was bullshit, I've tried to prove it."

"You haven't?" Mav asks, his brows drawing together.

"Not exactly. With the way everything is tied up with authorities right now, it's been more difficult. But I found something else while I was digging." Harrison pushes his tablet into the middle of the table so we can all see it. It's a listing for a cabin on a lake in Maine on a vacation rental website. "I already had Wolfe's financials from the time Ezra went missing. I gave them to my guy to trace the transactions weeks before the arrest."

"He rented a cabin?" Harlow asks.

"I did," Maverick says, his face pale. "I used my dad's credit card. Ezra and I were going to head there that night."

"Did your dad know that?" Harlow asks at the same time Harrison says, "Did you share that with Ezra?"

"Ezra knew, yeah. My dad didn't find out until the bill came the next month."

"The code to get into the cabin was used once three hours after Ezra was last seen," Harrison says.

Maverick goes so still and so pale I think he might faint.

I quickly reach across the table and grab his hand. "I can see what you're doing. Stop."

"I can't," he says though a pained whisper. "I should've gone there to look for him. I should've —"

"Stop, Mav. You can't live in that headspace. Why would you look for him there? You were supposed to go together," Belle says.

"When my dad died, I spent months blaming myself, saying that if I had just left school on time instead of stopping to talk to a cute boy, I could've been home to call an ambulance. I could've saved him." I squeeze his hand. "But I couldn't predict a heart attack any more than you could predict Ezra's actions." Mav nods and slides back into his seat, releasing my hand.

"We think Ezra went to the cabin?" Belle asks, eyes flickering between Mav and Harrison.

"I'm confident he did," Harrison says. "It's likely the first place he stopped. It doesn't give us much in a way of finding him, but it establishes a firmer timeline."

"So he ran there and then ended up in Green Peak, New Hampshire? Then went to Nashville with Jasper. Do we know anything else?" Harlow asks.

"I have a theory," Declan says, shocking almost everyone at the table.

"Uh, how much do you know?" Kai asks like he's nicely trying to tell Declan he doesn't know what's going on.

"He knows everything," I admit. Everyone nods in acceptance and turns their attention to Declan. Everyone except Belle, who is shooting daggers from her eyes at me.

"What's your theory?" Harlow is waiting with the face

she gets when she's in the middle of investigating some-thing. It's a mixture of serious and curious wonder.

"It wasn't Wolfe." He says it so casually, like that theory doesn't blow a hole in everything we've been thinking so far.

"It has to be my dad," Maverick argues.

"That's where the evidence points," Harrison agrees.

"Then why isn't Ezra sitting right there?" Declan points to the empty chair next to Maverick.

"The trial hasn't happened yet. He could be waiting for that. Or maybe he's worried about how everyone will react. Legally, coming back from the dead is going to suck," Jo says.

Declan leans forward in his chair, folding his hands and looking at Harlow. He knows she's the one he needs to convince because once she is, she'll dig into his theory better than an FBI agent.

"If I was in hiding to keep Willa safe and the bastard who was behind all of it was locked up, there wouldn't be a single thing on this fucking planet that would stop me from returning to her side." He reaches out and pulls me fully off my chair and into his lap, but his gaze never leaves Harlow's. They're having some weird stare-off. Like he's challenging her to disagree with him while she tries to find a way to do so.

"Or he doesn't love me the way I love him," Maverick says in a voice that sounds so defeated, it causes tears to burn in the backs of my eyes.

"No, Mav. He loves you like crazy. Jasper said as much when we had that call with him, unprompted. He was not only aware of how much Ezra loved you, but was affected by it enough to mention it to us," Harlow says, breaking her staring contest with Declan to look at Maverick.

Jo throws her arms around Mav as he sobs into her shoulder. She eyes me with a silent plea for help. I'm usually the one to comfort Maverick. I've known the most loss, which somehow made me the default grief friend. I smile sadly and nod, letting her know she's doing all she can do right now.

"So we need to find a suspect that isn't Wolfe, but would convincingly threaten Maverick's life," I say, leaning back against Declan's chest. He wraps his arms around me, holding me tight, like he's afraid someone is actually going to force him into hiding to protect me.

"It's possible he had a partner. I've been reading through all the drug trafficking allegations because those seem the most likely to be part of what Ezra witnessed to start this whole mess. The scope of the operation is huge. There's no way he did it alone, but so far, he hasn't rolled on anyone. Either out of loyalty or possibly fear that someone would take out his wife and child." Harrison scratches his chin. "My money is on the latter. I doubt Wolfe is loyal to anyone other than himself."

"I have to go see my dad," Maverick whispers.

"I'll go with you," I offer immediately. Declan stiffens. I put my hand over his mouth before he can argue. He knows what happened the last time any of us went to a prison, so I know there's no way he's letting me go without an argument. "I'm going with him," I say directly to Declan. I see the fear in his eyes, but it won't stop me.

"I can go alone," Maverick says, having seen the same fear in Declan's eyes that I have.

"When are you going?" Dec asks as soon as I remove my hand.

"Maverick is on the approved visitor list. It'll take me a few hours to make some calls to get Willa on there too." Harrison is already getting up and calling someone before I can respond to thank him.

"Tomorrow?" Mav asks, hesitantly looking between me and Declan. "He's being held in Auburn. So about three hours from here."

"I have weight training in the morning, but we can be on the road by ten. Does that work?"

"Declan," I start to say, but he shakes his head.

"I'm not letting you go alone, Princess. I'll stay in the car and wait, but I'll lose my mind if you make me wait at home for you."

"Okay," I agree. He kisses me softly before placing me back in my chair.

"I have to head to the arena. You're still coming, right?"

"Of course. Who else is going to yell at you for playing like a cocky idiot?"

Cal barks out a laugh while Declan just smiles.

"I'll see you there, Princess." He kisses me again quickly before saying goodbye to everyone else.

"That was really heavy for a lunch meeting," Jon says. I startle a little, having completely forgotten he was there.

I turn to him. "On a lighter note, I need your help with something."

"Belle!" I yell, running after her. She stops on the sidewalk between her house and Cal's.

"I don't want to talk right now, Willa," she says, her voice quiet.

"Please. You're my best friend —"

"No," she snaps, turning to face me. "You're *my* best friend. Your best friend is Declan."

"Both things can be true," I say sadly.

"They can, but they aren't. Declan knows you in a way that I thought I did. He knows everything about Ezra!" she exclaims. "Declan knows your heart, and I didn't even know he fucking existed."

"What about you and Kai?" I argue. "He knows your heart better than I do, and he should. I don't get angry at you for that."

"I gave you every ounce of me, Willa! I told you every hope and every terrifying fear. I told you what I felt for Kai. You held me while I healed from Brad. I whispered secrets in your ear at sleepovers when we were kids. I kept nothing hidden from you." Belle's eyes are glassy with unshed tears, her body shaking from anger and sadness. "I thought we were each other's person. But you've always been Declan's, and I just got the scraps." She turns on her heel and runs to her house.

I open my mouth to apologize or argue or beg her forgiveness. I don't know which, but it doesn't matter because I can't get a sound past my lips.

"Give her time to calm down. She'll come around."

"Will she?" I ask, turning to face Kai.

"She loves you. She's just hurt."

"Belle and Declan mean so much to me, but in such

different ways. There was never a competition," I try explaining to him because I can't seem to do it with Belle.

"You made her feel like she was in a competition she wasn't aware of and then lost. I'm not saying that was your intention," he adds quickly, seeing the protest forming on my lips. "I'm just telling you how she feels so you can work on fixing it. Which is probably more than I should say at all if I want to sleep next to her tonight."

"Thanks Kai." He nods and jogs after Belle.

I take a deep breath and try to get my head on straight.

declan

"BEN!" I shout, jogging to catch up to where he's standing by the entrance to the tunnel.

"Hey Dec." He's busy adjusting something on his camera and doesn't even look up.

"Can you do me a favor?"

He looks at me and raises an eyebrow.

"My wife is coming tonight, and I was wondering if you could get some shots of me interacting with her. Like the ones you got of me last time, but where you can see her too?" I ask.

Ben laughs. "I can definitely do that. Since we're on home ice, I have free rein of where I can shoot from."

"Can you get my wife too?" Gideon asks, having overheard our conversation on his way to the locker room.

"Are they sitting together again?"

"Sure are," Gideon answers.

"Easy enough."

"Perfect. I'll pay for your drinks after the next away game," Gideon says, clapping Ben on the shoulder and heading to the locker room. None of us married guys go out after home games. Even when Willa was away, I just wanted to be somewhere I shared with her.

"I'll . . ." I pause. Trying to think of something to thank him with. "I'll get you something I can't tell you about yet." I smile and clap my hands together. He said he likes Shattered Halo, and I'm sure Willa wouldn't mind giving him some tickets to one of their Boston shows. But it hasn't been announced yet, and I'm not going to be the one to spill the secret.

Ben laughs and shakes his head at me like I'm an idiot. "You don't need to get me anything, Dec. I'll happily get a picture of you and your wife. I'll already be taking pictures anyway," he says, gesturing to his camera like I forgot it was his job.

"I know. I want to," I shrug and head towards the locker room to get ready.

I practically run into the locker room, my teammates laughing at me. There's always a different energy surging through my body when I know Willa will be at one of my games. It's been like that since she went to a few with her dad when I was in college.

"Save it for the ice," Coach says, trying to get me to stop bouncing on the balls of my feet.

"Sorry, Coach," I mumble and take my seat on the bench next to Gideon.

I put my gear on and lace my skates while Coach talks strategy. Chicago is a good team. Both their offense and defense have been solid so far this season. It's going to be a tough game. But I'm ready.

The lights are bright, the ice is cold, and the crowd is

loud as we make our way out of the tunnel and onto the ice. The energy in the arena tonight is perfect for this type of game. We're surrounded by hometown fans on our own ice. They're wild and screaming and excited to see their team win.

Tonight is going to be a great night. I can feel it.

willa

"THE NATIONAL ANTHEM? REALLY?" Cal whines.

"It was the only way Jon could get me what I needed."

Cal glares at me as he paces. "Rockstars don't sing the National Anthem."

"There's no way that's true," Kai says, but he's smiling at how annoyed Cal is.

"Reba did it," I say.

Cal stops pacing. "Really? Reba did it?"

"She's telling the truth," Kai tells Cal.

"Well, if Reba did it, so can I," Cal says, puffing out his chest and starting his vocal warm-ups.

"Come on," I say to Kai. "Maggie is sitting alone waiting for us."

He follows me to our seats, adjusting his baseball cap to try to cover some of his face while I make sure my wig is still in place.

"It's weird seeing you blonde again," he says. "Not bad,"

he amends when he catches my questioning look. "Just different."

"There you are!" Maggie shouts. She jumps up from her seat and gives me a quick hug. "You must be Kai. I'm Maggie, Gideon Banks is my husband." Kai smiles and shakes her outstretched hand. The team is finishing up their warm-ups by the time we finishing greeting each other. Maggie was able to use the other two tickets her parents have for Cal and Kai. They're doing what Declan's parents are and traveling a lot. She said they've only made it to two games so far this season.

"Ladies and gentlemen, please stand for the singing of your National Anthem," the announcer says. "Tonight's performance is by Callahan Griffin of Shattered Halo."

Maggie's big brown eyes go wide as Kai and I descend into a fit of laughter that's luckily drowned out by the roaring of the crowd. We manage to get ourselves together in time for Cal's first note.

"He's going to get you back for this," Kai says in my ear.

"Worth it."

Cal does a great job. The crowd gets so loud it's deafening. You'd think he won a Grammy with the way they're cheering for him. Declan even skates up to the rug Cal is standing on and gives him a hug. I'm sure he was wondering what the hell Cal was doing here.

By the time Cal gets to his seat next to Kai, he's changed into a jersey with Declan's number on it and a baseball hat.

"Are you wearing a Chickadees hat?" I ask him, leaning around Kai.

"Jasper gave it to me," Cal huffs.

"Your funeral," I say and lean back into my seat. Boston is a serious sports town, and the Chickadees have beaten us in the World Series twice in the last five years. Cal is asking to get beat up in the parking lot.

"Does Dec have to score for this to work?" Cal asks.

"Ideally." Declan said Chicago was going to be tough, so him scoring isn't key to my plan.

"Why is Dec's teammate blowing kisses at you?" Kai's pointing at Martinez, who is in fact, blowing kisses at Maggie and me.

I snort at the same time Maggie giggles. We look at each other and blow him a kiss back. He smiles and gets in position for the face-off. Dec and Gideon both glare at him before turning back to the ref holding the puck.

"Cameron has a theory that if he flirts with us, it'll make Gideon and Declan play harder," Maggie explains. "Because of aggression or something."

Kai nods like that makes complete sense to him.

"Looks like it worked," Cal says as Gideon wins the face-off.

"Or not," Kai mutters when Chicago's defense immediately gets it out of their zone.

By the end of the first period, the score is at zero for both teams, but the frustration is tangible. Any time we were in scoring range, Chicago's defense stopped us. The same went for them, though. If they managed to get anywhere near our goalie, they were stopped. There hasn't been a single shot on goal. Which might be the first time I've seen that.

I pull my phone out to text Dec. He doesn't always check in between periods, but I'm hoping he does today.

29 on defense is keeping weight off his right leg when you guys aren't near him. I think he has an injury. Try to get to that side instead of the left.

Goalie has a blind spot, bottom right. He's missed most shots during warm up in that box.

88, left wing on the second-string reflexes are slower than the right wing. Tell your guys to outskate his old ass.

This is a guess, but I think the center on the first line is letting Gideon win the face-off. They're relying heavily on their defense. They're running an offensive defense, I think. It wouldn't surprise me if one of the d-men attempt to score the moment you give them an opening.

HOCKEY BOY

You're a fucking godsend, Princess. I showed Coach your texts. He might hire you after this.

Win the game, and you can show me your appreciation when we get home.

Fuck, Willa. Do you know how uncomfortable it is to get a boner wearing a jockstrap?

Head in the game, hockey boy.

Yes, Princess.

"I got popcorn, nachos, hot dogs, pizza, and beer," Cal says behind the pile of food he's holding. I can't even see his face. "Oh, and I got you a Coke, Kai." Cal turns around and sticks his butt out to show the bottle of Coke in his back pocket to Kai, who just sighs and grabs it.

"We had dinner right before coming here." I don't know why I bother. Cal eats nonstop.

"I'll take a beer and a hotdog. Oh, and nachos!" Maggie says. I hand her what she asked for from the stack.

"I like you, Maggie," Cal garbles around a mouthful of pizza. Maggie blushes into her beer, and I roll my eyes.

"I got you and Gideon tickets and backstage passes," I tell her.

"To what? Isn't your tour over?" I explain the added shows we confirmed today, and she squeals. "Thank you! I'm so excited!"

"They're back," Kai says. I watch the team skate back out onto the ice. Declan and Gideon make a few laps around the rink before stopping in front of us. Declan taps his heart, and I do the same, while Gideon and Maggie just smile at each other.

"Married people are weird," Cal mutters.

"You're married, dumbass," Kai points out.

"Yeah, but like not *that* married," he says, gesturing to the four of us.

"I have no idea what the means," Kai sighs.

"Obviously. You're not married," Cal says. "You're living in sin with my sister."

I mutter "Jesus Christ," under my breath right before Maggie starts loudly cackling.

"Your friends are so funny," she says once she calms down.

"You only think that because you don't know them," I

whisper. She laughs and lightly slaps my arm. She thinks I'm joking.

"Face-off!" she yells. I look at her beer to see it's already empty. Maggie is a lightweight. Noted.

Gideon is slow on the snap on purpose this time, letting Chicago win. Martinez gets the puck and passes to Declan, who easily breaks away from their offense and goes straight for 29's right side. 29 tries to stop him, but Dec checks him, and 29 goes down. Declan quickly takes the shot on the goalie's bottom right.

"Goal!" Maggie screams a second before the buzzer sounds and the goal lights up.

Declan throws his arms in the air, pointing the one holding his stick at me. He immediately skates over to me and puts his hand on the glass. Instead of doing the same on my side, I take my wig off, tip my head upside down to shake out my hair, and lift back up to meet Declan's eyes. Then I put my hand on the glass opposite his. The hand with the shiny diamond that will be unmistakable.

His smile is blinding. I know all the cameras are on us right now. It was what I asked Jon to arrange. This is a Saturday night game. A million people are watching. It's my way of showing the world Declan is mine. Of showing Declan I want the world to know I'm his.

Next to me, Kai and Cal take their hats off. Maggie is holding the sign I gave her earlier that says "Mrs. Monroe," with an arrow pointing at me. I didn't want anyone misunderstanding who I was. Declan's smile never falters, but he starts laughing when he looks up. I look at the jumbotron and facepalm. Cal has made his own sign that says "Declan

Monroe owns this bum," with a hand drawn picture of a peach.

"Told you," Kai says in my ear.

The ref blows his whistle, having let this go on longer than normal. Declan blows me a kiss and skates back into position. I'm still smiling as I watch him bend over and place his stick on the ice. I've always loved watching Dec skate. He flies over the ice with puck handling skills that could land him in the Hall of Fame. But now that things have changed between us, I'm suddenly seeing how powerful his legs are and the way his tongue darts out to lick the drop of sweat from his full lips.

I shake my head a little, snapping myself out of the thoughts that were quickly leading to visions of being naked with Dec. I need to focus on the game. The guys hold Chicago back and manage to keep the score at one-nothing.

"A bum?" I ask Cal after the second period ends.

He shrugs. "This is a family friendly event, Willa."

"I've seen men lose teeth at these games. I don't think you had to censor your sign," I point out.

"Shit, you're right," he says, sounding disappointed.

"Look," Maggie says next to me, pointing at the jumbotron. The camera is on me, Kai, and Cal again. So we wave and Cal blows kisses, mouthing hi to Harlow and Cora.

"How does it feel to have cameras on you like that all the time?" Maggie asks.

"You get weirdly paranoid that you're going to develop chronic nose picking or something equally embarrassing," I admit. "I'd love to say you get used to it, but when it's moments like this, where I know I'll never be able to watch my husband play hockey without attention falling on me more than it should," I shrug, "it gets old."

"You could watch from the family box with the other wives. The cameras can't see in to most of it. I'll even go with you," she offers.

"You're so sweet, but I'd like to stay down here with you for as long as I can. If it interferes with the game, I'll go up to the box." I've met some of the other wives and girlfriends and they all seem nice, but I like to be close enough to the action to smell the sweat. Not literally, but I like to feel like I'm a part of it.

HOCKEY BOY

What's the verdict, Coach?

Goalie is protecting his right. Leaves the top left open if you can be quick enough. I'd get the puck to Ivanov. He's faster at shooting.

That's not an insult to you before you go there.

. . .fine.

I don't have any other observations, but Chicago knows you're onto their strategy. They're a smart team, so I would expect something different for the last period. No idea what. You watched their tapes, so you should know.

I did, and they never played so defensively and effectively as they have tonight.

What did your coach say?

He said they cleaned house and got a whole new assistant coaching staff. So it's anyone's guess.

Dammit. He just said to get the puck to Ivanov.

I send him a smiley face and pocket my phone.

declan

"LISTEN UP," Coach yells between his cupped hands. "That was a hard-fought win, and I'm proud of you boys. Chicago was tougher than we were expecting."

"Monroe's wife saved our asses," Bouchard says.

Coach smiles. "She sure as shit did."

I grin, proud as hell of Willa. Sure, I scored and so did Ivanov, but it was only because of her careful observations.

"Mrs. Monroe also has two other members of her band with her, and they're asking for autographs."

"They want our autographs?" Fitz, the second line center, asks looking bewildered.

"Probably not yours," Martinez snickers.

"Cal will sign your naked ass if you ask him to," I say.

"He's right. I will!" Cal yells from the other side of the door.

"Get showered and dressed so they can come in here," Coach says, shaking his head and trying to hide a smile. "I won't have any of you traumatizing Willa."

"You'd have to try a lot harder than that!" Cal yells again.

I roll my eyes. "For fuck's sake, Callahan! Go do something for five minutes so we can get dressed!" I can hear my wife hysterically laughing in the hallway.

"Shower and get dressed. You have twenty minutes before press," Coach says and leaves for his office.

I've never seen the guys change so quickly. They're all presentable within seven minutes.

"Alright Cal, you can come in," I shout. He barges in and immediately makes a beeline for Bouchard. Kai and Willa follow at a normal pace until Willa spots me. She runs and throws herself into my arms, kissing me deeply.

The team chants her name, making her blush and laugh. "The only thing I did was pay attention. I'm not a coach." All my teammates come up to her and thank her, tell her how awesome she is for saving the game for us. More than half ask for her autograph. Cal and Kai seem more starstruck than they should be considering they're the more famous ones in this room. But I'm glad everyone is having a great time.

Coach pops his head back in. "Press in two minutes. They want Banks, Ivanov, Bouchard, and Monroe," he says, pausing when he looks at me. "They're going to ask about Mrs. Monroe. It's up to you two if you want to be out there together or not." Then he's gone.

"What do you want to do, Princess?" I ask Willa. I've been holding her hand the whole time, even when she was signing autographs.

She shrugs. "I'm used to interviews. I can go with you if you want me to."

"I always want you with me." I cup her cheek and kiss her lips gently.

Leroy is waiting for us outside of the media room. He's the manager of media coordination or some title like that. Basically, he's who we talk to before we talk to the press.

"Players will go in first. The media have been instructed to hold questions pertaining to Declan's relationship until the end," he says. He turns to Willa. "You'll stay here with me, Mrs. Monroe. Once the topic changes to you, you can make your way onto the stage. There will be an empty chair next to Declan for you. You don't have to answer any uncomfortable questions."

"Don't worry. I've had PR training. I've sat down for thirty interviews in the past two months. I've got this." She smiles at him, but he looks shocked.

"T-thirty?" he stutters.

"Oh. I thought you knew. I'm in a band. We're doing pretty well right now. We just finished our latest tour, but part of a tour is television and radio interviews. Usually at least one morning TV show and one radio show per stop, with an occasional late-night show thrown in. We had fifteen shows and thirty interviews this last leg."

I snort. "She's being modest. Their latest album just went multi-platinum."

"I'm the drummer from Shattered Halo," Willa offers the shocked man.

"Oh!" he exclaims. "You're Willa Prince!"

"The hair didn't give that away?" Gideon asks, amused by this whole interaction.

"I didn't want to assume," Leroy says, blushing. His phone buzzes in his hand. "They're ready for you. You know the drill."

We nod and make our way to our seats. The reporters ask their usual questions while peppering us with compliments. They think it softens us up to answering their questions in more detail. It doesn't. We just want to get out of here most of the time.

It's getting towards the usual end time for these things when one reporter asks Gideon, "You guys came out in the second period and exploited weakness in Chicago's defense that you didn't even see before. Where did that come from?" Gideon looks at me. Good enough segue.

"I can answer that. It was my wife. She's an avid hockey fan and texted me everything she noticed during the first period. I showed it to Coach, and we changed what we were doing."

"Your wife being Willa Prince?" another reporter asks. I smile and turn towards the door where Willa is standing.

"Wanna come out here, Princess?" I ask her.

She walks out on stage and goes to take the seat next to me, but I pull her into my lap instead. The clicks on the cameras go wild. The sound reminds me I need to ask Ben if he got any good pictures of us tonight.

Willa points to a female reporter near the front with her hand raised. She's definitely a seasoned pro at this stuff.

"When did you two meet?"

Willa smiles at me before answering. "I was four, Dec was six. We've been best friends since."

"When did it become more?" the next reporter Willa calls on asks.

"Around eight months ago, now. Have you ever realized the person you were meant to be with has been right in front of you your whole life, but you were blind to it? That was us for too many years to count." Shit. That answer squeezes my heart.

"How long have you been married?" the reporter Willa points to in the back asks.

"Almost two months. We didn't feel the need to wait. When you've been as close as we have for as long as we have, not being married felt like wasting time."

I'm just sitting here, holding my beautiful wife in my arms, and letting her describe this perfect love story we don't have yet, but we will. Several reporters start asking questions all at once, and I see Leroy move out of the corner of my eye, probably to shut things down, but Willa holds up her hand.

"Declan and I are more than willing to answer your questions, but you need to wait your turns. This isn't an elementary school classroom; we're all adults here." The room quiets and hands shoot into the air.

Willa calls on a few more reporters and kindly answers their questions. "It was great to meet you all, but I'd like to go home with my husband." She stands, takes my hand, and pulls me off stage.

"You really are a pro," Leroy says with a surprised laugh.

"It's not the eighties, Leroy," I say, patting him on the back. "Rockstars aren't all drugged out and drunk in front of reporters anymore."

"Take me home, Dec," Willa says as we walk away from

the media room. A low growl starts in my chest, and I scoop Willa up into my arms. She squeals a little before wrapping her arms tightly around my neck.

"You need to start warning me before you do that."

"Nah. I like that noise you make when you're surprised."

"Wait until you hear the other noises I can make," she whispers in my ear.

"Fuck."

We barely make it inside the door before we're on each other. Willa's in my arms, grinding against my stomach as I fuck her mouth with my tongue. My knees are screaming for me to sit down and ice them, but I ignore the pain.

"Fuck, Princess," I groan into her mouth.

"I need you inside me, Dec. Please."

"Fuck."

I let her down in front of the couch and quickly pull her pants down, taking her panties with them. She rips my jersey and her shirt off and pulls her bunched up jeans off along with her shoes. I bite my fist as I take in how fucking perfect she is standing in front of me in just a pink lacy bra.

Willa reaches for my belt, but I grab her wrist. "Sit on the edge, legs spread." She scrambles to do as I ask. I kneel in front of her, kissing my way up her thigh. "Do you taste as sweet as you smell?"

"Find out for yourself." Her voice is breathy as she stares at me with lust-filled eyes.

I don't need to be told twice. Licking my way from her

entrance to her clit, I moan at her taste on my tongue. "You taste even sweeter."

"Dec," Willa whines.

"I've got you, Princess."

I descend on her in earnest, sucking her clit and teasing it with my teeth. She grinds against me, trying to get more friction.

"I want you. Baby, please," she moans. I practically growl when she calls me baby. I didn't think I liked that, but from her lips, it's fucking everything.

I slip two fingers inside her, curling them towards me. I know I find the right spot when the noise she makes gets louder and deeper.

"Right there, Dec. Fuck. Right there," she mumbles with her eyes shut and head thrown back. I suck on her clit hard and then she's coming, screaming my name and pulsing around my fingers. I lick her through it until she's sensitive and pushing me away.

Willa runs her hands through my hair and pulls me towards her, kisses my mouth that's slick with her arousal and moans at the taste.

"Princess," I murmur as I pull away. My knees are throbbing so badly, they killed my hard on. "Can you get two bags of ice and the athletic tape?"

Willa's eyes go wide as she jumps off the couch. "Shit, baby. Your knees." She throws my jersey on and runs upstairs.

"Willa? The ice is down here!" I yell to her, gingerly pulling myself onto the couch and arranging my body so that my back is leaning on the arm and my legs are elevated.

Willa is running back down the stairs and into the

kitchen. I hear her curse while rummaging in the freezer. She reappears a few minutes later with two bags of ice, two cloth bandages and a pair of my basketball shorts. That at least explains what she went upstairs for.

"I couldn't find the tape. Will these work?" she asks, holding up the bandages.

I stand slowly and take my suit off. Willa helps me get my shoes off and my shorts on before making me sit back down on the couch and wrapping the ice in the bandages around my knees.

"I could've ridden you and this wouldn't have happened," Willa says, crawling between my legs and settling her head on my chest.

I laugh. "I told you, Princess. You're not ready yet." My dick, however, is taking notice of my wife wearing my jersey. Only my jersey. I know she feels me harden underneath her when she snorts. "Ignore that."

She wiggles, causing me to groan. Willa slides down my body and pulls at the waistband of my shorts.

"Princess," I warn.

"Let me take care of you." She looks at me and bites her bottom lip. I lift my hips, letting her pull my shorts down.

"Holy shit, baby," she says when she sees the size of me. My dick twitches. Willa smiles when she looks up at me. "You like when I call you baby?" she asks. My dick twitches again. Her smile turns sultry as she lowers her mouth to my cock.

Willa licks from my balls all the way to the tip without breaking eye contact. I almost come from that alone. "Take me in your mouth, Princess."

She does as I ask, sucking gently on the head before

taking me to the back of her throat. "Fucking Christ!" I yell, my hips thrusting up of their accord. "Willa, holy fuck." She pulls all the way off and then takes me to the back of her throat again, but this time she swallows. I moan louder than I ever have in my life. I can feel how wide my eyes are from shock or pleasure, I'm not sure which. She does the same thing two more times, and I'm done for. I never stood a fucking chance.

Willa swallows everything I give her and then licks her lips like she just had a tasty snack. I'm panting like I just ran a marathon. My jaw is hanging open, and I'm staring at my wife like she's the perfect surprise. Willa gently pushes my jaw shut with her finger and kisses my cheek. Then she helps me get my shorts back up. I haven't been able to utter a single word.

"I don't have a gag reflex," she says as she pulls the blanket off the back of the couch and throws it over us.

"Yeah, I'll say," I manage, my voice hoarse. She leans in and kisses me. It's slow and sweet, but dirty as fuck with the taste of me on her tongue. She snuggles into me, and I wrap her tightly in my arms. I fall asleep with a smile on my face.

I'm so fucking in love with this woman.

willa

I FORCED Declan to make an appointment with his physical therapist before his morning practice. I watched him try to walk around the house this morning looking like the tin man searching for his oil can. I'm glad I did too. The physical therapist wouldn't let him practice, which he would've pushed through and hurt himself more. She said he just needs to rest today, and he can be back on the ice tomorrow.

"Driving isn't going to bother my knees, Princess," Declan says, trying to take the keys from my hand. I snatch them away and glare at him.

"Yes, it will. You can stretch out in the back while I drive." I hop in the driver's seat of Cal's massive SUV and adjust the seat so I can reach the pedals. The man has one child and now he drives a car with a third row and every added safety feature that exists. Maverick's and Declan's cars only have two seats and mine is too small to comfortably fit two large men, so we're borrowing Cal's.

Declan climbs in the back as I adjust my seat. Maverick

is already in the passenger seat. I see the two of them exchange a look while I adjust my mirrors.

"What? What was that look?" They both glance at each other again, which just makes me mad. "I will sing the entire three-hour drive. Don't test me." They both look alarmed, which is satisfying, but I keep my face in a scowl.

"I just thought Declan would be driving," Mav says, but he's tapping his fingers on his thigh. It's a nervous tick of his. I'm sure he's nervous about having to see his dad, but I'm getting the feeling that's not the current problem.

"He has old man knees," I say. Mav turns a pleading look on Declan.

"It's just that your driving is a little scary, Princess," Dec offers, trying to lighten the blow.

"Scary?" My voice rises in pitch. I can see Mav flinch out of the corner of my eye.

"It's not scary, exactly," Mav says nervously. "Just. . . aggressive."

I curb my shock and smile. Declan and Maverick both look scared at the change, which just makes me smile wider.

"Buckle up, baby," I say, catching Declan's wide eyes in the mirror. "You too, Mav." I turn to him just in time to see him scramble for his seat belt.

This is going to be fun.

"We're here," I singsong. I spent the last three hours singing show tunes and driving like I usually do. Judging from the gasps and a few worried yelps from Mav, I might need to adjust how I drive. You'd think if I was that bad, I would at least have been pulled over or even been in an accident. But I haven't. Squeaky clean driving record over here, so I don't know what they're being so dramatic about.

After handing over our IDs to the guards at the gate and parking in the small visitor lot, Mav and I are led through a metal detector and into a bland room. The walls are eggshell white with a black linoleum floor that's old and cracked. The small white tables with their matching benches are bolted to the floor. Harrison told us what to expect, but it's depressing seeing it in person. Since the senator is being held on non-violent charges, he's allowed visits like this. I was expecting the kind behind glass where you have to talk into a phone. Drug trafficking doesn't seem non-violent to me either, but what do I know?

Maverick's fingers are tapping his bouncing legs. I put my hand over his and it stops the bouncing, but his shaking becomes more evident. "It'll be fine, Mav," I lie. He knows it's a lie, but he forces a smile, anyway. My heart aches for my friend.

Soon, a guard enters with James Wolfe in tow. He takes the senator's handcuffs off and takes his post by the door.

"No cuffs?" I mutter under my breath in shock.

"Non-violent, remember?" Mav whispers back.

"Maverick, Ms. Prince," Wolfe greets, taking the seat on the bench across from us. He folds his hands in front of him like he's conducting a meeting. His salt and pepper hair is immaculately styled. He's wearing beige pants and a shirt that resembles hospital scrubs. "Or is it Mrs. Monroe now?" The jerk smiles at me.

"You saw last night's breaking celebrity news?" I ask sarcastically. "I didn't take you for a fan of gossip."

"You'd be correct. I keep abreast of any and all news surrounding my son and the people he's allowed in his circle." Wolfe smiles using that politician smile that was plastered all over the state of Maine during his many campaigns over the years.

"Dad, what did you do?" Maverick asks, losing all pretense that this is a friendly visit.

Wolfe clears his throat and shifts in his seat, almost like he's uncomfortable, before looking at his son. "I did what I thought was best for my family. That's all I've ever done."

"I don't think insider trading, kidnapping, or murder are good for any family," I mutter.

Wolfe's eyes flair in surprise.

"What? No insider trading?" I ask with a casual shrug. I should probably be playing nicer with this man, but there's no way I was going to sit here and watch the way Maverick reacts to him without opening my mouth.

Wolfe leans forward, keeping his voice low. "While there may be some truth to the charges against me, I have never harmed or arranged harm of another person." Maverick scoffs, but Wolfe doesn't let up. "I know what you think I did, Maverick, and I can assure you that you're wrong."

"Which thing? Knocking Mom around or killing my boyfriend?" Maverick asks with so much venom in his tone that I have to double check it's actually him sitting next to me.

"*I*," Wolfe starts, "have never laid a hand on your mother or anyone else."

"You don't need to lie. I've seen your handy work," Mav says, shrugging casually, though his fingers are still tapping out a soundless beat on his leg.

"You're not listening, son. *I* have never caused physical harm to another."

"Then who?" I ask, but Wolfe's eyes immediately flicker to the guard and then to all the cameras in the room. He shakes his head when he meets my stare. I quickly glance at Maverick, who looks just as confused as I feel.

"So you didn't physically hurt anyone, but you still tried to force me into a career I didn't want and into a marriage I'd be miserable in."

Wolfe sighs and looks at his hands. "Believe it or not, that was to protect you." Maverick and I both scoff at the same time.

"You need to give me more than that." Maverick's tone is bordering on a plea, but he's still too angry to go there.

Wolfe's lips press into a firm line. "I can't," he says, looking at the cameras again.

"Give me something, Dad. Please." This time, the desperation bleeds through in Maverick's voice and expression. I grab his hand and grip it tightly in mine.

"He's here," Wolfe whispers and immediately stands.

"Who's here? In the prison?" Mav asks. Wolfe shakes his head almost imperceptibly. He's holding his hands out for the cuffs before we can ask him anything else.

"I love you, Maverick. I'm sorry." With those parting words, he's being led through the door and back into the bowels of the prison.

"Who was he talking about?" Harlow asks after we finish recounting our day to everyone from our usual seats around

Cal's table. Well, everyone else is in a seat. I'm in Declan's lap, tracing the lines of his tattoos on the arms he has wrapped around me. The one on his left arm is of the mountain range near the campground we grew up going to. It's the one I find my fingers tracing almost unconsciously all the time. He didn't enjoy letting me go into the prison alone and has been clinging to me ever since.

"His partner?" I suggest. "He kept glancing at the guard and the cameras like he was worried about saying too much."

"It's Ezra. It has to be," Declan says. "I had three hours in the car to think about this, and it's the only thing that makes sense. There's no point telling us his partner is here. That's a conclusion we would've jumped to, anyway."

Harrison looks at Maverick for a moment before speaking, like he's trying to weigh his words carefully. "Maverick, did you ever see your father hurt your mother?"

Mav blinks slowly. "You believe him?"

"It's not a matter of belief. I just want facts," Harrison says gently.

"No. I never witnessed it, but she would always call me to help her with her injuries after," he admits sadly, gaze turning down to his lap.

"I'm sticking with the Senator Wolfe theory. It's all we have right now and even if he's not guilty of some crimes, he isn't innocent." Harlow says, sharing a glance with Jo. "Our platform for the podcast is open and taking submissions as of this morning. Maybe we'll get lucky, and someone will have a lead on Ezra."

"I'll start digging into associates," Harrison says. "Are

there any old classmates or childhood friends your dad ever spoke about?" he asks Maverick.

Mav's face scrunches up in thought before he nods. "I don't know his name," Mav sighs and places his head in his hands. "There was one guy he just called an 'old buddy' that he would meet for drinks once or twice a year. I never asked because we weren't close, and I didn't care."

"Harlow, can you start pulling yearbooks? Look for any pictures of Wolfe with someone else. I'm in the middle of looking into his current known associates, but they're all corrupt and it's a lot of shit to dig through." Harlow nods to her dad.

The conversation switches to Harrison, Harlow, and Jo talking research strategy. I stifle a yawn, but Declan notices.

"Come on, Princess. It's been a long day."

I leap off his lap before he can stand with me in his arms. "No carrying me until your knees are feeling better."

His eyes narrow, but he listens and holds out his hand to me instead. I take it, enjoying the way his rough, warm hand feels against mine.

"Are you staying here or at my house?" I ask Jo. She's supposed to be moving into her own apartment in a few days, but I wouldn't be surprised if Harlow insists she stay here until we figure out who is working with Wolfe. Someone tried to silence Harlow. Trying to silence Jo next makes sense.

"Can you stay with me? Please?" Mav asks sounding so broken it breaks my heart.

They stare at each other for a moment before Jo nods.

"We're going to find Ezra," Kai says to Maverick.

"Whether he's here or in the jungles of Brazil, we'll find him. He's alive, Mav. Hold on to that."

"I'm trying. I'm trying so damn hard, Kai," Mav admits.

I glance up at Declan, but he looks just as helpless as I feel.

"Hey, Dec. Did your friend get pictures of me at your game last night?" Cal asks, changing the subject and causing Harlow to roll her eyes.

"I hope he did, and with your Chickadees hat on. I'll post it everywhere," I tease. The mood needs lightening, and no one is better at that than Cal.

"Not a single person tried to fight me in the parking lot for wearing it," he says, and crosses his arms smugly.

"Let's see if that still holds when I tag every Boston sports team in it."

Cal's eyes go wide. "You wouldn't."

"Your wore the rival team's merch to a home game? I don't like sports and even I know that's bad, Callahan." Belle glances at me and gives me a small smile before turning back to her brother.

"It's not even the same sport! Hockey and baseball aren't related!"

"I don't even know if Ben took a picture of you, Cal," Declan says.

"Why wouldn't he? Look at me." Cal stands and turns with his arms out like we need to get a good look at him to understand.

"On that note, I'm going home to get some sleep." I pull Declan behind me. Cal catcalls as we leave, but I ignore him.

Sleep never finds me. I spend the night wrapped in

Declan's arms, replaying the meeting with the senator, trying to find anything I may have missed.

TWENTY-EIGHT

I HAVE a string of away games that's keeping me from Willa for eight days. I'm not happy about it, and I wanted to ask her to come to at least one of them, but she's using this time to try to repair her relationship with Belle. I couldn't argue with that. Or the blowjob she gave me to hold me over as I was about to leave the house. I was almost late getting on the bus.

"Ben!" I yell, taking my seat next to him. He raises an eyebrow at me. Probably because it's barely seven in the morning and everyone else is still half asleep. Or in Slava's case, back asleep. "Just the guy I was looking for!"

"Why?" he asks, suspicious of me.

"I was wondering if you got any good shots from Friday's game," I explain. Usually he just texts me, but the game was the day after Thanksgiving, and I didn't know if he had some family stuff happening. I didn't want to bother him.

"Oh! Yeah, I did, actually. I forgot to send them to you.

My dad flew in for the weekend, so I was occupied." He quickly pulls out his tablet. I get comfortable while he navigates to what he's looking for. "I did some editing to remove the reflections of the surrounding people."

"Holy shit, Benny boy." I snag the tablet and swipe through the pictures. "These are amazing." There are a few shots from where he must have been standing somewhere behind Willa. But there's one that stands out. I'm standing in front of my wife, my hand on the glass to meet hers on the other side. The awe on my face is front and center while you can see her smiling in the reflection on the glass.

I bark out a laugh, making Ben look at me in confusion. "Cal is going to be so pissed you erased him." Ben rolls his eyes at my explanation. I tilt my head and watch him. Something in that movement itches at my brain. Like it's familiar. Which I guess it probably is, since he's my roommate when we're away. Willa's visit to the prison and the subsequent meeting has my brain overthinking everything.

"What? Is there something on my face?" He wipes his cheeks and then scratches his beard.

"No. Sorry. I'm just out of it today." I keep swiping until I find a shot from the other side of the rink. This time my back is to the camera, but Willa's face is in focus, smile wide and eyes sparkling.

"You really love her," Ben says, his blue eyes assessing my face.

"I really fucking do," I say.

"Here." Ben swipes through a few more until he gets to one of Cal, arms up, eyes practically popping out of his head, and mouth wide open on a shout. He looks like a complete maniac.

"I love this," I laugh. Ben got a few good shots of the three of them watching my game, and a cute one of Willa and Maggie cheering. "These are great, man. I appreciate it."

"Anytime." He takes the tablet and sends them all my way.

"I talked to Willa and got you two tickets and backstage passes to a Shattered Halo show in Boston that hasn't been announced yet. I thought you might want to take your boyfriend. Gideon and Maggie will be there too."

Ben's eyes go comically wide, and his face pales. He said he was a huge fan, and I think I just blew his mind.

"As a thank you for the photos and for being a good roomie," I explain. He's still staring at me with a dumbstruck expression. "It's not for another few months, but we don't have a game that night if that's what you're worried about."

Ben shakes his head, snapping himself out of it. "That's very generous, Declan."

"We're friends, Ben," I shrug. "It's the least I can do."

Ben nods, a strange expression crossing his features. He settles back in his seat and closes his eyes.

I pull my phone out to text the group chat Cal added me to last night.

> Ben freaked out when I told him about the tickets.

KAI

> In a good way?

> I thought he may have stopped breathing, or he saw a ghost.

PRINCESS

Most people aren't used to the price tag on
your presents, Dec.

Technically, I didn't pay for anything.

PRINCESS

Not the point. It's a gift that would normally
cost a lot of money. That makes some
people uncomfortable.

BELLE

Cal tried to buy me a car once, and it made
me so uncomfortable I almost threw up.

CAL

I'm your brother. I can buy you a car if I
want to.

MAV

Why does she get a car, and you got me a
ten-pound block of cheese last Christmas?

CAL

You love cheese!

MAV

I'm lactose intolerant!

JO

I watched you eat pizza last night.

MAV

Got me there.

I snort. Seems Maverick is doing better this morning,
thankfully. Willa was really worried about him last night. I
was too, if I'm being honest.

Willa texts me in our private chat.

PRINCESS

> Belle and I are getting dinner tomorrow
> night.

That's awesome!

> I'm nervous. I didn't mean to hurt her, but
> I'm not sure she sees it that way.

Her agreeing to dinner means she's
working on forgiving you, right?

> I think so.

It's only been a few days. Let her work
through it.

> That's the problem. Belle forgives within
> minutes. Hours at most. Days never.

See how dinner goes before you freak out.
She may have just needed longer because
it was a pretty big bomb you dropped.

> I'll try.

> I miss you, baby. Can't wait until you're
> home.

I groan and look out of the window. We're not even out of Massachusetts yet. She makes me want to jump off the bus and run home. Hockey be damned.

"You better not be sexting your wife right now," Ben mutters.

"I'll save that for the room," I tease him. He grumbles and turns so his back is to me.

I miss you too, Princess. I'll call you after
the game tonight.

I'll have my list ready.

I smile and lean my head back. The next eight days are going to be the longest of my life.

TWENTY-NINE

"ARE you sure you guys don't want us to bring something back for you?" I ask Jo. She's in my living room setting up her laptop. She moved all her stuff into the guest room at Maverick's. Harlow wouldn't let her get her own apartment, and Jo didn't want to stay with any couples. We all still have safety concerns with the idea that Wolfe wasn't working alone. I think we all feel better knowing Mav isn't alone too.

"I'm sure. I have a ton of these submissions about Ezra's case to go through. I'm just going to order a pizza," Jo says. Harlow is meeting her here once she puts Cora down to bed and Cal's dad, Jason, takes over. The guys are all hanging out at Maverick's tonight. Which is why Jo is here. "Thanks for letting me use your space."

"You can come over whenever you need to, Jo. You didn't even have to move out."

She scrunches up her nose. "I don't need to overhear what you and Declan are getting up to."

I laugh. "Fair."

"Ready?" I turn to see Belle standing in the doorway, a tight smile on her face.

"Ready."

The ride to the restaurant is quiet. Belle is driving since apparently everyone agrees about my skills behind the wheel.

"Why is no one here?" I ask, looking round the empty parking lot of the usually very busy restaurant. Belle pulls into a spot right out front. The door to the restaurant immediately opens, and a server stands out front, holding the door open.

"Ms. Griffin, Mrs. Monroe," the server says, gesturing with his arm for us to go inside.

"Where is everyone?" Belle asks him.

"Mr. Irons and Mr. Monroe bought out the restaurant for you for the night," he explains, leading us to a table in front of a window. We picked this restaurant because it overlooks a lake, and this table has the perfect view.

"Of course they did," I sigh. My phone vibrates in my pocket at the same time as Belle's pings.

HOCKEY BOY

Try to have fun tonight, Princess. Belle wouldn't be there if she didn't love you and want to talk through this.

"Kai?" I ask Belle.

"Declan?" she asks me in turn. I bite my lip and nod, trying to suppress my smile since I know he's a sore spot for her right now.

We sit in silence, only speaking when the server comes to take our orders.

"I'm sorry," I say the moment he leaves our table.

Belle sighs and stares at her hands. "I know you are, Willa. I've had a really hard time trying to sort through my feelings, even with my therapist's help."

"Is there anything I can do to help?"

Belle shakes her head. "I think I understand now why you kept Declan separate."

"If you understand, why do you look so sad?"

"Because I feel like I failed you," she explains, lifting her eyes from her hands. There's no anger there, only hurt.

"You lost me."

"I didn't see it. You started hiding parts of yourself after your mom died. Replacing your smile with a scowl unless you were with people close to you." She holds my stare, waiting for me to deny her words, but I can't. "Then your dad died, and you closed yourself off even more. You dyed your hair purple, wore mostly black, and pretended like nothing could crack your armor."

"I didn't want you to see it," I whisper. Belle reaches her hand out and takes mine.

"I know, and that hurts." I open my mouth to apologize, but she speaks before I can. "I understand it, though. But why did Declan get all of you? That's what I'm still struggling with."

"I don't have an answer to that because I honestly don't know. Maybe because there was always physical distance between us, or because he always made me feel like I was perfect." I squeeze her hand and smile softly. "What would you say to me if I said I wanted to quit the band and start an elephant sanctuary?"

Belle's eyes go wide. "That you should take a step back

and think this over. You don't even like animals. Or the outdoors. Or being in charge of things."

I nod and hold up a finger, pulling out my phone and quickly dialing Declan on speaker. He picks up on the second ring. I can hear the noises in the locker room filtering through the phone before he even speaks.

"Hey, Princess. Is everything alright? You should still be at dinner." I smile at his sweet concern.

"I'm fine, hockey boy. Belle and I were just talking, and I'm thinking about quitting the band and starting an elephant sanctuary."

"We'll need to find a really large piece of land for that. Have you done a pros and cons list for this? Do elephants like snow?" He answers immediately and then pauses for a moment. "I need to do some research, but if you're serious, I'm all in, Princess. I'll go on whatever adventure you want me to."

"I think I'll stick with this adventure for now," I say with a smile.

"This one is pretty great," he agrees. "I have to get on the ice, but I'll call you after my game."

"Tell Slava his passes were too slow last game, and he needs to be faster if you want to win tonight. Detroit's offense is fast and aggressive. They're going to be on him the moment the puck hits his stick." I can hear Declan repeating what I said to Slava at the same time Belle snorts from trying to hold in her laugh.

"You got it, Willa!" I hear Slava yell.

"Kick ass out there tonight, baby."

"You know I will, Princess." We quickly say our good-byes, and I turn to Belle.

"You know I support you no matter what, right?" Belle asks.

"I do. That wasn't the point I was trying to make. You both support me, but you're more cautious. Dec has always been more balls to the wall. I need you both. It's never been one or the other for me." I squeeze her hand again; grateful she hasn't taken it back. "I've never felt like I gave him more of me than I did to you. I have so many more memories with you, Belle. I just kept him to myself because I wanted to be selfish. I'm so sorry that it hurt you."

Belle's lips curve into a small smile. "I'm sorry it's taken me so long to come to terms with you and Declan."

"What else?" I ask, making a circle around her face with my finger. "I can see there's something else."

She sighs. "I was supposed to be your maid of honor. It's probably a stupid thing to be upset about, but Kai pointed out that it's potentially what I'm actually the most hurt by."

I just stare at her, not sure what to say. We promised to be each other's maids of honor when we were kids. That never wavered over time, either. "I'm such an asshole," I mutter.

Belle laughs. "Well, at least it wasn't something you thought about, judging from your reaction."

"I'm sorry, Belle. I didn't even think about it. We didn't even have a real wedding."

"Why did you get married so fast?" she asks, the humor leaving her face as she looks down at my stomach.

"No! Don't look at me like that. I'm not pregnant!"

The server takes that moment to drop off our food. He's nice enough to pretend he didn't just hear me shouting about my empty uterus. "Can I get you anything else?"

"Gin and tonic. Two limes. Please." He nods and quickly scampers off to get my drink. Or to avoid any more shouting.

Belle eyes me suspiciously. "You don't need to prove it."

"I know. I need it after that question." She laughs, but doesn't touch her food, waiting for me to answer her first question.

"It was my next adventure," I say softly with a small lift of my shoulders.

Belle smiles sadly and nods. "Can we agree on no more secrets?"

I plaster on what I hope is a convincing smile. "No more secrets." She must believe me because she returns the smile and then digs into her dinner.

I eat as much as I can, the guilt of keeping one more secret turning sour in my stomach.

Belle and I sing along to her Top 40 playlist the whole ride home. Which, luckily for her, was only about fifteen minutes. Knowing I can't sing has never stopped me from doing it.

"What the hell?" Belle mutters, turning the radio down. I look where she's looking.

"Is that Harlow?" Red hair flashes in the beam of our headlights as Harlow runs barefoot down the sidewalk in front of our houses.

"Why is she running?"

"Wait. Jo is chasing her. Pull over!" Belle stomps on the brakes and throws her car into park. We quickly get out and run after them. Harlow is already inside Maverick's house with Jo hot on her heels. Another woman walks in calmly behind them. "Okay, maybe we could've parked in Mav's driveway," I pant.

"Oh shit," Belle says. She's in front of me but stops suddenly. I barely prevent myself from crashing into her.

"What?" I ask, looking around and seeing what she saw. "Oh, shit!"

Standing in the doorway is Eva Wolfe, Maverick's bitch of a mother.

"What the fuck are you doing here?" Mav shouts from inside his house.

I rush around Belle and shove my way past Eva to get to Maverick. Which turns out to be unnecessary when I see everyone already here. Kai and Cal are standing in front of Maverick like they're ready to protect him with their bodies. Harlow is staring at Eva with wide eyes while Jo is bent over and huffing air from running over here. I stand next to Cal, trying to get in front, but he pulls me slightly behind him.

"I'll take out the trash," I offer, even though Eva is about half a foot taller than me. Belle walks in behind her, not hiding the disdain from her face, before standing next to me. Harlow and Jo move to Kai's side, all of us a wall between her and the son she hurt.

"How did you get in here?" Harlow asks. "There's a guard at the gate."

Eva doesn't spare a glance at any of us, her beady gray eyes zeroed in on Maverick. "Your father was arrested, and I don't hear a word from you, yet you have time to visit him."

"I have nothing to say to you," Maverick answers her.

Eva scoffs and crosses her arms. "Your father ruined this family, and you have nothing to say?"

Maverick pushes his way through Kai and Cal. "We're not a family. Never have been. You made it clear that I was only alive to marry and make connections for you. Just a pawn in your scheming."

"What have I done? All I did was support my husband. How was I supposed to know he was breaking the law?" Eva scoffs again. I forgot how much I heard her do that over the phone when Mav met her for lunch over the summer. It's grating on my ears.

"Breaking the law? He's been accused of trafficking drugs, Mom! Drugs that killed thousands of people!" Maverick shouts, but she doesn't even flinch.

"I'm very aware of the charges against your father. Which is why you need to come home and —"

"No. I am home." I smile at how strong Maverick is right now. His parents have done a good job chipping away at his confidence for most of his life, but he's finally fighting back.

"We need to show a united front if we hope to beat the charges. The prosecutor has a son that shares your. . .tastes." She scrunches her nose like she smelled something rotten.

"You're not pimping out your son to save your murderous husband, you psycho," I snarl, trying to get around Cal, but he keeps his arm firmly in front of both me and Belle. I look around him to see Kai struggling to keep Jo back too. Harlow is still really pale and staring at Eva like she's seen a ghost.

"Dad is taking a plea deal, and I'm releasing a public statement condemning his actions and making sure the public is aware of the distance between us," Maverick states, shocking everyone in the room if the gasps are anything to go by. Even Eva shows a brief flash of shock on her face. If I blinked, I would've missed it.

"Your father isn't taking a plea deal, Maverick. There isn't one on the table." Eva takes a step forward and reaches out like she's going to grab Maverick and drag him out of his own house. I dart under Cal's arm and stand next to Mav, slapping his mother's hand away before she can touch him. She sneers at me.

"Oh, hi Mrs. Wolfe. So nice to see you again. Please feel free to fuck right off," I say, smiling sweetly.

"Let's go, Maverick," she says like she hasn't heard a single thing he's said.

"You misunderstand. You are not welcome here. This is Maverick's home, and we are his family. Leave." I say the last word through teeth clenched almost as tightly as my fists. I've never punched someone before, but now feels like a good time to start.

Eva scoffs, looking down on me like I'm beneath her. My smile widens, and I step towards her. Maverick grabs me around the waist and hauls me back against him, but the look of fear on Eva's face, as quick as it was, satisfies me enough not to fight him.

"Call Dad if you don't believe me. From your car because Willa is right. You're not welcome in *my* home with *my* family. Come back here, and I'll be pressing trespassing charges against you."

"Sorry I'm late. Whose car is in the. . ." Jon freezes in his tracks as he walks through the door, carrying a box of chicken wings and a case of beer. "Street." he finishes. "What's going on?"

"You will come home, Maverick," Eva says, spinning on her heel and slamming the door behind her.

"Should I leave?" Jon asks.

"It was her," Harlow says, her eyes wide. Cal wraps her up in his arms and murmurs something in her ear. Jo's eyes go wide and everyone else looks as confused as I feel.

"Stay, Jon. We need to have a family meeting," Maverick says, leaving the foyer and sitting on his couch. We decided to keep Jon in the loop since he's become close to the guys and is the one handling anything band related. It's easier to explain delays to an agent that understands what's happening.

"I need the laptop," Harlow says, making a break for the door, but Cal doesn't let her go.

"You're not wearing shoes, Firecracker. I'll get it," he says. I leave them to talk and sit next to Mav on the couch.

"Thank you," he says.

"Should've let me at her," I mumble. He laughs and pulls me in for a side hug. I hug him back instead of questioning how he's so happy right now. I peek up at him and see him smiling. I meet Belle's eyes across the room where she's standing with Kai. She looks just as confused as me.

Everyone is silent while we wait for Cal to get back with the laptop he went to get. I'm snuggled between Mav and Harlow, the latter bouncing her knee so much I reach out to stop it. "Sorry," she whispers.

"Can we call Declan?" Cal asks while Jo pulls something up on the computer.

"He's playing right now." And losing. I haven't been able to watch any of it, but I get the alerts on my phone.

"We can watch the rest of his game if you want," Mav offers.

I shake my head. "There are eighty-two games in a season. I can miss one. This is important."

"Who wants to go first?" Kai asks, looking between Mav and Jo.

"You first," Mav says to Jo.

"I was going through the submissions to our new platform when one of them got my attention," Jo explains.

"It's why I ran here shoeless," Harlow adds.

"And said it wasn't my dad," Mav says.

"Listen first and then hopefully Harlow can explain because I don't know how she jumped there either," Jo says, clicking on an audio file.

"You got rid of the boy?"

The voice is muffled, but clear enough to understand the words. I can't tell if it's male or female, though.

"I told you I did."

My heart stops. That's Maverick's dad.

"Then why is his brother trying so hard to find him?"

That's the first voice again.

"It's his brother. What the fuck were you expecting?"

Senator Wolfe.

"You could've left a fucking body."

First voice.

"You told me to make sure no one could connect it to us!"

Senator Wolfe.

"Did you hear that?" Harlow asks. "Play it again, Jo," she says before anyone can answer. Jo does as she asks.

"So my dad either thinks he killed Ezra, or he pretended to?" Maverick asks.

"Not that," Harlow says and makes Jo play it again. She replays a noise after the muffled voice twice more.

"The scoff!" I yell, making Harlow jump next to me, but then she smiles.

"Exactly!"

"Harlow, you need to call your dad," I tell her. "How the fuck did she get in here? Someone call the gate."

"I'm going to need this explained," Kai says, scratching the stubble on his jaw.

"Eva scoffs. It's pretty much her favorite thing to do," I explain. I watch as all the pieces click into place on Kai's face.

"Fuck!" he shouts and runs his fingers through his hair.

"My mom. All this time, I thought she was just a puppet for my dad, but it's the other way around, isn't it?" Maverick sighs and leans back.

"I was still focusing on the senator since we had no evidence to point us anywhere else," Harlow explains.

"A noise that might be a scoff or a million other things on a recording isn't exactly evidence," Belle says gently.

"I know, but Wolfe is clearly the other voice. Which means he either is terrible at murder or faked Ezra's death. And who would he be answering to?" Harlow asks. "I need to call my dad." She jumps up from the couch and makes the call while heading into the kitchen.

"It makes sense," Maverick says.

"It does?" I ask.

"My dad was always strict and definitely disappointed in me for my choice of career, but he was never cold in the way my mom is." He picks at the hem of his shirt. "I've been thinking about my childhood a lot since we went to visit him. Every comment he made about Ezra was after my mom said something."

"What about the weird, arranged marriage thing she seems so focused on?" Jo asks.

"Political marriages are more common than you'd think."

"Gross," Cal mutters.

"She's power hungry. I always thought it was because my dad hit her, and she was compensating by becoming the woman standing by a powerful man," Mav says. "But what if he wasn't lying? What if he never hit her?"

"Then who did?" I ask. Mav shrugs as Harlow takes her seat.

"So," she says. "Plea deal?"

"I said that to see her reaction."

"She seemed surprised, but I think we all were," I say.

Mav smirks at me. "That's because you don't know her. She was surprised at first, but she turned angry really fast," he says. "And not at me."

"Because she thinks he's about to roll on her," Harlow says.

Maverick shrugs. "Or at least embarrass her more."

Everyone is quiet, letting the chaos of the evening sink in. It's a lot and nothing at the same time. Harrison is going to do a lot of digging to figure it all out. But the biggest question that no one wanted to voice hangs heavy around us all.

Are we safe?

declan

WE FOUGHT like hell against Detroit and still lost. It's a shitty start to this road trip. It was made even shittier when Willa told me everything that went down at Maverick's house. I've been tossing and turning for over an hour. What if something happened, and I wasn't home?

The lights in the hotel room turn on, making me groan and bury my face in my pillow. "Why?" I complain.

"What's going on? I can't sleep while you're over there cosplaying a rotisserie chicken."

I laugh and throw my pillow at Ben. "I'm just really worried about things that went down at home," I explain. I really like Ben. He's become a good friend. I don't know him well enough to let him in on everything, though.

"Is Willa okay?" he asks, genuine concern in his tone.

"She's good, man." I smile, so he knows I mean it. "She just had a rough night, and I'm not there."

Ben nods. "I get it. She's strong, though. She can handle it."

"Did you guys meet at the last game?" I ask him.

He shakes his head. "She's a female drummer in an industry dominated by men and married to your dumbass." I laugh at his accurate and insulting assessment. "I also overheard her letting the ref know exactly what she thought of his calls at the last game."

I belly laugh at that. "You're right. I wouldn't cross her."

"Can we sleep now?"

"Yeah. Sorry for keeping you up." He turns the light out instead of answering me. "Can I have my pillow back?" My face catches it with an oof a moment later.

"Gideon!" I yell, jogging after my team captain. He stops and waits for me. I had another concern last night that I didn't think Ben could help me with.

"Hurry up, Dec. You're delaying breakfast, and I'm starving."

"How close are you with your agent?" I ask him when I get to his side.

"She's nice, and I've been working with her since I signed eleven years ago. I don't talk to her outside of work-related things, if that's what you mean."

"Would it be weird if you did?" I ask.

He frowns. "Are you trying to ask Diego to be your friend?"

"Fuck no. He's great at what he does, but I don't like him."

"I'm going to need your help on this one, buddy."

"Willa's agent is always with them. Well, not always. But like kind of a lot." When she told me he was there last night, I got weirded out. "They haven't even known him very long. He was at Thanksgiving with us." I leave out that he was invited, and I wasn't.

"Are you worried about him and Willa?" Gideon asks slowly.

I roll my eyes. "Not in that way. I'm just worried he's taking advantage or something."

"Why don't you talk to Willa about it?"

"I needed another opinion."

"Just talk to her. But try to make more sense when you do." He claps me on the shoulder and walks away. I go to follow him, but just as I take my first step, my phone rings. My stomach growls in protest, but when I see it's Willa, I answer it.

"Good morning, Princess."

"Dec," she says, her voice sounding strange. I freeze in my tracks.

"What's wrong? Did she come back?"

"I'm okay, Declan. But the night guard, Dean, was found dead in the guard house this morning."

"What happened? Did he have a heart attack or something?" I ask. Dean was a nice guy, but he was in his sixties and always eating cheeseburgers.

"Uh, no." That's all she offers, and I can tell it's something much worse that she doesn't want to tell me.

"I'm coming home." I turn on the spot and march back to my room.

"You're not coming home. You have three more games," she protests.

"Fuck hockey. You're in danger." I plow through the door to my room, almost knocking Ben over. He looks like he's about to let me have it until he sees my face. His brows shoot up, and he follows me back towards the beds.

"I'm fine. Hey! Callahan, give me that back!"

"Hey Dec, it's Cal. I've got our girl handled. You don't have to come back."

"I can't stay here while my wife could be in danger, Cal," I say while throwing my clothes into my duffel bag.

"I get it, but I hired around the clock security, and Willa agreed to stay with Belle and Kai until you're home."

"Agreed isn't the right word. Forced is better. Or threatened. That's a better one," Willa yells.

"How did Dean die, Cal?" I ask, pausing my packing. "Cal," I repeat when he doesn't answer right away.

He sighs. "His throat was slit."

"I'm coming home." I hang my phone up and throw the last of my things into my bag.

"Is everything okay?" Ben asks, following me out the door.

"Someone killed the security guard at our gated community last night. Maverick's mother also showed up last night. And I was playing a fucking game." I'm aware the anger I'm feeling shouldn't be directed at Ben, but I can't stomp it down right now.

Ben grabs my elbow to stop me. "I'm your friend, Dec. Let's figure this out."

"What's there to figure out?" I ask, taking a deep breath to calm myself.

"Today is a travel day, right? Your game isn't until seven tomorrow night. If we get you on a flight soon, you can be back in time to play. We just need to talk to Coach."

"We? Are you coming with me?" It would be nice to have someone with me while I panic the entire flight to Boston.

Ben shakes his head. "I'll go with you to talk to Coach, but I have to coordinate with the social media people. We're doing some travel stuff so they can post behind-the-scenes content. Kind of like what you guys are like off the ice."

I nod and take off at a brisk pace to find Coach. Which isn't too hard. He's always at breakfast with the team. He sees me coming and immediately gets up from the table and meets me.

"What's going on, Monroe?" he asks.

"I need to fly home. I'll be back by tomorrow night's game." I think. "You can bench me if you need to." Coach frowns, and I can see Ben roll his eyes.

"Declan is trying to tell you that there was a murder in his neighborhood, and he's freaking out and needs to check on his wife." Ben explains for me.

Coach's eyebrows fly into his hairline. "Is Willa alright?" he asks. I appreciate him more than he knows. There are plenty of coaches who would be far more concerned with the game, but he genuinely cares about his players.

"She says she is."

"He needs to go see her or he's going to keep freaking out. Then he'll play like shit for the rest of the time we're on the road." Ben says, holding up his phone. "I got him a flight out in two hours. The return flight lands three hours before he needs to be on the ice."

Coach examines Ben with keen eyes before turning them on me. "What were you going to do if I said no?"

"Go anyway," I say immediately.

Coach nods, spinning the gold band on his left hand.

"Check on Willa and get your ass back here. Bring her with you if you need to, but you will be on that ice tomorrow night."

"Thank you, sir!"

"I sent you your tickets. There's an Uber waiting for you out front. You need to go now," Ben says, shoving me towards the door.

"You're a good friend!" I shout over my shoulder as I run out of the hotel.

I'm coming, Princess.

willa

"DO I really have to stay here?" I complain as I sprawl out on Belle and Kai's couch.

"You don't want to have a sleepover with me?" Belle asks teasingly. We left dinner last night on much better terms.

"I don't want to snuggle with you *and* Kai."

"He can sleep in the guest room," Belle says.

"No fucking way. I'm sleeping with you," Kai says, pulling Belle into him. She laughs, but he's frowning like he actually thinks I'm going to try to take her from him.

"I'm up for a snuggle party." I shrug casually, like I'd ever get into a bed with the two of them. I'd barely be able to lie down before they'd go at it.

"I sleep naked," Kai says immediately.

"Gross." I scrunch up my nose. "You'll have to put clothes on tonight, so I'm not uncomfortable."

"You're not sleeping in my bed, Willa!" Kai shouts.

"I'm sleeping in Belle's bed."

"That's my bed!" I snort at how angry he's getting. I'm

about to rile him up some more when the doorbell rings, followed by an aggressive knock.

"I'll call security," Belle says. Cal forced everyone to agree to a lockdown while the gatehouse was still a crime scene. They're keeping the gates open while the authorities do what they need to do, and he's freaked out about people being able to get in. But that also means no one we know could be at the door.

"Willa!"

"Declan?" I fly off the couch, trip over the side table, bump into a wall, and run straight for the door. I open it as quickly as I can to my husband's panicked face. The moment he sees me, he pulls me into his arms.

"Fuck, Princess," he sighs into my hair. His strong arms are tight around me, squeezing so tight it's hard to breathe. Yet somehow, it feels like the first time I've been able to take a deep breath.

"I told you I was okay," I say into his neck.

"I need to see for myself. I had to have you in my arms, or I was going to lose it. I almost lost it on the fucking plane over here." He fists my hair, pulling my head back just enough to claim my lips.

"Does this mean I get to sleep in my bed?" Kai asks.

Declan ignores him, carrying me out the door and into our house. He wastes no time carrying me through the house and up the stairs to our bedroom. He tosses me on the bed and quickly shucks his jacket and shoes, followed closely by the rest of his clothes. I do the same until we're both naked and staring at each other.

"I need to feel you inside me."

Declan ignores me, dropping to his knees at the end of

the bed and yanking me to the edge. Instead of spreading my legs like he wants me to, I sit up and hold his face in both my hands, forcing him to look at me.

"I need you to listen," I tell him. "When my mom died, I measured time by days after her. When we went camping that first summer without her, it was two hundred and forty-six days since she died. When I turned eleven, it was one thousand one hundred and sixteen days without Mom. But the summer that year, I don't know if you remember," I say and Declan smiles, "it was the first year my dad finally started letting us go off on our own. We hiked, swam in the lake, went to those square-dancing nights the campground held every Friday." We both laugh at the memory of us tripping over our own feet. I stroke Dec's cheeks with my thumbs. "That's when I started measuring my life in moments. What I didn't realize until recently was that those moments were you. I measured time from the moment we said goodbye until the moment I jumped into your arms to say hello again. The moments in between goodbye and hello were so small compared to the ones between hello and goodbye."

"Willa," Declan says, voice thick with emotion.

"I don't know what you're waiting for me to be ready for or what moment you think we need to be in. But I'm here, Dec. I'm here in this moment with you. I'm with you."

Declan surges to his feet, pulling me with him. His mouth crashes into mine. The urgency and desperation in his kiss is a stark contrast to the gentle way he lays me down in the middle of the bed. I've never wanted anyone as much as I want Declan in this moment.

"Please," I moan into his mouth, trying to grind myself against him, desperately seeking the friction of his body.

"You're beautiful when you beg, Princess."

"Please, baby." I watch how feral my words make him, his pupils so large they're almost completely blocking out the green of his irises. Declan grabs my hips and thrusts, burying himself inside me. "You're going to split me in half," I gasp.

"No, I won't. You were made for me, Princess. Look how well you take me." He leans back on his heels, eyes glued to the spot where our bodies connect. His hips move slowly, hitting a spot so deep inside me I'm seeing stars with every thrust.

"Holy fuck, Declan," I moan.

"That's it, Willa. Let everyone know who you belong to."

I dig my heels into his ass, urging him to go faster.

He chuckles, picking up his pace. "This what you wanted? Your husband's cock drilling you into the mattress?" His dirty words and the hot kisses he places along my neck have me so wound tight I could go off at any moment. "Don't come yet. You'll come when I tell you to."

"What? I can't," I pant. "I need to come."

"You're doing so good, Princess. Wait until I tell you to." I nod at his command, frantic to do whatever he tells me to.

"Please please please please," I mutter, begging.

"I've never been able to say no to you," he whispers in my ear. Declan kisses his way across my jaw and takes my lips. "Come," he commands. I shoot off like a rocket at his command, screaming his name as I convulse around him. He keeps a steady pace, fucking me through my orgasm before he stills with a low groan, emptying himself inside me.

Declan flips us so that I'm collapsed against his side, our sweaty bodies fused together, chests heaving. I look up at him, my hair a mess against his chest. He kisses me softly, his fingers gently caressing between my legs before they still when they find the mess he left. He breaks the kiss to look down. After less than a minute of hesitation, he scoops his come with his fingers and pushes it back inside of me.

"Do you have a breeding kink?" I ask him.

He shakes his head. "I didn't. It might just be you." He meets my eyes. "We didn't use a condom."

I nod. "I'm on the pill." He looks at my stomach, splaying his large hand across it, seeming lost in thought. "Dec?"

"I'm in love with you, Willa," he says when he looks up at me. "I know you're not ready and that's okay, but I couldn't let another moment go by without you knowing how I feel about you."

I can't do anything except gape at him, my heart racing. I so badly want to give him those words, but they're stuck in my throat. He takes my hand, gently kissing my palm.

"It's okay, Princess. I can wait until you're ready to tell me."

I snuggle into him, letting his warmth, his love, wrap me up and lull me to sleep.

I've been pouting on Belle's couch for the better part of three days. Declan still has two more games to play before he can come home. I've never missed him the way I do now. He tells me he loves me every day when we talk, but I still can't get the words out. I don't know if it's because I don't love him like that yet or if I'm too broken to love him at all.

Part of me wants to be selfless and let him go. Tell him to run far away from the broken girl with only shattered remains for a heart. But it's well established that when it comes to Declan, I'm selfish. I won't give him up for anything or anyone.

He's mine.

"What time does Declan's game start?" Harlow asks, sitting next to me.

"In an hour. You like hockey?" I ask, pretending I knew she was here and didn't startle me.

She smiles at me like she knows I'm trying to play it cool but doesn't mention it. "Nope. Well, I might. I've never watched it."

I laugh and shake my head. "You're escaping Cal, aren't you?"

"I love that man, but if I spend one more minute with him hovering over me, I *will* kill him."

"Have you or your dad found anything?" I ask her. The cameras around the gate were wiped. When Belle and I pulled up to the gate that night, we assumed Dean was on break and just used our code to open it. All the residents have a unique one in case we need to get in when a guard isn't there. The police pulled the log, and Belle used her code four minutes after the gate was opened using Dean's button. Which lines up with Maverick's mom showing up. But that's all they have right now.

"He's following a money trail that doesn't add up. The ports the drugs were funneled through were purchased under a fake name. The police are aware and investigating, but they have to do it legally." Harrison knows a guy that can hack into almost any system, so he's able to find things the police either can't or have to jump over a bunch of red tape to find. "He thinks he can connect the movement of some money from the Wolfes' account around the time of purchase, but the problem is it's a joint account."

"So it could still be either or both of them."

She sighs. "Pretty much. My dad is hoping he can trace the money to whoever sold it and get answers from them. That name was false in the purchase agreement too, though. So who knows?"

"Pizza!" Kai yells.

"You left to get pizza?" Cal asks, following him inside with Cora on his hip. "We agreed to stay behind locked doors!"

Harlow sighs loudly next to me. "Sorry," she mutters.

"I did. It was curbside. I only had to open my window," Kai says.

"We let a viper into our den! You can't just leave!" Cal exclaims. Belle takes Cora from him, allowing his arms to fly into the air in exasperation.

"You're being dramatic," Jo says, walking around him with Maverick on her heels. We're all watching Dec's game together tonight since Cal won't let us go anywhere without this very thing happening.

"I'm being the exact right amount of dramatic!" Cal screams. Cora starts laughing at her dad's antics.

"Don't encourage him, Cora girl," Harlow says, trying to hide her own laughter.

"So, how did your day of research go?" I ask Jo. She

texted the group chat this morning saying she was spending the day going through professional sports teams websites trying to find someone who could be Ezra. Our only real lead on him is Jasper, but he swears he hasn't heard anything from Ezra in over two years. That leaves us with someone who worked for an MLB team in social media who also likes to pick first names that start with 'e' and last names that could be first names. Which seems better than nothing, but somehow also feels like nothing.

"There's an Easton Derrek who works in marketing for a team in Seattle, and an Eli Frank working in public relations for a team in Colorado, but neither panned out. Easton is in his fifties, and Eli's picture was on the website." She turns her phone so we can see. Eli has a sweet smile, but he also looks nothing like Ezra.

We drown our disappointment in greasy pizza while watching Declan play. Harlow gets really into it. "I like that one." She points at the screen. Cal growls next to her and pulls her onto his lap.

"Martinez is a big flirt." Although, I don't think all the flirting in the world would get Declan to play better tonight. He's skating slow, missing passes, and shooting right at the goalie. The cameras keep catching his face. He looks frustrated. I don't know what's going on with him.

> What's going on, hockey boy?

I know he can't text me right now since he's currently on the ice missing a pass from Ivanov. I'm hoping he'll look at his phone when the period ends.

"Umm, Willa? I know nothing about hockey, but I think

Declan is blowing it," Harlow says. The period ends after a few more agonizing minutes. Utah is up by three already and there are still two more periods to play.

I watch Declan make his way down the tunnel. His head hung low. The camera catches Gideon, who makes a typing gesture like he's using a keyboard and points at Declan while looking directly at the camera. He's telling me I need to talk to my husband.

"I did text him," I mutter.

HOCKEY BOY

I can't keep my mind on the game when I've left you alone to deal with everything.

I'm fine, baby. Get your head in the game and show Utah what you're made of.

I'll try, Princess.

I sigh. "Alright, everyone. Get in close and smile like you're having fun." I hold up my phone and my friends do as I ask. Cal ends up having to hold my phone since his arms are the longest, but he gets a picture of all of us smiling. I send it to Declan immediately.

I'm not alone. I promise I'm okay. We all are. Just focus and do your job. Then come home and do me.

Fuck, Princess. You have no idea how happy that picture just made me.

Or how hard your words made me.

Tonight and tomorrow night and then you're home.

> I'm counting the minutes until I can bury
> myself in my perfect wife.

I shiver with anticipation as I read his words.

"Please tell me you're not sexting him right now," Maverick says, leaning away from me.

"Send him nudes if it gets him to shoot at the fucking net," Kai mutters.

I ignore them both.

> I have to get back out there. I love you,
> Princess. I'll call you tonight.

I watch Declan return to the ice; a renewed determination clear in the way he's skating. I have a love hate relationship with the way I can affect his game without even being there.

Gideon wins the face-off, passing it to Declan who skates around everyone and scores within the first eight seconds of the period.

"I'm going to need you to sext him between every period if they make the playoffs," Cal says. I snort, but don't argue.

I watch my husband skate around Utah like their players are just minuscule obstacles. He scores again right before the end of the second period. This time, when his team enters the tunnel, their heads are held high.

declan

I LOOK at the picture Willa sent of her with her family. People who are very quickly feeling like family to me too. She's home, and she's safe. Her smile ignites a fire in my chest. I never thought I could love someone the way I love her, but now I'm starting to think I couldn't love anyone else because I was always in love with her. My love for her doesn't feel new. It feels like it's always been there, but my eyes are just now opening to it.

"We need two more, Monroe," Gideon says, skating up to me while I make a lap around the ice before the period starts.

"They're expecting me. I'll pass. Just make sure you're open." He nods and skates to the bench just as the ref blows his whistle.

Gideon loses the face-off, but Rogers is quick getting the puck back to him. He misses his first two shots but gets the puck by the goalie's left skate by a hair. Utah goes from a team playing a clean game to dirty really quickly after that. I get it. They thought they had the win clinched, but we came back and tied it up.

The entire period is full of penalties and wasted power plays. We keep getting the advantage, but they're aggressive and violent. Martinez got five for fighting. I've been in the box twice for two minutes each for charging one asshole. To be fair on the refs, that was a valid call. He started it by tripping Gideon behind the ref's backs, though.

"No overtime," Ivanov says next to me on the bench. We're watching our second line fight for their lives out there. It's my fault we're working so hard to claw our way back from an almost guaranteed loss. I start to apologize, but he stops me. "No apologies. No overtime."

The moment we're back on the ice, we fight for the puck like it's the last roll at Texas Roadhouse. Time is quickly counting down on the clock. One minute. Utah has stopped every attempt by Ivanov, Gideon, and me.

I have the puck again, but Gideon and Ivanov are covered. I spot the massive form that is Martinez out of the corner of my eye. Looking at the goalie like I'm about to shoot on him, I fake the shot and slip the puck back to Martinez. He slaps his stick so hard against the puck I barely see it fly past my head. The lights flash and the buzzer sounds. That son of a bitch did it.

I want to drop to my knees right here on the ice. I'm that tired. But we still have twenty seconds to run down before heading directly to the airport. This trip has been long and emotionally draining.

We keep Utah away until the last buzzer sounds. I barely hear Coach going over the game, even though he glares at me a lot. I already know it's my fault. I already apologized to my team.

By the time I make it onto the bus and collapse next to Ben, I'm ready to sleep. The exhaustion I feel is bone deep.

"One more game, Dec," Ben says.

"It's so hard to be away from her when I can't stop thinking about her being in danger, you know?" I ask him, not expecting the look he gives me. Like he completely understands.

"Call her before we get to the airport."

I pull out my phone and dial her. She picks up immediately. I'm sure she was waiting.

"Hey, hockey boy."

"I miss you, Princess. Ask me to retire. I'll do it right now and come home to you." She laughs, but I'm completely serious. I love hockey, but not as much as I love her.

"One more game before you're home. You can handle it."

"That's what Ben said."

"I think Ben and I will get along very well," she says. I turn and see Ben smiling. He can probably hear her. "Ask him if he wants to come by on Christmas. We're hosting this year." I smile at how domestic this is. Discussing a holiday we're hosting at our house with my wife. It's everything I never knew I wanted.

"I'm flying out to spend it with my dad, but thank you," he says into the phone.

"Oh, he has a sexy voice!" she exclaims.

"Hey! My voice is sexier!" I yell, earning a bunch of glares and shushes from the rest of the team. Then I turn to Ben. "No offense, man."

"I'm gay, Dec. There's no threat here," Ben says, laughing at me.

"Oh, right."

"Darn it," Willa says. "There go my dreams of a threesome."

"Princess," I grumble into the phone, trying to stay quiet.

"Don't worry. I'm all yours, baby." I smile victoriously at her words. Ben rolls his eyes and stands. I didn't even realize the bus had stopped.

"I have to board the plane. I'll call you tomorrow. I love you, Princess."

She hesitates like she has been the last few days since I first told her how I felt. "Have a safe flight."

And just like every other time she hasn't told me she loves me too, I swallow down the hurt. I know she feels it. I can see it in her eyes when she looks at me. I just need to be patient and continue to tell her and show her how much I love her.

We lost last night, but I'm not sure how much any of us care. We know we should, but we all just want to be home with our families. Thankfully, that was the longest trip of the season for us.

My knee bounces as I stare out the window of the bus. Coach insists we park at the training center and take a bus as a team to and from the airport for team bonding or something. It's the first time I wished I could've gone straight from my plane to my car. I'd be getting home right about now. Even Gideon seems pretty antsy to see Maggie. He's usually the calm one.

"Dec."

"Yeah?"

"Dec," Ben says again, shaking my shoulder.

"What?" I ask, turning to him.

"Look." He points to the window opposite us where Bouchard and Ivanov are sitting. The bus pulls into the parking lot and there, leaning against the hood of my car, is Willa.

I jump up and practically fall over Ben, trying to get past him. I mutter an apology under my breath. Ripping my bag from the overhead compartment, I charge towards the front of the still moving bus. Everyone on the team is laughing at me, and Coach is sighing into his hand. I ignore them all. The moment the bus is in park, and the doors are open, I'm running.

Willa runs to meet me, throwing herself into my arms and wrapping around me. "I missed you, hockey boy."

"I missed you so fucking much, Princess."

I hear the click of a camera. Willa looks over her shoulder, ready to tell off the paparazzi, but I pinch her chin and turn her to face me. "That's Ben."

She smiles and wiggles to get her feet on the ground. I watch her strut right up to Ben and hold out her hand. "It's so nice to finally meet you, Ben. I'm Declan's wife, Willa."

Ben smiles and shakes her hand. "I've heard too much about you," he says.

"Dude! Don't tell her that," I whine and slip my arm around Willa's waist.

Willa laughs and snuggles into my side. "He talks about you all the time too. I feel like I know you."

Ben looks at his feet, like he's feeling awkward. "Maybe in another life," he says before looking back up. "Have a good night, guys."

"He doesn't speak much, does he?" Willa asks as we watch his retreating form.

"He does, but it took him days of being stuck with me to open up."

"You ready to go home?" she asks, smiling up at me.

I grab her and throw her over my shoulder, causing her to squeal. I smack her ass, and she gasps. "Save those noises for home, Princess. I plan on staying buried inside you until I have to leave for practice tomorrow afternoon."

"Fuck, baby. Hurry up and take me home." She scrambles to get into the passenger seat as I throw my duffle bag in the trunk. I slip into the driver's seat and start my car. I pause with my hand on the gearshift.

"How did you get here?" I ask her. She smiles, a little guilty.

"I had to sneak out when the guards Cal hired traded shifts. Then I took an Uber from the gate."

I want to smile and frown at the same time. My mouth is twitching so much that Willa bursts out laughing. I join her, deciding to drop it for now. I barely make it out of the parking lot before my phone rings.

"Uh oh," Willa mutters when she sees who it is.

"Hi, Cal," I say.

"Dec! I can't. . . I lost. . .she's —" The poor guy is in a panic.

"Willa is with me, Cal."

The breath he lets out is so loud over the speakers I flinch. "I thought your plane was landing around now. I didn't know you came home to get her."

"Sorry about that, man. I should've let you know. That was my bad." I look over at Willa to see a breathtaking smile on her face.

"Totally cool. She's your wife and all. Just, uh, maybe next time tell me? You know, until we don't have to keep track of each other anymore."

"You've got it."

I quickly say goodbye and glance at my wife again. "You owe me, Princess."

She smiles and slinks her hand up my thigh and to my belt.

"What are you doing?" I ask, my eyes darting back and forth between the road and her hand.

"I don't like being in debt," she says, her voice taking on a sexy note as she quickly undoes my belt and pants.

"Willa, this is a bad idea."

"I don't know what you mean," she says, rubbing her hand over my erection.

"Fuck! Take me out, Princess." I lift a little to help her. The moment she's able to get me out of my pants and in her hand, she lowers her mouth and takes me to the back of her throat. "Holy fucking shit."

"Mmm," she hums around me. It's taking everything I have to concentrate on driving. I throw my directional on and quickly pull over onto a dark side street. Leaning my seat back, I grab her hair and direct her head.

"Just like that. Fuck, Willa you're so good at that." She sucks me like she's being paid to do it. She takes me down her throat, swallowing every time. "I'm going to come. Swallow everything." I moan and unload into her soft, perfect mouth.

She smiles as she pulls off me with a pop.

I cradle her jaw in my hand, pulling her to me and kissing her senseless. "Let's get home, Princess."

willa

CHRISTMAS IS TOMORROW. I've spent the entire month of December either in Declan's arms, at his games, or doing promotional stuff for the upcoming tour. I've never been more busy or more happy than I have been since I married Dec. I still haven't told him I love him. I know I do. I had that revelation one night while he was sleeping, and I just watched him, loving every little twitch and noise he made. If only I could get the words out instead of struggling like they're physically thick in my throat.

I wish this was something I could talk to Belle about. Trying to explain to her that I haven't been able to tell my husband I love him without also explaining that I lied to her about why I married him is impossible. We leave for the tour in two weeks. I need to tell him before we leave. Our time together will be limited for two whole months.

"Blue with snowflakes or elves loading Santa's sleigh?" Declan holds out two rolls of wrapping paper.

"Snowflakes for adults. Elves for Cora."

"Duh. That was so obvious," he mutters to himself,

making his way back to the stack of boxes he needs to wrap. He got everyone his jersey, but he's extremely excited about the small one he found for Cora. He also bought her a plush hockey puck and a mini stick. Uncle Declan has quickly become her favorite person without really trying.

I watch as he wraps each gift with care before placing it under the tree. I usually decorate my tree with silver and red ornaments, but Declan wanted black and gold to match his team's colors. I have to admit; it looks really good.

"I don't see any presents under here for me." I look up from the monster romance Jo let me borrow to see an exaggerated pout. He smiles when I laugh at him.

"I hid them. I didn't trust you not to peek."

Declan gasps and clutches his chest like he's appalled by the accusations. I laugh at his antics, watching the amusement in his eyes morph into pure love. The way he looks at me simultaneously stops my heart and kickstarts it. It melts every doubt I have about our relationship. Declan took a wrecking ball to the walls I built around my heart without me noticing. Or maybe he was already behind those walls before they were built.

"Why are you looking at me like that?" he asks. I can see the smile in his eyes. He knows exactly how I'm looking at him.

"How am I looking at you, husband?" I tease, getting off the couch and making myself comfortable in his lap where he's sitting in front of the tree.

"Like I'm all you see."

I cradle his face in my hands, feeling the scratchy stubble along his jaw. "You've always been all I could see."

Declan surges forward, kissing my lips so desperately I'm sure they'll bruise.

"You better have made room in your fridge!"

Declan growls against my lips but doesn't move away from me.

"You say that like there was anything in there to begin with," I call back to Belle. I move to get up to help her put the food for tomorrow away, but Declan's arms tighten around my waist.

"Gross," Cal complains. I look over my shoulder and glare at him.

"I have a doorbell. If you used it, we wouldn't be in this situation," I point out uselessly.

"A minute later, and you would've seen things I'd have to remove your eyes for." I snort at how possessive Declan is being. He still hasn't loosened his hold on me. "I'm not kidding, Princess."

Cal looks alarmed and then thoughtful. "Yeah, I get that. I'd kill anyone who saw me balls deep in Harlow."

"They wouldn't find the body if it was Belle," Kai says, walking by us with his arms full of grocery bags.

"You all have issues," I yell, making sure Cal and Kai can hear me in the kitchen. I finally pry myself away from Declan, giving him a soft kiss. He pouts, but it just makes me smile.

"I kind of like it," Harlow says. Cora is on her hip and making grabby hands at Declan.

"Unca Deeeee!" she squeals, squirming to get to him. Harlow laughs and hands her over.

"How's my favorite niece today?" he asks her, swinging her around. She giggles and flails her arms.

I watch them, warmth blooming in my chest at the sheer joy on both their faces.

"He'd make a great dad," Belle says, coming to stand next to me. She laughs at the sudden panic on my face. "You'd be a great mom, you know. Doesn't have to be right now. Just don't rule it out because you lost yours."

I glare at her.

"Hey, don't be mad at me for knowing you're scared you'd either be a bad parent or die and leave them. You're my best friend, and I know you." Belle pauses. "I think I know you better than I thought I did when everything with Declan went down."

I smile and wrap my arms around her. It's still a touchy subject, but not as much as it once was.

"You do," I promise. "Speaking of dying."

Declan freezes, and I can feel Belle stiffen from where my arms are still wrapped around her. Probably wasn't the best way to break this news.

"I called the hospital and got my mom's medical records," I explain. Which does little to erase the worry on Belle and Declan's faces. Cal, Kai, and Harlow make their way over to me, the worry clear on their faces too. I've always been terrified I'd get breast cancer like my mom did and die early. At twenty-five, I'm already close to how old she was when she died. So I contacted the hospital last week, and her records were in my email this morning. I read through them twice while Declan was at the gym with his team. It was a relief as much as it was heartbreaking.

Declan hands Cora to Cal and comes to stand in front of me. I let Belle go, but take her hand in mine, Declan's in the other. "She apparently had diabetes since she was a child and never really took care of it. She technically died from end stage renal disease. Her kidneys were so damaged that they stopped functioning, and she didn't want to be put on a donor list. Her death wasn't as sudden as it felt."

Declan and Belle both throw their arms around me, sighing with relief.

"I also called my doctor, and she said that there's always a chance I could develop it later in life, but it's becoming less likely as I get older. As long as I do my yearly bloodwork, I'm in the clear."

"You just scared the shit out of me, Princess."

"Yeah, that was a really fucked up segue," Belle mutters.

"Sorry," I say into Declan's chest, Belle still clinging to my side. I look up and see the love shining in Dec's eyes. I smile as he leans in to kiss me. I feel Belle back away as he does, which makes me laugh into his mouth.

"Thanks for the heart attack, but we need to get Cora to bed," Cal says. "Have fun watching your terrible movies." I stick my tongue out at him at the same time Belle pinches his nipple. He screams and runs away from her.

"Where are you going?" I ask Declan. He was following Kai to the door.

"I have something I need to finish for tomorrow over at Kai's. You and Belle can have your night and watch your Hallmark movies. I put the popcorn on the counter for you and there's margarita mix in the pantry." He kisses me. "I love you, Princess. I'll be back in a few hours."

I watch him walk out the door, admiring how good his butt looks in his jeans.

"He didn't have to leave," Belle says.

"I know. I think he wanted to let us have our tradition." I

have a lump in my throat just from how thoughtful he is. The man is turning me into an emotional mess.

Belle and I have always watched cheesy Hallmark Christmas movies on Christmas Eve every year. Maverick started to join in with us.

"Where are Jo and Mav?" I ask, just realizing they weren't here with the rest of the group.

Belle sighs and flops down on my couch. "Mav volunteered to go check on Adira for Kai. Jo went with him."

I flinch. Kai and Ezra's mom has been in a hole of depression and alcohol since Ezra was legally declared dead. Kai has tried really hard to get her help and maintain a relationship with her, but all she sees when she looks at him is Ezra.

"Have you checked on the house recently?" Belle asks. She knows I haven't. We're still keeping track of each other, even though there hasn't been an incident since the night Eva was here.

"Ask what you really want to know," I say, giving her a small smile to let her know it's okay.

She sighs. "When are you going to sell it?"

"I don't know. I've been thinking about it, and it's not the house I want to keep. My memories behind those walls are mostly sad. But I don't want to lose the walls my mom painted. I have nothing of hers. Those walls and the blurry images in my head of my mom painting them herself are all I have left."

My dad kept all her things for years. He locked them away in the spare bedroom, not letting me in to see them. Then one day, he had a breakdown and donated all of it. There wasn't a single shirt or stray hair tie left. I was so devastated I didn't speak to him for months.

Belle remembers how upset I was, so she just nods and grabs the throw blanket on the back of the couch to toss over our legs. I snuggle up to her, grateful that some things never change.

"Merry Christmas, Princess."

I snuggle into Declan, not wanting to wake up and leave the warmth of his body. He chuckles but holds me tightly anyway.

"Merry Christmas," I mumble into his neck.

"Can I have my presents now?" He sounds so eager it makes me laugh.

"They're under the tree. I moved them while you showered last night."

I squeal as he scoops me up and drops me to my feet just long enough to throw one of his shirts over my naked body, then I'm right back in his arms. He runs down the stairs, tosses me onto the couch and starts dropping presents at my feet as he gathers his into his arms.

"How many gifts did you get me?" I ask him, looking at the small mountain at my feet.

"No idea." He sits next to me with this pile next to him and waits.

I roll my eyes. "Go ahead, hockey boy."

After maybe ten minutes, Declan has opened all his presents and helped me with mine because he was too excited to wait. I got him more shirts since I keep stealing his, band merch for when he comes to our shows, a new game day suit in a deep green to match his eyes, a watch with our wedding anniversary engraved into the back, and a bunch of other small things I picked up when I went shopping with the girls. Declan got me my favorite perfume, oval cut diamond earrings to match my ring, a gold necklace that says Mrs. Monroe, team t-shirts and his jersey that also says Mrs. Monroe, a pile of books from my Amazon wishlist, and tons of lacy lingerie.

"There's one more thing," I tell him. He starts to get up to check under the tree again, but I stop him by climbing into his lap. "It's not under there."

"Is it here?" he asks, grabbing my ass with his hands and squeezing. I shake my head and look into his eyes. They're twinkling with happiness and burning with lust at the same time. It's been a pretty common look on him lately and I love it. I love him.

"I love you."

Declan's whole body tenses. "Say it again," he whispers. His eyes are wide and there's an uncertainty there that makes my stomach hurt. I know I put that look in his eyes. He's worried he heard me wrong. That I didn't just tell him what he's been waiting to hear.

"I love you, Declan. I love you so much that love might not even be the right word to describe what I feel for you. I'm sorry it took me so long to tell you."

"I love you so much, Princess. I always have, always will."

I knew I couldn't wait any longer to tell him. Watching the relief on his face when I told him the odds of me getting sick were less dissolved that thickness in my throat that kept stopping me from telling him how much I love him.

But the look in his eyes, that unconditional and all-encompassing love that's there whenever he looks at me, broke every last barrier I had. I love him with everything I have and everything I am. And maybe I always have.

I kiss him fiercely, showing him how much I love him with every touch of my lips and graze of my fingers. Declan grabs my hips and pulls me down to grind against his erection. I moan at the feel of his hard length against me, only a few thin scraps of fabric between us.

"I need to be inside you," Declan moans, shifting so he can get his pants and boxers off. "Please, Princess." I was already wet, but his desperation would've soaked my panties if I was wearing any. I rip Declan's shirt over my head and position myself above him, slowly easing myself onto his erection.

"You're so big, baby," I moan. "I feel so full."

"Fuck, Willa. This pussy was made for me," he groans, his grip on my hips bruising as he helps move me up and down his length. "Does my wife love her husband's cock?"

"I love my husband, and his monster cock." Declan groans at my words and slams me down on his massive length over and over. I'm panting, my head thrown back and so close to my orgasm I could cry.

"Look at me when you come, Princess."

Lifting my head, I look into Declan's lust-filled eyes.

"Good girl. You're doing such a good job riding my cock. Look at how fucking sexy you are taking all of me."

The dirty words mixed with his praise do me in. I come screaming his name and looking into his eyes. Declan keeps pounding into me, maintaining eye contact.

"Give me one more, Princess. You can give me one

more." I shake my head. There's no way. "You can, Princess. Look into my eyes and soak my fucking lap."

I gasp as he roughly circles my clit with his thumb, wrapping his other arm around my waist to pull me down as far as I can on him.

"Come with me," he pants. "Now, Princess." It's as if his command went straight to my clit and set me off like a bomb. I come even harder than I did the first time, watching Declan fall apart with me, my name sounding like a prayer on his lips.

I fall onto his chest, both of us trying to catch our breaths. Our sweat glues us together, but I don't care.

"I love you," I whisper, peppering his neck with kisses and tasting the salt on my lips. His arms tighten around me as he buries his face in my neck.

"Fuck, I love you. I love you," he murmurs, pulling back just enough to capture my lips. "I love you."

I smile against his mouth and push against his chest. He frowns, not wanting to let me get off his lap.

"We're going to be caught if we don't get dressed, and I'd like my friends to keep their eyes."

Declan throws his head back and sighs, but he lets me stand. He laughs as I rush to the bathroom to clean up the mess we made as it runs down my thighs. "I'm going to lick you clean next time," he calls after me, causing a full body shiver.

Letting myself love Declan is the best and scariest thing I've ever done.

declan

IT'S my first time backstage at one of Shattered Halo's shows. The reason for that still stings a little when I think about it, but then I remember I have her. I have Willa. My wife. The love of my fucking life. And suddenly the sting fades away and all I see is her.

It's crazy behind the scenes. Staff buzzing around everywhere in a way that looks like chaos, but considering the opening band was on stage right at eight and now Willa is about to go out exactly at nine like was scheduled, I guess it's working.

"There's a VIP you need to meet after the show," Nate tells the band as he flies past us. They all roll their eyes.

"That's bad?" I ask.

"They're usually a spoiled brat that has a hissy fit when they realize daddy's money doesn't get them into our pants," Kai says.

"You're joking," I say, looking at the lack of smiles on their faces.

"Nope. There was one guy who is the son of some airline

tycoon that honestly thought he could buy a night with Willa." A growl escapes my throat at Mav's words, my fists clenching at my sides. Willa makes her way over to me and places her hands on my chest. She looks like a fucking badass in her tight black jeans and low-cut purple body suit.

"I told him I didn't like men with such little penises they had to use their daddy's money to get laid."

"She also said she forgot her microscope at home so she wouldn't be able to find his dick anyway. He cried a little," Kai adds, looking like a proud brother.

"Don't worry. The fans and VIPs are kept on the other side of the stage. We get to be on this side. So you won't risk your marriage and career by murdering someone for saying they want to screw your wife," Harlow says.

Willa sighs and grabs my face in her hands. "No murder. I only screw you," she says, lips twitching when she uses Harlow's phrasing. "I'm surrounded by fans who want to sleep with you at every one of your games, and I haven't killed a single one of them. I think you can handle this without committing a crime."

"Fine," I grumble and lean down to kiss her.

"One minute," Nate yells as he power walks past us in the opposite direction.

"Have fun out there, Princess."

"Always do, hockey boy," she says, getting up on her toes and kissing me before making her way out onto the stage.

"What?" I ask Harlow when I catch her staring at me.

"You make her happy."

"Not as happy as she makes me," I say, turning and smiling as I watch Willa. Her eyes are closed as she beats her sticks on her drums. She's so fucking beautiful when she's engrossed in her music like that.

"Maybe happy isn't the right word. Soft? That might be closer."

I turn my attention back to Harlow, raising a brow in question.

"Willa and I weren't super close in high school, but we were friendly enough. Even when she smiled, she was hard. Like she was always ready for a fight or to jump in and defend someone."

"And now?" I ask, curious about what point she's trying to make.

"Now she's happy. She doesn't seem like she's constantly waiting to wage war or something. Like her shoulders are finally relaxed, and her smile reaches her eyes. You know?"

"Yeah," I say. I know what she means. I noticed it on Christmas after she told me she loved me. I don't know why it was so hard for her, not that I can't guess. But I don't need to, and I'll never ask her because just knowing she loves me as much as I love her is enough. Hell, it's more than enough. It's everything I never knew I wanted and always needed. The moment the words passed her lips, I felt like my life finally clicked into place. She was always the missing piece.

I'm glad I wore jeans. I had to excuse myself to the bathroom after the first song to strap myself down behind my zipper. I couldn't help it. Watching my wife out there was hot as fuck, and all I wanted to do was take her back to the dressing room and show her.

The second they were finished and made their way to us, I had Willa in my arms. She wrapped legs around my waist, which did nothing to stop the painful erection I'm still sporting.

"I'm sweaty," Willa says, trying to pull away from me.

"I don't care." I grab the back of her neck and bring her closer so I can take her lips. She gasps at how hungrily I kiss her, and I want to swallow every sound she makes.

"I've never felt so fucking single."

I break away from Willa to see Maverick scowling at all of us. Harlow is in Cal's arms, and Kai has Belle tucked closely to his side.

"Sorry, man," I say, putting Willa down gently, but still keeping her in my arms.

"VIP meet and greet, now," Jon says, coming up to us, looking pissed.

"Try that again but ask nicely, or you can explain to them why the band is refusing to meet with them," Willa says, scowling at him. I try to hide my smile. It's such a turn on when she puts people in their place.

Jon sighs and runs his hand through his hair. "I'm sorry. I've been stuck with her the whole show. She's a real piece of work," he says. "Can we please go get the meet and greet over with so I can get a beer?"

"Yes," Willa answers. Jon lets out a breath and motions for us to follow him.

"Should I wait?" I ask, realizing the woman didn't pay to see me.

"Nope. I won't see you for a week, so I'm not wasting

any time I have." I smile at her answer and kiss the top of her head.

"Was Jon the best option for entertaining her?" I ask quietly. Not quietly enough because he turns his annoyed face on me.

"No. Jo usually does it, but she stayed home to edit the podcast episode since there were no VIPs. This was last minute, so I got stuck with it."

"I'm surprised she's still here," Cal jokes. Jon snorts and turns back to lead us to a room down the hall from the dressing rooms. I looked at Willa's longingly as we passed it. She caught me and laughs. Jon opens the door and moves aside so we can step in.

"What the fuck are you doing here?"

MY EYES FLY between the blonde bombshell in the tightest red dress I've ever seen sitting on the black leather couch in front of us, and my suddenly furious husband. His hand grips mine so tight that it verges on painful, but I don't try to pull away. Declan is never angry, not like this.

And suddenly I know who this is.

"Don't pretend you're not happy to see me, Decky. I paid a lot of money to see you tonight."

"How did you know I would be here? This is a meet and greet for my wife and her band. Not me. Do I need a restraining order?" I can feel the tension in Declan's body. He's on the edge of snapping.

"We're in Boston, and you don't have a game until tomorrow. It wasn't that hard," she says, standing and trying to saunter towards him, but I quickly step in front of her. She sneers down at me from her towering heels just as Declan tries to pull me back.

"Bethany I assume?" She doesn't answer me, just

continues to glare at me like she can make me disappear with her hateful thoughts. "I'm Willa. Declan's wife."

"Yeah, I heard all about your façade of a marriage," she says to Declan. "Don't worry, Daddy can get it annulled so we can be together."

Belle grabs my arm and holds tight, probably knowing I'm about to launch myself at her. Harlow takes her lead and grabs the other one while Declan wraps an arm around my waist.

"She's not worth it, Princess," Declan says, pulling me against his chest. I instantly relax against him.

"Not worth it?" Bethany screeches, her face turning as red as a tomato.

"Nope," Declan says. "One drunken night with you could've cost me everything and it wasn't even memorable."

"Uh, do I need to call security?" Jon asks because he's terrible at reading the room.

"Yes," I tell him without looking away from Bethany.

"What makes her so fucking special? Mediocre band whores are your thing?"

I watch Kai grab Belle before she can throw herself at Bethany. Cal has a solid grip on Harlow too. If the moment wasn't so tense, I would be happy to have friends like them.

Declan holds me even tighter and takes a deep breath, trying to calm himself. I wrap my arms around his that are still around my waist and thread our fingers together. He squeezes them before speaking.

"Willa is and always has been everything to me. She's always been the most important person in my life, and she will be until the day I die. I don't have to justify my relationship to anyone, especially you. But since it seems you don't understand, I'll put this as simply as I can." Declan turns me in his arms so I'm facing him. He looks at me as he speaks his next words. "Willa is the love of my life. I married her because I love her and want to spend the rest of my life showing her how much. She is my forever." He looks up at Bethany as security sweeps in to remove her. "There is no ending where you and I are ever anything to each other."

Bethany screams and fights as security removes her from the room. She shouts about her dad killing our careers, but I barely notice her.

"I know she forced our hand and made us get married faster than we would have naturally," Declan says as he lifts his hands to cradle my cheek. "We're inevitable, Princess. We would've always ended up here."

I wrap my arms around his neck and pull myself up his body so I can be face to face with him. "I love you." He kisses me like no one is watching.

"She's the reason I didn't get to be your maid of honor?" Belle asks. I break the kiss to look at her, thinking she's going to be upset I didn't tell her, but instead she's looking out the empty doorway like she's considering following Bethany out.

I nod, choosing not to explain everything.

Because what Declan said was right. We are inevitable. This love I feel for him isn't new. It's not a new sensation in my chest or a foreign feeling I got when I looked at him. It was always there, waiting for me to acknowledge it. The reason we got married no longer matters and it would just hurt feelings. The reason we're married now and will hopefully stay that way is what matters.

"Damn," Cal says, scratching his jaw and looking awkward. "Not your best decision there, Dec."

"You had a baby with a stranger, Callahan. You don't get to comment," Harlow says, putting him in his place. I laugh because she has a point.

Declan laughs and claps Cal on the shoulder with me still in his arms. "You're not wrong, man."

"Alright, she's gone," Jon says. "I called Jo to give her a heads up. She's getting in touch with the PR team to make them aware in case Bethany goes to the press. But you should probably call your PR team, Declan. Get them on it from your end too."

"Thanks. I'll call them," Declan says to him.

"We have your backs," Belle says, coming to stand next to us, Kai still attached to her side. "Anyone with eyes can see your marriage is real, and you love each other. Don't let some crazed bimbo get to you."

I snort and slide down Declan so I can hug Belle. "I'm sorry," I whisper to her. She squeezes me.

"I understand. I wouldn't want to try to explain that woman to anyone. Luckily, Kai is too much of an asshole for anyone to chase him."

"Hey!" Kai complains.

"Except for me, obviously," she says, grinning up at him. His fake frown cracks, and he smiles back before kissing her.

"Someone, please smother me in my sleep and put me out of my misery," Mav mutters before leaving the room. I watch him leave, the sadness weighing his shoulders down.

"We need to find Ezra," I say. I've been having the small moments of guilt. Like being happy is somehow a betrayal to Ezra. I snap myself out of it pretty quickly, but then that's followed by guilt for not dedicating more time to finding him. It's a cycle that's getting old and needs to end soon. I can't keep feeling guilty over living my life and finding happiness.

"Jo and I are planning on spending our time on the bus going through more leads that have been submitted to the platform. My dad is still trying to find anything to lead us to Gavin Irons. That man is a ghost, though," Harlow says, her eyes trained on the doorway where Mav disappeared.

"Bus is leaving in twenty minutes!" Nate yells as he breezes by.

I sigh and snuggle into Declan. "I wish you could come with us."

"I do too, Princess."

"We'll see at you at your game next week," Kai says, patting Dec on the shoulder as he leaves the room with Belle. Cal does the same thing as he leaves with Harlow.

"I meant everything I said," Declan says when we have the room to ourselves. "I believe with everything I am that we would still fall in love and get married. We're lucky we got to do it sooner."

I laugh and shake my head. "Oh yeah? What else do you believe?"

"That we're going to have kids, and you're going to be the best mom to them. That we're going to bring them back to the campground where we met every summer." He kisses me, his lips barely brushing mine before he speaks again. "We're going to go on so many adventures, Princess."

"I can't wait," I whisper against his lips. The idea of kids is still terrifying to me, but I can see the picture Declan is painting, and I want it.

Declan's lips crash into mine. I kiss him back with equal ferocity. I want him to feel how much I miss him on his lips for days.

"Willa! Bus!" Nate yells.

"Fuck," Declan curses. He kisses me again, gently this time. "I'll call you on the way to the airport tomorrow." I nod, holding back tears. It's so much harder to leave him this time around. "I love you, Princess."

"I love you too, baby."

We separate in the parking lot with another steamy kiss. He walks me to the bus, leaving me after telling me how much he loves me again before heading to his own car.

This is going to be the longest week of my life.

declan

"HOW ARE you doing with all this?" Gideon asks me while we change before our game. By 'all of this' he means Bethany causing a stink with the press with claims my marriage is fake. She tried telling them my marriage was fake, but no one bought it, so now she's trying to make Willa out to be a home wrecker. She even cried in front of a poster of me that I did for Nike. It's picking up more traction than it should.

"Worse than Willa. She's not bothered by Bethany at all."

"She loves you and is secure in your relationship. That's not a bad thing."

"I just hate that this is happening at all."

My phone vibrates next to me, and I grab it.

PRINCESS

I won't see you before you get on the ice.
I'm so sorry, baby. The traffic sucks.

I sigh and hang my head. I haven't seen Willa in a week. Not since the event with Bethany.

> Cora is in your jersey. Look how cute she looks!

I smile when a picture of Cora sitting in her car seat wearing my jersey comes through.

> She's going to be my lucky charm tonight.

I'm nervous. The last time we played New York, the team was blatantly targeting me. To the point where Coach considered benching me tonight. He agreed to let me start as long as I didn't argue if he made the call to pull me. It was the best I was going to get.

> I love you. Kick ass tonight, hockey boy.

> I love you too, Princess.

"Monroe."

"Yeah, Coach?" I ask warily. He better not have changed his mind.

"Mr. Sinclair wants to talk to you," Coach says. His face is stone, and I can't tell if this is bad or not. Anderson Sinclair owns the Boston Bruisers. If he wants to talk to me right before a game that isn't even at our home arena, it has to be bad. Right?

"Stop panicking. He didn't seem mad," Coach says.

"Did he seem happy?" Martinez asks.

"No."

"Great," I mutter. I'm in full uniform, skates included. I stand and look down. "Uh."

"He's right outside. Stay dressed."

"Thanks, Coach." I take a deep breath and ignore the stares of my suddenly quiet teammates.

Mr. Sinclair is standing right outside the locker room. His arms are crossed over his chest. Anderson Sinclair is a large and intimidating man. He's my height, in good shape, and smells like money. His black hair is slicked back, and his brown eyes find mine immediately. He's not much older than I am. He inherited the team from his dad.

"What can I do for you, Mr. Sinclair?" I ask, trying to keep the nerves out of my voice.

"Is your marriage fake?"

My eyes widen at first, but then I get mad. "I'm really sick of that question. I'm sick of everyone questioning if I love my wife or if I'm using her."

Sinclair's eyes narrow on me, but then I point to the gold band on his left ring finger.

"How would it make you feel? Knowing you made a single mistake before you even started dating her and that mistake keeps publicly telling people your relationship isn't real and that you don't really love her. I'm lucky enough to have a wife that is in the spotlight too and knows it's absolute bullshit, but I still fucking hate it." I scrub my hand down my face. "I have loved my wife since I was six years old. My head was up my ass until recently, but it's on straight now. She is everything to me, and if you're here to kick me off the team because some spoiled brat isn't getting what she wants, then go right ahead. I still get to walk away with the best thing that's ever happened to me."

Sinclair smiles. "I just needed to hear it from you."

I blow out a breath. "Sorry," I mutter.

"Don't be. But you should know," he says, stepping closer to me while looking around, "I know Bethany. Unfortunately, we came in contact a lot growing up. She won't give up, Declan."

I sigh and drop my head. "I don't know what to do."

"Fuck," he mutters. I look up to see him looking at his phone. "She's here. She's in the owner's box. My wife just let me know. This isn't my arena, so I can't kick her out."

"Uh, my wife is almost here. What do I do? I don't want anyone causing a scene. Willa won't unless she's provoked, but Bethany is definitely going to provoke her."

"Where is she sitting?"

"Willa prefers the stands to a private box. She and Maggie are going to be sitting there together. The rest of the band is going to be in a private box." I give him the box and seat numbers.

"I'm going to have my guys watching her. I have an idea." With that, he turns and leaves.

"Should I be worried about your idea?" I call after him. He just chuckles.

"You get fired?" Gideon asks, handing me my helmet and sticks as he leaves the locker room with the rest of the team.

"Nope, but Bethany is here."

Gideon freezes. "Shit."

"Yeah."

"Listen up!" Gideon shouts.

Everyone stops and turns to us, including the coaches.

"The psycho bitch trying to take Willa from us is at the game tonight," Gideon yells. Everyone boos, and I tear up. I thought it would be difficult to get close to a new team after being with San Diego for so long, but it wasn't. They took me into the fold immediately. "We're going to make our boy look good in front of his wife and then we're going to make sure the world knows who Declan belongs to!"

Everyone cheers. Even Coach is smiling.

"What does that mean?" I whisper out of the side of my mouth.

"You'll see."

willa

"SORRY! I swear I'm not usually late," I say, taking my seat next to Maggie. Considering this is the second time I've been late meeting her at a game, we both know I'm lying.

She laughs me off. "You didn't miss anything yet. They're still warming up."

"I know, but I wanted to see Declan before the game and introduce you to my niece."

Gideon skates in front of us and holds up a paper that says, "Operation Claim the Prince" on it.

"What the hell?" I ask. Maggie's eyes are wide as she nods. Then she looks around until she finds whatever it is she wanted and glares at it. I follow her line of sight and groan. "Why is she here? I just wanted to watch Dec annihilate the team that tried to cripple him while drinking a beer with my friend."

Maggie turns to me and grabs my hand. "Pretend she isn't here." She bites her lip nervously.

"What? What was that operation thing about?"

"Giddy and I came up with a plan when all this came out this week. You're just going to have to trust me."

I narrow my eyes at her but decide I do trust her. "Fine. I trust you, but if it's something embarrassing, I'll cook for you and guilt you into eating it."

Maggie looks horrified. As she should. Cal told her all about how terrible I am at cooking when we were at the last game together.

We settle in and watch the game. Declan skates up to me whenever he can. The worried look on his face kills me. He clearly knows Bethany is here and the cameramen seem to keep trying to get him looking at her, but he never does. If his eyes are anywhere other than the puck, they're on me or Cora. He's been waving to her whenever he can, and I know she's loving it.

"I love you," I mouth to him. The first period just ended with the score at one to zero. Gideon scored the only goal.

"I love you too," he mouths back. He's about to skate off when a carpet is rolled out and the announcer asks for everyone's attention. Dec turns around, confusion marring his face. I turn to look at Maggie, who seems equally confused when Anderson Sinclair walks out onto the carpeted ice.

"Hello, New York. I'm Anderson Sinclair, owner of the Boston Bruisers," he says into a microphone. He gets a good mixture of cheers and boos. "I have a player on my team being targeted by the daughter of another owner. You may have seen it in what my mother likes to refer to as the trashies, or tabloids, if you'd like." The arena quiets down, either in confusion or interest. "As a favor for not reporting your team after the way you played against us last time and getting you thrown out of Stanley Cup contention, I've been allowed to show you a video his teammates made for him."

The lights dim, and Gideon's face lights up the jumbotron. "Declan and Willa are close friends of my wife, Maggie, and myself. Willa might know hockey better than a lot of hockey players, and she has no problem telling Dec when he messes up," he laughs. I probably would laugh along with him if I wasn't so dumbstruck. "They're the most supportive couple I've ever met. She's busy being a multi-platinum artist, yet she always watches his games and comes to as many as she can. He's busy getting us the cup, but he calls her the moment he can to check how her show went."

Gideon's voice continues while pictures of Declan and me flash across the screen. Some of them I recognize as ones Ben took, including the one of me in Declan's arms in the parking lot of the training center. The pictures fade into a video of Martinez.

"The first time I met Willa and Declan, I told him his wife was," he pauses like he's searching for the right word. "Hot." I snort, knowing what was actually said. "He had me up against a wall for disrespecting her like that. I knew we'd be best friends right then and there." He talks about moments he noticed as more pictures flash across the screen. These are ones I don't recognize. Pictures the guys must have taken in the locker room. There's even a bunch of Dec on FaceTime with me in his hotel room.

"Willa is like a sister to me." I gasp when I see Cal's face on the screen next. "Declan quickly became a brother to me, and my daughter's favorite uncle." Unlike the nice stories from the Bruisers, you can see the anger in Cal's face. "I don't take threats to my family lightly. Willa is family. Declan is family." Instead of flashes of pictures across the screen with a voiceover, a video of Declan and me on Christmas greets the crowd. We're snuggling in our Christmas PJs while everyone opens gifts. I turn to look at him after Cora squeals her excitement over the hockey stick he got her. Even I can see how in love with him I am at that moment.

The next video is of me watching one of Declan's games and screaming at the screen, then immediately texting him about something. I laugh. I know this one. Harlow took it because she thought I looked crazy.

She's not wrong now that I'm watching it on such a huge screen.

Then I hear my voice even though the screen is black. "I love you, baby."

Declan's voice comes through right after. "I love you, too, Princess."

Everything fades and the lights come on, but then I hear another voice and notice there's a video playing. The arena goes dark again, and Bethany is on the screen.

"I don't care what you have to do! Drug him if you have to, but you will get him into my hotel room after the game tonight!"

"You want me to drug Declan Monroe and get him to your hotel room? He's the size of a horse. I don't have a fucking horse tranquilizer, Bethany. And how the fuck would I get him out of the arena and into the hotel with no one noticing?" I can't see who the man is that's speaking, and his voice is distorted, but it's clearly Bethany on the screen plotting to drug my husband.

I'm out of my seat, but Maggie grabs my hand. "Wait. I don't think it's over."

"Then just drug him and get him into a janitor's closet or something," she huffs.

"What are you going to do with him?"

"I have someone who is going to walk in on us and take pictures of him naked with me. Then he'll have to be mine. Daddy will make sure of it." Bethany smiles like a psychopath.

The video stops and the lights go back on. I'm trying to get out of Maggie's surprisingly strong grip so I can rip Bethany's head off her shoulders and use it as a puck.

"Oh dear, how did that get in there?" Sinclair says; the edges of his mouth twitching. "Officers, I do believe you have a job to do." He nods towards the owner's box. I can't see what's happening, but I can hear Bethany screaming in frustration. So I can assume she's being arrested.

Maggie lets me go, and I bolt for the tunnel. Declan was being led off the ice by Gideon. I need to get to him if it's the last thing I do. Security doesn't stop me, probably understanding what I'm doing.

"Declan," I yell when I see him. He turns immediately and catches me as I launch myself into his arms. "Are you okay?"

"I don't know," he says, his voice shaking.

"I love you. I won't let her touch you. I'll rip off her fake boobs and beat her with them before I let her near you again," I promise. Declan snorts and relaxes.

"I love you so much, Princess," he says into my neck. "I'm done after this."

I pull my head back and frown.

"I'm going to retire after this season."

My frown deepens. We've talked about him retiring already. It was pretty much a definite with his knees, but I don't want what happened with Bethany to force his hand.

"The only person I want to be valuable to is you. You and any children you give me," he answers my unvoiced thoughts.

"Oh, baby," I say, my heart breaking for him. "So many people value you for the right reasons. Not just me."

"You're the only one that matters, Princess."

I kiss him. "Retire for you. Not for anyone else."

"I am. I'm retiring because being with you is what I want. I'm sick of all these trips away from each other. We've spent most of our lives being separated by distance, and I'm done. I want to be stuck to your side like glue, Princess."

I laugh and kiss him again. "If you make the finals, you've got another six months, hockey boy."

"What's six months when you have forever after that?"

I smile and kiss him again. "Get in there with your team and then show New York who's boss."

"Yes, Princess."

***

"Was the video your idea?" I ask when I take my seat next to Maggie.

"Yeah," she says, her cheeks turning pink. "Not that last part. Is Declan alright?"

"Not really. He will be."

"Bethany's arrest has already gone viral. Her dad can't

control the amount of people that took videos of everything tonight. Everyone knows what she wanted to do to Declan."

"It's so fucked up," I say and pull on my hair in frustration.

The guys are back on the ice warming up. Declan looks sad, and I wish I could jump the boards and hug him.

"Do you think he could still play with me holding onto him like a koala?" I ask Maggie. She laughs but thinks about it.

"Probably, but not well. He wouldn't want you getting hit."

"You're right. Damn."

My phone goes off like crazy. I pull it out of my pocket, assuming it's my PR team or possibly Dec's wanting to talk about tonight. It's actually the family group chat.

CAL

Tell Dec we love him!

MAV

Yeah and tell him to beat New York because fuck them.

KAI

Let him know he's family. We won't let anything happen to our family.

BELLE

We love you both so much!

JO

I'm working with both PR teams. You can both focus on the game. We'll be good with the videos going viral. No one will come after your marriage again.

HARLOW

Cora says "Yay Unca Deeee!"

I smile at my phone and then wave down Declan when he skates near me. I hold my phone against the glass so he can read all the messages. Declan's smile is so bright it's blinding, and a single tear escapes from his eye. He looks behind me at the box our family is in and makes a heart with his hands. I can see them return the gesture on the jumbotron. Belle has to elbow Kai to get him to do it, but he does. Cora is bouncing on Cal's hip and waving at Declan so aggressively, he has to switch his hold on her so she doesn't fly out of his arms. Declan laughs and blows her a kiss.

I put my hand up to the glass and he puts his on the other side.

"I love you, hockey boy!" I shout as loud as I can.

"I love you, too, Princess," he yells back. The ref blows his whistle, and Declan skates off.

THIRTY-EIGHT

declan

"THANKS FOR THE VIDEO, man. It was great," I tell Gideon after the game. We won two to zero. I got the only other goal in the third period.

"That was actually Maggie. She somehow managed to get ahold of Sinclair, and he agreed to help her with it."

"How?" I ask, shocked. I don't even know how to get in touch with him, and I work for him.

"I have no idea," he says with a laugh. "Not the end, though. I don't know how that happened."

"Sinclair said he had an idea," I say.

"You think that was his idea?"

I shrug.

"If the video was Maggie, what were you talking about before the game?"

Gideon rubs the back of his neck, looking embarrassed. "It's lame now. It was cool before the video and arrest."

I snort. "I'm sure it was great."

"Just give it to him," Slava says.

Gideon sighs and reaches behind him, grabbing a jersey

252

and throwing it at me. I open it up and laugh, hard. It's my number, but the back says Mr. Prince.

"I love this. I'm taking it home with me."

"He's so going to fuck Willa wearing that," Martinez says.

I glare at him. "I am, but you don't get to talk about it."

He laughs and continues to undress in the methodical way he has.

"Monroe. Sinclair wants to see you," Coach says.

I'm half-dressed but make my way into the hallway in my socks, anyway. Sinclair may have done me a favor tonight, but he's not a man to keep waiting just because you're half in hockey gear and smell like sweat.

"Bethany is being charged with stalking and attempted kidnapping, among many other things," he says without greeting.

"Was that video you?" I ask him.

"It was actually the body cam footage from the under-cover officer she hired."

My mouth hangs open in shock.

"I was her target before you were. It's not the first time she tried this. You sleeping with her got her to stop harassing my wife. Getting her away from yours was the least I can do."

"Thank you, sir," I tell him. He nods and walks off, but then pauses and looks at me over his shoulder. "You should also be aware that she was the reason behind the last New York game being dangerous for you. She blackmailed the coach. That's been taken care of as well."

I scratch the back of my head, both confused and thankful for Anderson Sinclair.

"Dec!" I look up to see Ben walking quickly in my direction. "How are you doing?"

"I'm okay." He raises a brow in question. I laugh. "I really am. Still trying to sort through everything that happened tonight, but I'm also happy to have friends like you and the guys."

Ben smiles and nods. "Good to hear it. I just wanted to check on you before I left."

I frown. "You're leaving?"

"Yeah. My dad lives in New York. I'm going to stay and visit with him this weekend. I'll be back Monday."

"The band is going to be down here any minute if you want to meet them."

"I'd love to, but I'm already running late, and my dad is a stickler for punctuality." He waves and jogs to the door that leads to the parking lot.

I head back to the locker room and shower quickly so I can hold my wife without sweating all over her.

wolfe

I WATCH the time tick down on my watch. I was surprised they allowed me to keep it in here, but then I realized why. They want me to watch the last minutes of my life countdown. *She* wants me to know my time is at an end.

I frantically write down everything I can into the palm sized notebook I've managed to keep hidden. Maverick is coming to visit me today, and I need to give him as much information as I can to keep him safe. He needs to know what I've done to get the power I have. Had. And what I've done to keep him safe from *her*.

I've been writing in this book every chance I get, but only when I'm alone. I know there are eyes on me everywhere. My cellmate pays too close attention to me not to be reporting back on all my movements. He's in state mandated therapy right now and shouldn't be back until after I meet with Maverick.

I hear the loud steps of heavy boots coming my way.

A guard.

It's time.

Frantically, I write every last thing I can think of and shove the small notebook into the waistband of my pants. Standing, I wait for the guard to take me to my son.

"Ready?" I look up to see Peters. At least I got one of the nice guards. Holding my hands out, I let him cuff me and lead me to the visitor's area. The walk there is unusually quiet. Like the rest of the prison knows, this is the end for me. *She* owns the prison, just like she owns everything else. Me included. But she doesn't own Maverick, and I'm giving my last breath to make sure it stays that way.

I see him, my son, sitting at the table in the rundown old room, waiting for a man he despises. His shoulders are back, and his eyes find mine, a wariness in them that's always been there when he looks at me. But this time there's a fire too.

Peters takes my cuffs off, and I take the seat next to Maverick instead of the one across from him. His eyebrows shoot up at my proximity, but he quickly schools his features.

"What did you want that couldn't be discussed over the phone?" he asks me, keeping a chill to his tone.

I look at Peters, who looks at the camera above my head, then back to me and nods. He turns away to give me a moment of privacy.

"I had one favor left, and I called it in," I tell Maverick, the look of confusion back on his face. I grab the small book from my waistband and shove it into his hand. "Put this in your pocket and read it once you're safely back home. It's the best I could do." I hug him quickly and kiss his temple before standing and making my way back to Peters.

"What? Dad?"

I look over my shoulder and see him shove the book into his pocket and make like he's going to follow me, but I shake my head.

"We're supposed to get twenty minutes."

"I'm sorry, son. I don't have that kind of time left."

Maverick frowns and looks at Peters, who takes the cuffs back out and secures them around my wrists.

"I love you, Maverick."

"Dad!" I hear him call after me, but I don't look back. Peters leads me back through the door and to my cell.

"The debt has been paid. Goodbye Senator," Peters says and locks the cell behind him. My cellmate is back, and he's not alone.

"Sorry, Jim," Aaron says. He's been my cellmate since I was brought here after my arrest. "He'll make it quick." He pulls my arms behind my back with a grip that's bruising, but I don't fight them.

The other man pulls out a large hunting knife and quicker than I can follow, slices it across my throat. It's not until I look into the eyes of my killer than I realize I recognize him. Panic fills me, not from the pain or my quickly approaching death, but the knowledge that my son is even less safe than I thought he was and there's nothing I can do about it.

The taste of my own blood fills my mouth at the same time it leaves my body. Within seconds I'm on the floor, choking on it, cold seeping into my skin. The edges of my vision blur and soon everything is black.

willa

BELLE SMACKS my hand away from my mouth. I've been biting my cuticles and it's driving her nuts.

"He's fine. He's already on his way back."

"I don't like that he wouldn't let anyone go with him," I complain. I know Maverick is an adult and can handle himself, but his dad asking to see him and demanding it be today isn't sitting right with me.

"Cheese or no cheese?" Harlow asks, popping her head into the kitchen from the back deck where she's grilling burgers. It's a random warm New England day in the middle of February, and we happen to be home to enjoy it, so we're taking advantage.

"Always cheese, Harlow," Belle says.

"You're right," she says to herself and heads back outside.

Declan, Cal, and Kai come barging through the front door. They were playing with chalk on the driveway. Cora is snuggled in Declan's arms, which would be adorable if it wasn't for the look of horror on all their faces.

"What? Is it Maverick?" Jo asks, rounding the island and abandoning the salad she was making.

"No? Not exactly. Where's Harlow? She needs to call her dad," Kai says. I point to the sliding glass door that leads out back. Cal immediately goes outside to get her. He's out there for less than ten seconds before they're both back with a plate of cheeseburgers in Cal's hand and Harlow on her phone.

"Dad? Yeah, I just heard. When can you get here?" she pauses for his answer. "Okay, I'll see you soon."

"Can someone please tell me what's going on before I lose it?" I ask. Declan comes to me, pulling me into his free side while Cora naps on his shoulder.

"Senator Wolfe is dead. Murdered by his cellmate," Kai says.

"Where the hell is Maverick?" Jo shouts.

"Here," Mav says, going to her to give her a hug. I watch the way she clings to him, and I can't help worrying. I think Jo could be good for Maverick, but if we actually find Ezra and he comes back. . . I look over at Belle to see the worry on her face too. She's thinking the same thing I am.

Maverick will choose Ezra. He will *always* choose Ezra.

"Sorry for your loss," Declan says, but it almost sounds like a question. Maverick looks at him and frowns.

"What loss?"

"Your dad?" Cal says.

"I just saw him. He's not dead," Mav says.

"Uh. . ." Kai starts.

"Harlow?"

"In here, Dad!" Harlow calls.

Harrison comes into the kitchen, his laptop in his arms. He sets up at the island without so much as a greeting.

"Is my dad dead?" Maverick asks him.

"I'm afraid so, son," Harrison answers. "His throat was slit within minutes of your visit and then conveniently leaked to the press immediately."

All the color drains from Maverick's face before he hunches over and grabs his knees.

"Breathe, Mav," Jo says, rubbing his back.

"I'm going to need you to tell me what happened," Harrison says once Maverick has pulled himself together.

He recounts the short trip and how odd it felt, then pulls a small book from his pocket.

"He slipped me this when the guard's back was turned and made some comment about having called in his last favor."

Harrison takes the book from him and flips through the pages. His eyes widen and brows shoot to his hairline. "Have you looked at this?" he asks Maverick.

Mav shakes his head. "No. I got in the car and drove right back here. This is the first time it's been out of my pocket."

Harrison hands the book back to him. "I need that back when you're done with it, but I think you should read it first."

Mav takes the book and opens it to the first page. His eyes scan the words, but his expression is unreadable. Once he's finished, he puts it on the counter and turns it to face us. "I think you guys need to read this too."

I grab it and read it out loud.

My Dearest Son,

I know what you think of me, but all my actions since the moment you were born were to protect you. I didn't always succeed, but I tried. This journal is all I can leave you. I will detail as much as I can before my expiration date.

I stumbled into a world of violence and blood that promised me power and wealth. While I received those things in spades, they were not worth the price. Everything I have been accused of is true and so much more. Everything except what you have accused me of.

In my line of work, love is weakness, and weakness means death. I couldn't show you love and affection, for it would make you my weakness. I had hoped over time you would harden your heart, but I should've known you could never. You are so much like your mother in that regard. Not Eva. She is no mother to you. You'll soon find that out once you read this journal.

I need you to know; I loved your mother with everything I was capable of, and I will until my last breath. She was a light in this world, just like you are. And because of that, I couldn't take your light from you.

Ezra is alive, Maverick. Eva wanted me to kill him, to take what you loved so that you would break and bend to her will. Instead, I staged it to look like he was killed and paid off judges and police officers to have him legally declared as such. I cannot tell you where he is, as I made sure I wasn't aware of his movements after I got him out of the state.

That being said, I have written a phone number at the end of this journal. Call it when you're ready to bring him home. Eva must be taken care of before you make that call, Maverick. You will both be in danger if you jump the gun. Ezra saw something he shouldn't have, something even Eva won't tell me about, and I believe he has proof to back it up. If she even thinks he's alive for a moment, she'll kill him.

Trust in the family you've built. They've protected you so far and will continue to do so. Ask Harrison for help. Make Eva pay when I failed to. Bring Ezra home to you.

I'm so proud of you, Maverick. You chased your dreams and fought hard for them. You love even harder and have a loyalty that runs deep. You are everything I hoped you could be and everything I wish I was. I love you, and I'm sorry.

Always,

Dad

I look up and see tears in Maverick's eyes and confusion in everyone else's.

"So Eva isn't your mom," Cal says. "But you look like her."

"Where's the number?" Kai interrupts, grabbing for the journal, but Maverick snatches it to his chest.

"We can't, Kai."

"Give it to me, Maverick." Kai's voice is low and scarier than I've ever heard it.

"Malikai," Belle says, grabbing him and forcing him to face her. "I know you want your brother, but if bringing him home means his death, we can't." Her eyes plead with him to understand, and I watch as his resolve waivers.

"We can hide him. Protect him," Kai says, but the uncertainty in his voice gives him away.

"We can't. You know we can't," Belle tells him, her voice soft.

"I want him back more than I want my next breath," Mav says. "But we have to make sure it's safe."

My eyes flick to Jo's just in time to see her quickly wipe a tear from her cheek before going back to rubbing Maverick's back.

I clear my throat and turn my attention to Harrison. "So what's with the Eva thing?"

"I don't know for sure, and I'm hoping James's journal has more answers, but it looks like there's evidence showing she's at least connected to the Bratva. So far, it seems like she got in with them when she was young. Probably a classic case of dealing drugs to survive. Her family was dirt poor."

"The Russian mafia? We're dealing with the Mafia?" Cal screeches out the last word.

"At least the arranged marriages make sense now," I say.

"How?" Belle asks.

"If Eva was trying to make herself more powerful, she'd

need to form connections. Mav's probably valuable as an asset in that way."

"I'm not an asset. I'm a fucking person," Maverick says, looking appalled.

"Eva had an older sister," Harrison says. "Her name was Abigail. I think it would make sense you were her son, considering you do look like Eva, as Cal pointed out."

"Wolfe kept referring to her in past tense. Is it safe to assume she's dead?" Harlow asks.

"She died twenty-five years ago. It was ruled as a suicide. Maverick would've been one at the time," Harrison says. "I'm hoping the journal gives us more insight into that. Let me show you what I've been working on since James's arrest."

We all gather around Harrison as he pulls up notes and pictures on his computer. "The feds already have a case against her. It's enough to arrest her, but not enough to keep her behind bars or to threaten her with to get her to out her accomplices."

The file Harrison has is extensive. He explains that Eva is the contact point for drugs coming into ports in Maine. She runs the drugs in all of New England, not just Maine, like we thought. Recently, she's been dipping her toes into weapons, but the Irish have a problem with that. So she's trying to force Maverick to marry one of the Irish mafia princesses to smooth it over. His files are reading like a mafia novel and if it were anyone else other than Harrison, I would think he made it up to mess with us.

"To summarize," Harlow says when we get to the end of the files. "Eva married James because she saw the potential to have a political pawn, claimed her nephew as her son, and is trying to use him to form an alliance with the Irish Mob. Ezra saw something that could be her demise, but we can't get in contact with him because if she even smells him near us, she'll kill him."

"I'm not great at this super detective stuff," Declan says, "but we're not talking about taking on the mafia right?"

"No," Harrison says immediately. "I think whatever Ezra saw pertains only to Eva. Which means we only need to take on Eva. I'm going to continue working with the feds on this and hopefully they'll do it for us. The DEA is obviously involved, but I don't have contacts there. Probably Homeland too."

"Take this," Maverick says, holding the journal out to Harrison.

"You should read that before I do."

Maverick shakes his head. "I'll read it, but I can't right now. Knowing that number is there will be too tempting." Harrison nods and takes it from him.

Harrison packs up, promising to get the journal back to Maverick as soon as he can.

"The burgers are cold," Harlow says.

"I'll order pizza." Cal grabs his phone and calls our usual order in.

I snuggle into Declan. We're back on the road tomorrow for the final two weeks of the tour, and I can't find it in me to want to do it right now. I just want to stay in the warmth my husband's arms offer me. With Declan, I feel safe.

But it seems like Maverick isn't safe. I catch Jo's eye, and I immediately know she's thinking the same thing I am.

Will he ever be safe?

declan

"THIS IS AMAZING!" Maggie says, while bouncing on her toes and clapping. "Willa is the coolest person I know."

"Hey!" Gideon says. "You're married to the captain of the Boston Bruisers and the best center in the league."

"I said what I said." Maggie shrugs and keeps watching Shattered Halo. They just finished the first song of their last show.

"Sorry!"

I turn and see Ben rushing up to us with Nate pointing him in our direction.

"Turns out you're not the only one planning to announce their retirement at the end of this season. I had a meeting with media to plan an announcement. They want you both together for a photo op," Ben explains.

I give Gideon a questioning look. He holds up his hands and shakes his head.

"Who?" I ask Ben.

"Can't tell you," he says with a grin.

We watch the rest of the set in relative silence. We're all

singing along, obviously, but there's no conversation happening. Maggie keeps clapping after every song while Gideon holds her against him, smiling at how happy his wife is. Ben is smiling too, but it's almost sad. Or maybe wistful. I'm not as good at reading people as Harlow, but she's home with a sick Cora tonight.

"You good, Benny boy?" I ask him.

"Yeah, I'm good," he says and sighs. "You know that guy I've talked to you about?"

"Of course."

"He'd love this."

"I gave you two passes," I point out.

Ben nods. "You did, but we're not exactly on speaking terms right now."

"If you love him like I love Willa, you'll work it out."

He laughs. "Is that the scale?"

I shrug. "I love her epically. Like the entire reason my heart beats is for her."

"You're practically a poet," he jokes.

"What do you love most about your man?"

Ben's smile is so sad I want to hug him, but he's not really a physical affection type of guy.

"He hears me when I'm quiet."

"Fuck, dude."

"Yeah."

"I hope you work it out," I tell him honestly.

"Me too."

I turn my attention back to my wife. Her eyes are shut as she beats her drums and just feels the music. It's fucking erotic. I could watch her do anything and find it erotic, but when she's like this, in her element, it does something to me. It's a particular mixture of pride and lust that gives me a high for her like no other.

"Fuck," Ben mutters next to me. He answers his phone quickly. I can't hear what he's saying, but the call ends quickly.

"What?" I ask. He's looking down at his phone with a scowl.

"The alarm on my house went off. The company is sending the police out, but I have to go meet them."

"Shit, man. I hope everything is alright. Do you want me to go with you?"

He hesitates, looking out at the stage briefly before turning back to me. "No. Thanks for offering, though."

"It's not an issue. I can go if you're uncomfortable."

"I'll call you if I need you. Does that work?"

"Only if you mean that," I say.

"I promise."

I nod and wave to him as he rushes back towards the exit to the parking lot.

"Declan, have you seen Nate?" I turn to see Jo.

"Not since he brought drinks over for us about an hour ago."

"He's not organizing the meet and greet like he usually is. I don't have the list to figure it out."

That seems odd. I haven't been to enough shows to know much about Nate, but he seems to always be on top of his job. If someone told me efficiency was his middle name, I would believe them.

"Thank you, Boston! You're perfect as always. We are Shattered Halo, and we'll see you soon! Drive safe!" Cal says, ending the show.

I catch Willa when she throws herself into my arms. Kissing her in a way that's inappropriate in front of our friends.

"We have to go meet the people that paid for a meet and greet, but then I want to do that dressing room fantasy of yours," Willa whispers in my ear. I groan and kiss her neck.

"Where's Nate?" Kai asks.

"We can't find him," Jo explains. Cal calls over security and asks them to locate Nate.

"Where's Jon?" I ask, realizing I haven't seen him in a while either.

Security rushes up, surrounding us all. "We need to lock you and your friends down in one of the dressing rooms while we await police assistance," the one closest to Cal says.

"Why?" Cal asks him.

"We found Nate, Mr. Griffin. His throat was slit."

Willa gasps and pushes herself closer to my side. Belle is crying into Kai's shirt. Poor Maggie and Gideon look shocked and confused. Maverick looks like he wants to throw up.

"Fuck!" I shout. "Let's go where they want us to. Cal, call Harrison."

We're only in the room for a few minutes before the police come in and question us. It must be protocol since the band members were on stage and the rest of us were right next to it and very visible the entire night.

"We're still questioning the staff, but it looks like he was really only missing for a thirty-minute period before security found his body," the detective tells us after taking our statements. "Is there anyone else that was with you tonight that isn't here right now?"

"My friend, Ben. He left maybe two minutes before the end of the show. Someone broke into his house," I say. The detective nods and takes Ben's information from me. He hands it off to the other detective that's been standing there while this one questions us. The second detective takes out her phone and goes into the hallway.

"That's really easy to confirm since home security companies call the police when alarms go on for too long. They'll have a timestamp," the first detective explains.

"Our manager Jon is missing too," Maverick adds. His brows are furrowed like he's working hard to figure something out. "He was here when we went out on stage."

Jo frowns and pulls out her phone. "I'll call him." She dials his number and puts it on speaker.

"I can't talk right now," Jon says as a greeting.

"Well, you don't have a choice," Jo says.

"I have a personal matter I'm dealing with. Unless the stage blew up, I really don't have time for this."

"Nate was murdered, and you disappeared," Jo says, not beating around the bush.

"Well, I'm clearly alive," Jon says, completely missing the accusation in Jo's statement.

"You need to report to the Boston Police to give a statement by tomorrow afternoon or they're going to find you," Jo says and hangs up on him.

The detective tries to hide his smile, but his lip twitches. The second detective reenters the room, my eyes darting straight to him. I don't think Ben is a murderer, but I am worried about his break-in, and I haven't been able to check on him.

"Ben is clear. The timestamp on the alarm is around ten minutes before Nate was last seen. Ben arrived on the scene thirty minutes after the phone call and the police were already there. It's a thirty-eight-minute drive from here to his address. He definitely broke some speeding laws, but there's no way he could commit a murder in that time-frame," she says.

The detectives give us their cards and ask us to call if we think of anything. Gideon and Maggie head home after Willa apologizes for their night ending this way.

"Do you think Eva has a thing for throats?" Jo says. We all freeze.

"You think it's related?" Belle asks her.

"Dean's throat was slit. Wolfe's throat was slit. Now Nate's? That seems unlikely, doesn't it?"

"I need to get home to Harlow and Cora. Everyone needs to get behind the gates and security. We'll talk about this in the morning," Cal says, and I agree with him, scooping Willa into my arms and walking out into the hallway. Security is there waiting to escort us to our cars.

"We're locking down at home and never leaving," I tell Willa as I pull my car onto the road.

She laughs, though the sadness is clear in it. "You have a game tomorrow."

"I don't give a shit. I'll retire right now." I mean it.

"You have two months left. Four if you go all the way. Finish your career like you want to."

"Fuck my career, Willa. You're what matters to me. You.

Nothing else. Not hockey. I will never pick hockey over you. Ever."

She sighs. "That may be true, but I still want you to finish the season."

"Princess. . ." I start.

"Baby, stop. I'll stay home unless I'm at your games. I'll even agree to bring security with me if that makes you feel better. But we don't know that this is related to anything. No threats have been made against any of us."

I squeeze the steering wheel so tight my knuckles pop. "I can't lose you, Willa. I won't fucking survive it."

She reaches over and squeezes my thigh. "I swear I won't put myself in danger, Dec. Cal already told Isla and Logan we wouldn't be discussing a new album or new tour dates until everything settles down. And that was before tonight. I'm going to be a trophy wife until further notice."

"I love you, Princess."

"I love you, too, hockey boy."

My shoulders don't fully relax until I have her behind the locked doors of our house.

FORTY-TWO

"WHY DO YOU LOOK SO NERVOUS?"

"I'm not sure this is the best time for the surprise I planned for Dec," I tell Maggie.

"You said you weren't in any danger." She's frowning at me and looking around the arena like she might find the invisible danger lurking there.

"I'm not." Probably. "But Declan was ready to hang his skates last night and now I'm probably going to stress him out more."

"I'm sure he'll be happy," she says, smiling. Her smile quickly turns into a frown. "Is that them?"

I turn and stifle a groan. Declan's parents are making their way to us. They're in his jersey, each sporting matching Bruisers winter hats and foam fingers, while telling everyone they walk past that Declan is their son and then winking at them, leaving a trail of confused faces in their wake. I love Sally and Ted, but they're over the top at all times. And considering what happened last night, I can't say I'm in the mood for it. I was surprised when I finally tracked

273

them down and got them to come home long enough to watch Dec play on his new team.

I also had to break the news of our marriage to them over the phone. They had been backpacking in South America and didn't bother even turning on their phones. Which is another thing I don't want to get into with them, but if something had happened to Declan, they wouldn't have known. You know, like a whole wife and marriage.

"There she is! Our new daughter!" Sally squeals and practically runs over the other people in our row to get to me.

"Hi, Mrs. Monroe, it's great to see you again," I tell her as she crushes me to her chest. She's tall, probably at least a half of a foot taller than me. Ted is Declan's height and is grinning at me over his wife's head. Declan looks just like his dad, green eyes, strong chin, muscular build. But he got his light brown hair and kind smile from his mom.

"It's Sally, Willa. You're Mrs. Monroe now too." She was ecstatic when I told her over the phone. Swore she was just waiting for us to figure it out.

Sally sits, and then Ted pulls me into a hug. His hugs are warm and comforting like Declan's are. "We're so happy you're officially family now," he says before letting me go.

I introduce them to Maggie. She and Sally get along immediately and before I know it, they're exchanging recipes.

"What's going on, W?" Ted asks me. He's the guy that needs to give a nickname and it's always just the first letter of your name.

I bite my lip and stare at him. I don't want to freak him out, but they're going to be staying with us for the next week until they fly out again, so it's not like they won't hear about it. Leaning closer to him, I whisper a short, condensed version of what's been happening and why I'm now nervous about how Declan is going to react to it. To his credit, Ted nods along and doesn't freak out like I thought he would.

"Text D. Let him know we're here before he hits the ice. He's an emotional player, always has been."

I pull my phone out and text him immediately.

> I had a surprise for you, but after last night the timing is bad.

HOCKEY BOY

What is it? Does it involve you being naked?

> Your parents are here. They're sitting with Maggie and me in her parents' seats.

What? How? Why?

I'm excited and worried and nervous and sad it's not you naked, but happy because I miss them.

> It was going to be a happy surprise. I talked to them last week.

I am happy, Princess. Thank you for telling me before I got out there.

> Your dad told me to.

I have to get on the ice. I love you, Princess.

> I love you too, baby.

"Well?" Ted asks me when I put my phone away.

"He's happy you're here but thanked me for warning him."

Ted smiles like he knew that was going to be exactly what Declan said. He probably did.

Boston piles onto the ice, and I watch as Declan skates a few laps around the rink before coming to a stop in front of us. He smiles at me before turning and waving to his parents. His smile is happy, but I can see the concern in his eyes. He misses them, which is why I called them in the first place.

"I love you, Princess," Declan shouts so that I can hear him through the glass and over the crowd.

"I love you too, hockey boy!"

He blows me a kiss and skates back to warm up with his team. Martinez shoots me a wink and then one to Maggie. Gideon glares at him, but then waves to Maggie with a sweet smile on his face.

"Your mom knew the two of you would end up together," Sally says from my right. Ted is to my left, and I'm just now realizing they may have wanted to sit next to each other.

"She did?" I ask, surprised.

Sally nods. "She did. She would always say our little darlings were destined."

"Sounds like her," I say with a smile. It's not often I get to speak with people who knew my mom. My friends did and so did Declan, but we were all so young when I lost her that there isn't much they remember.

"She's part of the reason we've been traveling so much. She was always one to love to live life. Any curveball the world threw at her, she would take in stride and turn it into something new and beautiful."

"New adventures," I say in agreement, feeling a little choked up.

"I worry that I'm stuck sometimes," I admit before I think to stop the words. "I signed on the dotted line when Cal presented us with the recording contract because it was a new adventure. Marrying Declan was a new adventure. But what now? What's the adventure after this?"

Sally smiles. "You're worried whatever the next thing is will be negative, aren't you?"

I think about it, realizing she's right. "Yes," I whisper.

"It could be, but you're never alone, my love. We're here for you. Declan is in your corner and always has been. You have some great friends. So take that negative and find the positive."

"Sally and I were having some marital trouble one year. My job was taking me away from home a lot, and it put a real strain on our relationship," Ted says. I turn to look at him, but he's smiling at his wife like she's the only person he can see. "Your mom said something to me that I'll never forget." He turns his gaze to me. "She said that love is life's greatest adventure, and what's an adventure without a few challenges?"

I quickly wipe the tear from under my eye.

"I think that's when I realized that, even in the tough times, loving Sally would always be the greatest adventure of my life."

"You're not on the ride alone anymore, Willa," Sally says, squeezing my hand. I try my best to keep the tears from falling, but one escapes and, of course, that's the moment Declan comes back over.

His eyes are wide as he rips off his helmet and looks between me and the exit, like he's thinking about getting off the ice and coming over to me. I stand and put my hand on the glass and shake my head.

"Happy tears!" I yell at him. I can see the way he breathes out and relaxes. He puts his forehead to the glass, so I do the same on my side. "Kick Minnesota's ass, baby!" I yell when I back away from the glass. Declan smiles and puts his helmet back on.

"I'm so happy you two finally found your way to each other," Sally says, clasping her hands together over her heart and looking genuinely happy.

"Me too," I tell her.

Because if there's anything I've come to accept these past few months, it's that Declan and I were always going to find our way.

FORTY-THREE

"THIS WAS A TERRIBLE FUCKING IDEA," I say, biting the inside of my cheek while I watch the men I hired cut out parts of walls in Willa's childhood home.

"I think it's perfect," my dad says, patting my shoulder. Willa and my mom are out exploring some new shops in the small town. I told them Dad and I were going fishing. Instead, I'm standing in my wife's old bedroom watching as part of the wall her mom carefully and lovingly painted is cut out.

I take in a deep breath of relief once the piece of the wall is gently, and in one piece, placed into the windowed boxes I had made just for this. I had one made for each of the rooms her mom hand-painted designs on.

"She'll either love this or divorce me," I say, scratching at the scruff on my face.

"I think you're about to find out."

I look up to see my dad looking over my shoulder, his eyes wide and nervous.

Shit.

I turn slowly, plastering a happy smile on my face.

Willa looks around at the mess of tools and dust, her face frozen in an unreadable expression. I watch as her eyes rake over the missing rectangle of wall. I can see the anger creeping up, but thankfully the workers pick that moment to lift the box.

"I, umm," I start, scratching the back of my neck. "I wanted you to be able to take this back home. Have some part of your mom in our home without having to keep a whole house you rarely get a chance to visit."

I can't see Willa's face, but she hasn't moved. Her entire body is so still she could be a statue.

"Princess?"

Willa spins and launches herself at me. I flinch until I realize her arms are wrapped tightly around my waist.

"Thank you," she murmurs into my chest. She pulls back to look at me, her eyes shiny with tears, but there's a smile on her beautiful face.

"He thought you might divorce him," my dad says, unhelpfully.

Willa throws her head back and laughs. "I would never."

I take her mouth in a quick kiss, knowing if I linger, it will quickly become inappropriate for present company.

"They're going to replace the drywall and paint the whole house in neutrals to resell it. As long as you're ready for that. Otherwise, I can have them just replace the drywall and wait."

Willa looks around, her arms still wrapped tightly around me. I squeeze her hips gently.

"There's no rush," I tell her.

She shakes her head. "No. I want to sell. It's long overdue. I couldn't handle painting over the artwork and never seeing it again, but you solved that problem for me." She turns in my arms so she can run a finger along the glass of the box. "I didn't know this is an option."

"It's not," Hugh, one of the guys I hired, says. "Your man had these frames specially made and then made me prove I could get the piece of my own drywall out without damage before he even hired me."

"Declan!" my mother admonishes. I look over my shoulder at her and shrug.

"It was a wall in his office. I paid to replace it."

Willa laughs, the sound so light that I can't help but smile, knowing this is taking some of the weight off her shoulders.

"Thank you," Willa says, turning back around. "This is the most amazing thing anyone has ever done for me."

"Anything for you, Princess."

She leans up on her toes, kissing me. I give into the kiss, pulling her tighter to my body. A throat clearing is the only thing that breaks through enough to separate us.

Willa laughs again, stepping back from me. She laughs even harder at the pout on my face. Grabbing my hand, she pulls me along through the house and out to the car.

"Come on, let's grab dinner before we go check on Adira." Willa's smile falters when she mentions Kai's mom. We offered to check on her while we were up here. Kai pays someone to look after her, but he jumped on the offer for us to check too. Adira has been horrible to Kai since Ezra went missing, but she's still his mom, and he still loves her.

"We're already here," I point out. She looks down the street to the small blue house. "My parents can go ahead and get us a table." I look up and see my dad nod as he leads my mom to their rental. They're heading back home to Vermont tonight before jumping on a plane to their next back packing trip.

Willa's shoulders slump as she sighs and walks towards Adira's house.

"Is she really that bad?" I ask, taking her hand as I walk beside her.

"To me? No." Willa pauses and bites her lip. "Adira was like a mom to me. She insisted I come over for dinner and study time every night after my dad died. She brought me to the mall to buy my first bra and helped me through my first period."

"She sounds amazing." I squeeze her hand, and she smiles sadly.

"She is. Was. Everything with Ezra wrecked her. I used to blame Gavin for leaving, but if he was protecting his son," Willa says, pausing and then shaking her head, "I guess I still blame him a little. His wife needed him too."

"I don't think there was a correct answer for Gavin," I say. I can't imagine ever having to make that choice, and I never want to.

Willa nods slowly. "No. I suppose there wasn't." She continues walking towards the house, her steps slow. It's only a few houses down from hers and really should have taken a minute or two to get there.

"Come on, Princess. Introduce me to her." I pull her the last few feet to the stone pathway leading to the front door. Willa takes a deep breath and knocks on the door. She doesn't wait for a response before using a key to unlock it and letting herself in.

"Adira? It's Willa."

"In here," a raspy voice calls. I follow my wife inside. The house looks like it hasn't been updated in a few decades, but it's clean. A frail-looking woman with dark curly hair and blue eyes smiles at Willa. Kai looks just like her except for his nose and the tone of his skin. He's much paler than her.

"I just wanted to stop in and see how you were doing," Willa says, bending over to give Adira a hug.

"Did my son send you?" Adira asks, her tone changing to something close to resentment.

I see Willa's shoulders stiffen. "No. I'm here with my husband and wanted you to meet him."

I walk into the room, coming out from the shadow of the kitchen I was standing in.

"I'm Declan. It's nice to meet you." Reaching out, I shake her small, cold hand. Her eyes assess me from head to toe. She doesn't smile or say anything. "I've heard a lot about you."

Adira scoffs and glares at me. "I'm sure Malikai has nothing nice to say about me."

I open my mouth to argue, but Willa beats me to it. "I can't do this!" she yells, throwing her hands in the air. "I love you, Adira. I really do, but you need to stop. You can't keep blaming Kai for something that was out of his control. Kai does nothing but make sure the people he loves are happy and safe. He's a good person. I won't listen to you bash him anymore."

"Obviously not," Adira says, her face red with anger or embarrassment, I'm not sure.

"Ezra was an adult! He was twenty years old! Kai was not responsible for his actions, nor was he responsible for looking after him like a babysitter. Stop putting your guilt on him!" Willa's chest is heaving, and Adira looks like someone slapped her.

"It was nice to see you again, Willa." Adira turns in her seat, giving us her back, and she stares out of the window.

"I know you know something, Adira," Willa says, her voice back to a normal volume. "Why else would you need to drink yourself stupid every day? Why else would Gavin leave you? And why the fuck else would you treat your only remaining child like dirt?" Willa spins on her heels and marches right out the front door.

I'm about to follow her but stop when Adira speaks up.

"A mother will do anything to protect her children."

I look over my shoulder, but Adira is still staring out the window. Her eyes look blank in the reflection.

"Secrets never stay secrets," I counter.

"No," she says softly. "No, they don't."

FORTY-FOUR

DECLAN HAS BEEN quiet most of the drive home. I know he's giving me space to think, but I'm already feeling guilty for yelling at Adira and being less than engaging at dinner with his parents.

"I'm sorry," I say eventually.

Declan glances at me before turning his attention back to the road. "Do you believe what you said to Adira?"

"I think I do. I just blurted it out in the moment, but I've been thinking about it more, and it makes sense."

"You probably always had that thought in the back of your head, but didn't want to even consider it being true," Dec says, reaching over and placing his hand on my thigh.

I watch the street lights fly by my window. "What if she does know something? What if she knew how to help Ezra this whole time?"

Declan squeezes my thigh. "She said something to me after you left that makes me think otherwise. I could be wrong, though. I don't know her."

I turn in my seat so I'm facing him. "What did she say?"

"That a mother would do anything to protect her children."

I snort.

"What if she's trying to keep Kai away to protect him?"

I stare at the side of Declan's face. He keeps his eyes on the road, but shrugs, knowing my eyes are on him.

I know my mouth is hanging open, but it feels like my mind just went blank. What if he's right? What does she know?

"I don't think it's worth mentioning to Kai. At least not right now. If she really is protecting him, maybe we let her."

I nod and lean back in my seat, trying to wrap my brain around the idea that everyone in Kai's family abandoned him to either protect him or protect Ezra.

"She better have a really good fucking reason once we get Ezra back," I mutter.

Declan stays quiet for the rest of the drive home, just the occasional thigh squeeze to let me know he's still there with me. Part of me wants to immediately run to Harlow and ask what she thinks. Or make Dec turn the car around and go confront Adira.

But the more I think about it, the more I realize it wouldn't matter. If Adira really is protecting Kai, and I hope more than anything that she is and hasn't actually turned into a horrible person, then I need to let her. She won't tell us what she knows if she thinks she's saving him.

Just another layer added to this case. I can't help feeling like the whole thing is about to come toppling down.

declan

IT'S BEEN TWO MONTHS, and Willa is getting sick of being stuck at home. I get it. I really do. She hasn't been anywhere since the trip to Maine with my parents. But I still travel all the time or at the very least go to the training center. She sometimes comes with me to watch practice just to get out of the house. We made the playoffs with our first game happening tomorrow. I'm both excited and nervous because I'll be officially announcing my retirement at the end of the season, whether that's at the end of this seven-game round or in June while holding the cup. Either way, it's the end of this part of my life.

Harrison is still going over the journal Mav's dad gave him. He's been sending information to all his contacts in various government agencies to help with the case against Eva. Maverick has asked to be left out of all of it unless it pertains to him personally, and I really can't blame the guy for that.

Harrison was able to confirm that Abigail was Maverick's biological mother and James had suspicions that Eva arranged her death and staged it to look like suicide. Maverick took the news better than I was expecting, but I wouldn't be surprised if the poor guy had a complete breakdown after all this was over. He earned it, honestly.

"Can I come with you?"

I look at my wife. She's fidgeting with a throw pillow on our couch and giving me her best puppy dog eyes.

"You want to come with me to physical therapy?" I ask with a smirk. She thinks anything outside of this neighborhood is exciting at this point.

"They can give me tips on how to help you at home," she tries to reason.

"You help me plenty," I tell her, leaning in and giving her what was supposed to be a quick kiss. Willa grabs my shirt in her fists and holds on, deepening the kiss until I'm groaning. "I have to go, Princess."

"You have fifteen minutes before you need to leave," she says, her voice raspy. I can't deny her when she sounds turned on like that.

"Clothes off. Now." She obeys immediately, shedding the t-shirt and sweatpants she was wearing with nothing underneath. I strip as quickly as I can and sit on the couch, pulling her onto my lap. "This is going to be quick and dirty."

"I want you inside me."

I lift her and guide her over my already throbbing length. Willa has taken to walking around braless, knowing exactly what it does to me. I pretend to complain, but I love every minute of it. Especially the evil little laugh she does when I point it out.

"Fuck," I grunt out when she seats herself fully. "You take me so well, Princess."

"My husband has such a big cock."

The sound that comes from my throat when she says that can only be described as animalistic. "Say it again."

Willa leans forward, slowly rotating her hips in a way that has my balls tightening already. "Cock."

"Fuck, Willa." I grip her hips and plow into her from below. "Does my wife have a dirty fucking mouth?"

"Yes," she moans, her head thrown back.

"I'm going to fuck that dirty mouth when I get home."

"Harder, baby," she groans, leaning into me and biting down on my shoulder.

"Yes, Princess." I fuck her even harder, gritting my teeth as I feel that familiar tingle at the base of my spine. She's clenching around me, so I know she's right there with me. "Come. Come on your husband's fat cock."

Like the good girl she is, she comes hard, clenching around me so tightly I have no choice but to follow her right over the edge. We're panting, our sweaty bodies stuck together. There's nowhere else I'd rather be.

"Do you really want to come with me?" I ask her. She nods into my shoulder.

"Alright. But only if you put a bra on. I don't need anyone checking out my wife."

"People check me out all the time. A bra isn't going to fix that," she says, laughing as she pulls back to look at me. The happy, post-orgasm glow on her face makes my chest warm. I love every version of Willa, but this is my favorite.

"You're right. You can wear my clothes. Then they can't see anything."

She laughs and pulls off me, walking to the bathroom with her legs glued together to stop the mess running down her leg. I'm getting hard again just thinking about the mess we made. I shake my head to get my thoughts in order because I actually do need to leave.

"Can you text Cal while I get ready?" she calls from the bathroom. "I don't want him freaking out because I left without telling him again."

I sigh and grab my phone from my pants pocket before pulling them up. I know why he wants us all checking in, but it's getting old. It's not like I can't take care of my own damn wife.

> Willa is coming to physical therapy with me. We should be home around five.

CAL

I roll my eyes. I throw my shirt on and grab my jacket. "I'm going to leave without you, Princess!" I call.
My phone vibrates again.

MAV

Family meeting.

> I have physical therapy. Can you update me later or is it an emergency?

MAV

It can wait until you're home.

CAL

Can you pick up dinner, Dec? I'll call it into the Indian place next to the training center.

KAI

Get extra garlic naan. You always forget
and fucking eat it all.

CAL

Yeah yeah.

Sure, I can get it.

BELLE

Should we be worried?

MAV

No, but I think I figured something out.

HARLOW

Mysterious. I like it.

I snort and pocket my phone.

"Willa!" I call again.

"I'm coming!" she yells, running into the room. She's wearing jeans that hug her in all the right places. She's paired it with a Bruisers long sleeve that has "Mrs. Monroe" on the back. Her lilac hair is up in two buns. I think I heard her call them space buns before. I want to fuck her again. Right now. Screw physical therapy. Who needs functioning knees?

She smirks, knowing exactly what I'm thinking. Laying her palm over my heart, she gets up on her toes and kisses my jaw.

"We're running late," she says and then leaves the house.

I follow right behind her. The invisible tether that ties her heart directly to mine pulls me along like a dog on a leash.

Woof.

Willa sat quietly during my appointment, occasionally asking questions and taking notes. I didn't think she was serious about wanting to know more about helping me at home. It was easy to assume it was an excuse to get out of the house, but I should have known better. My woman has always been my greatest supporter, and she always will be.

"What do you think Maverick wants to talk about?" I ask her.

"No idea. He's still refusing to read the journal. Harrison gave it back to him a few days ago, and Jo said he won't even touch it."

"Maybe it's related to the charity stuff he's been doing with Millie. He mentioned some sort of fundraiser at the last guys' night. He asked if I could get some signed merch from the team to auction off." I was surprised when he told me he was still working on his charity initiative, even after finding out Eva was never a victim of domestic abuse. He still feels strongly about it, though. Probably because of what happened to Belle, or because he's genuinely a good guy.

Willa blows out a breath. "I hope so. I miss when family meetings were just Cal complaining about someone eating all his snacks."

"Harlow's been blaming it on Cora so he can't say anything."

Willa laughs. The car falls into a comfortable silence until we pull into Cal's driveway.

"I should've eaten the naan on the way back," Willa says, slapping her palm against her forehead. I chuckle, grabbing the bags of food and following her into the house.

"Finally!" Kai says, snatching the bags from me and bringing them into the dining room where everyone is already sitting. He goes right for the garlic naan, taking a giant bite out of it and glaring at Cal.

Once everyone has food in front of them and has at least taken a bite, Maverick speaks up.

"I got a call from Millie earlier," he says. He looks down at his hands and swallows audibly. I look at Willa. She looks just as confused as I do. "She wanted to give her condolences for the death of our manager."

"Jon's dead?" I ask. "Was his throat slit?" I'm halfway out of my chair and ready to scoop Willa up and move to an island somewhere with new names.

Maverick shakes his head. "Well, yes, but not recently."

"Huh?" Cal says.

"Are you saying Jon isn't Jon?" Harlow asks, catching on faster than the rest of us, as usual.

Maverick pulls a news article up on his phone and shows us. It's a picture of someone that isn't Jon who also had his name, birthday, and occupation, but died almost two years ago. His body was found in his car in a lake in New Jersey. Scuba divers came across it and contacted the police.

"Millie just heard he died. She hadn't read the article before calling."

"How did she hear?" I ask, lowering myself back to my seat, but pulling Willa onto my lap.

"The agency called Logan. She overheard as she was calling me for something related to our fundraiser. So she gave her condolences."

"They've been billing us for two years for Jon's salary," Kai says.

"Millie actually has Logan looking into that one, since his label works so closely with them," Maverick says. "I've had his entry revoked at the gate. Assuming that would stop him, anyway."

Jo's frowning, and then suddenly jumps up from the table. "Harlow," she says. "It's him. It's been fucking Jon this whole time."

Harlow's eyebrows shoot up. "He was here the night Dean died and arrived after he was dead. He said he was with his other clients the day James was killed and went missing the night Nate was murdered."

Jo grabs her phone and looks at the screen. "He's calling. Should I answer it?"

"Answer it," Willa says. I want to disagree and talk all of them into running somewhere he can't find us, but I know that's not really going to work.

"Hello?" Jo says, putting the call on speaker.

"You know my secret," Jon says.

"You sound pretty good for a dead man," Jo answers.

"Why, Jon? Or whatever the fuck your name is," Belle asks.

"My name is Patrick. And you haven't figured out the why?" He chuckles, and it sounds dark.

Harlow is typing furiously on her phone. I'm assuming she's talking to her dad right now to update him and hopefully get the police after this asshole.

I knew something was off with him. I just thought he was into really weird porn or liked to collect dirty socks. Murder wasn't on my list.

"Dean wouldn't let Eva in and probably threatened to call the police. James was actively a threat against her. If he flipped on her, it would be over. But why Nate?" Jo asks.

Patrick chuckles again. "Nate has been in this business a long time. I did a good job avoiding him at your shows for the most part. Unfortunately, I didn't do a good enough job, and he realized I wasn't who I said I was. He cornered me at your last show, said he was going to tell you. Couldn't have that, now could we?"

I watch all the color drain from Harlow's face as she realizes something. "You're a plant. Eva planted you here. You've been listening to our meetings," she says.

"And I know Ezra's alive. Thanks for that little tidbit. I've been funneling all that to Eva. She's very impressed with you, Harlow."

"Fuck you," Cal growls.

Patrick laughs again. "I tell you what, you find him first and you can keep him. If I find him first, I get to slit his pretty little throat in front of you. Happy hunting." The line goes dead, and we all just stare at each other. I hug Willa tighter to my chest.

"We can't," Harlow says, answering the question we were all thinking. Do we call the number James left?

"Calling it would lure Ezra to us. Jon," Jo stops and shakes her head. "Patrick, would be waiting."

"We could call it and warn him," Willa says.

"Then we would have no other way to contact him after that. It's probably a one and done number. Using it will burn it," Harlow says.

"I think we leave it for now," I say. "No one knows where he is still. That keeps him safe. If we get even a hint Patrick knows where he is, we'll have to call."

"He said if we find him first, we can keep him," Maverick says, his voice so low I barely hear him.

"He probably meant his body," Kai says, his face filled with grief.

"Fuck!" Mav yells, jumping up from the table and storming off.

"I've got him," Jo says, running after him.

"I recorded that conversation on Cal's phone and just sent it to my dad. He's turning over everything he knows plus the video to the police," Harlow says. Cal looks down to where his wife is holding both phones and pats his pockets.

"How did you do that?" he whispers. She just shakes her head and kisses his cheek.

"Did he say how close authorities were to getting Eva?" Willa asks.

Harlow sighs. "They're close to an arrest, but they need something ironclad that will put her away for good. If she's out, she's a threat to Maverick."

Cal's phone rings in Harlow's hand. "It's Logan," Cal says, taking his phone from her and answering. He quickly puts it on speaker.

"I'm with my brother, Theo," Logan says. "I think he can help you guys out."

"Hey," a deeper voice says through the phone. "Logan caught me up on what's going on, and I'm going to do my best to help you out."

"How?" Harlow asks.

"Theo's a hacker. He does it legally, but in certain circumstances, he doesn't mind bending his morals," Logan explains.

As far as I know, Logan isn't up to date on everything

that's been happening. Just what's been public in the news and now with the Jon thing. Having a hacker help us with all of it could be a game changer for us.

"Hey, Theo. Logan. This is Declan. Do you think we could set up a meeting? Everything that's been happening has made me wary of even talking on the phone."

"Absolutely. I'll give you all my number, and we can figure out when and where to meet. Is there more than just Jon you need me for?" Theo asks, probably reading between the lines of what I said.

"Yeah," is all I offer.

"I'll shoot Cal a text and get this set up," Theo says after giving us his number.

"Thank you," Cal says. The call ends, and we're sitting in silence once again.

"I didn't even think to ask Theo about any of this," Belle says.

"I knew he owned a cyber security company, but it never occurred to me to ask a guy that prevents hackers to hack," Cal says.

"I'm going to coordinate the meeting with Theo and my dad so that everyone is on the same page," Harlow says, snatching Cal's phone and leaving the dining room. Cal watches her go, looking like he wants to go with her, but stays put. She's been moody recently. She hates being stuck in the house as much as Willa does.

I get up, Willa coming with me since she was still on my lap. We silently help Cal clean up the food, all of us still processing everything.

"I don't know what to do," Cal says, his hands gripping the sink, shoulders hunched and head bowed. "How do I keep my family safe? I let that man into my home! I let him around my daughter! My wife!" He spins, so much anger and panic on his face I immediately go to him and crush him against me.

"We're going to get him, Callahan. Theo is going to help us. Jon, Patrick, whatever the fuck his name is, will be taken care of. Eva will be behind bars with him, and then we can bring Ezra home. It's almost over."

Cal sobs into my shoulder, and Willa comes over and hugs him from the side.

"It has to end, Cal. This is it, I can feel it," she tells him.

"I'm so tired," he admits, backing up from us and wiping under his eyes. "I'll give Theo a chance, but if nothing comes of it, I'm done. I'm going to leave the band and move my family away from here. I won't risk them anymore." He drops his head into his hands and whispers. "Not even for Ezra."

Willa comes to my side and wraps her arm around my waist. "I agree."

I look at her, surprised. She meets my gaze and smiles sadly. "I want to find Ezra, but not at the risk of everyone I love. At the risk of any family we create. He wouldn't want that for us."

Cal hugs her quickly and heads to find Harlow. Willa and I slowly make our way back to my car and our house. There are so many things running through my mind, but there's one thing that keeps coming to the forefront.

"You want kids?" I blurt out the moment the front door shuts behind me.

Willa turns and looks at me, alarm on her face. She must

think I've changed my mind since we last talked about having a family. "You don't?"

I walk right into her space and grab her face gently. "I want everything with you, Princess." I kiss her. "Fuck yes, I want kids. It would be the greatest honor of my life for you to be the mother of my children."

I kiss her again, her melting right into it. "Not yet," she breathes. "Not until I know they're safe."

I nod against her lips. "We can still practice."

She giggles when I sweep her up and throw her over my shoulder.

I take her to the bedroom and practice all night long.

willa

BOSTON CRUSHED Buffalo in the first round of playoffs. They took them down four games to zero. Because it went so fast, Declan has a full ten days off before he plays whatever team wins in the other division.

Harrison and Theo have been exchanging information. We're all finally meeting up tonight at Theo's wife's coffee shop. We didn't want to risk Theo coming here and getting him mixed up in all this just by sight. Harrison said to assume our movements are being watched. Logan had the idea to stage a label party at the coffee shop so it doesn't look weird we're there.

It's May, but the nights are still cold. I'm bundled in Dec's hoodie, in the back of Cal's massive SUV. I'm in the middle of Harlow and Belle in the third row since the guys couldn't fit back here. Kai, Jo, and Mav are in the row in front of us, with Cal and Declan in the front. Cal refused the idea of two cars, so we're all squished in here. Cora is home with Cal's dad and a small army of security guards.

"Cora's really been into cars recently, so I was thinking of a two fast theme for her party," Harlow says.

"I like bad two the bone better!" Cal yells from the front.

"He hears that, but not me asking him to take out the trash," Harlow mutters.

"Cora's birthday is in August," Kai points out, unhelpfully. Harlow glares at him, and he turns around quickly.

"Even I know you have to plan these things early," Maverick says. "What if they need to book a caterer or like a racecar driver or something?"

"You can hire a real racecar driver for a party?" Cal asks. "If that's the case, I'm back on board with the car theme."

Harlow sighs and rubs her temples.

"I like it. Does she still love pink? I bet we can mix all the car decorations with some pink. It'll be easy if we do solids for the plates and tablecloths," I say.

Harlow smiles at me and pulls up what she was thinking. It's pretty close to what I just said except she found an Etsy shop that will make custom car decorations that will already have some pink in them.

"I think it's perfect, and Cora will absolutely love it," I tell her and bump my shoulder into hers. Harlow smiles in relief. Not being Cora's biological mom gets to Harlow sometimes. She thinks she needs to try extra hard to be her mom because of that. She doesn't. But telling her that doesn't help.

"This place is adorable," Jo says. I look out of the window and see a brick storefront with a large picture window that has "Sweet Buns" in a curvy font. There are flowers and butterflies painted on the window to go with the spring season.

"Sweet Buns," Cal snorts.

Harrison's car is already here, along with another black SUV that I'm guessing is Theo's. We all pile out of the car and into the bakery. It's cozy and very pink in here. There are pink overstuffed couches that look comfortable in front of the window, but Declan pulls me away from them when I go to sit.

"We're meeting in the kitchen," he tells me. I follow him but turn with the little bell on the door chimes. A bunch of people file in and take the couches and other small tables around the bakery.

"Logan hired actors to pretend to be at a party. He's really covering all the bases," Belle says.

We all pile into the kitchen in the back. It's all stainless steel and squeaky clean. A real contrast to the vibe out front. Logan is standing and talking to two men dressed casually in jeans and t-shirts, but they're huge. They nod and walk out the doors we just came through.

"They're security. No one will be getting in here while we are," Logan explains. "This is my brother, Theo." He gestures to a man leaning over the large metal table in the middle of the kitchen talking to Harrison. Theo is tall with brown hair pulled into a bun at the back of his head and dark-rimmed glasses around his green eyes. He lifts his head when he hears his name and comes around to introduce himself to everyone individually.

"Alright, let me fill you all in on where Harrison and I are," Theo says, wasting no time. "Patrick Gibson, thirty-eight. As far as I can tell from his text and email exchanges, he's Eva's second. She assigned him to you when Maverick wasn't bending."

"If I do what she wants, will this stop?" Maverick asks, sounding defeated.

"Honestly?" Theo says. "It's unlikely. Now that she knows Ezra is alive, she's been sparing no expense trying to find him. Even if you do what she wants, she won't stop looking for him. I'm sure that includes using his twin, at the very least."

Maverick bangs his head down on the table, covering it with his hands. Jo takes the spot next to him, murmuring something in his ear.

"Patrick has gone off-grid. I've been monitoring Eva's communications and the last one from Patrick was from the night you spoke to him. He called her right after and then his phone disconnected."

"Theo was able to find his address, and the police raided it. He was long gone. Likely fled after he killed Nate," Harrison adds.

"What's the plan?" I ask, knowing they wouldn't ask us here if there wasn't one.

"We have enough information to put Eva away forever. Once I send this to the authorities, they'll arrest her, and she won't have time to run," Theo says.

"But...?" Declan says. Theo looks at him and nods.

"But we think it will draw Patrick out, and he's clearly unstable. There's a good chance he'll go straight for Maverick or any of you." Theo turns to Maverick. "I've been reading all Patrick's communications along with anything else I could find on him. I'm not qualified to analyze his behavior, but I can tell you he likes revenge, and he likes it bloody. And that's just from reading the file the FBI has on him."

Cal looks at all of us and then back at Harrison. "What do we do?"

Harrison pulls out a folder. "Do you know who your boss is, Declan?"

Declan frowns. "Anderson Sinclair."

"The Sinclairs are old money earned through some very questionable avenues," Harrison says.

"Great," Declan mumbles.

"They've been running the underworld along the East Coast for too long to let Eva take over," Harrison says. "I think if you approached him, he might help."

"At what cost?" I ask.

"I think the Sinclair family is who Eva is afraid of. I think whatever Ezra knows is something they'd want," Theo says. "I'm still working through years of Eva's emails, but that's the idea I'm getting from them."

"But that means calling him back here. Which means his death if we do it wrong," Maverick says, pain lacing every one of his features.

"If you can get Sinclair's protection, we can do it with a high probability of success," Theo says.

"We think we should wait until after the Stanley Cup Finals," Harrison says. "Sinclair will probably be more likely to help if you win it for him, but it also gives authorities the time to verify the evidence we've gathered. They won't make an arrest until they're able to do that."

"No fucking pressure," Declan says, running his fingers through his hair.

I turn to Cal. "Get your family out of here." He stares at me for a moment and nods.

"I'll find you somewhere hard to find and completely off the gird," Theo offers.

"Anyone else?" Harrison asks.

"Princess," Declan says, but I shake my head and grab his hand.

"I'm not leaving you, so don't even ask." He sighs but squeezes my hand. I look away from him to see Belle shaking her head at Kai, and Jo doing the same with Maverick.

"Go home and pack, Cal. I'll have everything you need by morning. If we get you out now, there won't be a reason to look for you when everything goes down," Theo says.

"I can stay and just send Harlow with Cora," Cal says, but I can see in his eyes that leaving his wife and daughter right now would kill him.

"We're good, Cal. This is just a precaution for Cora's sake," I tell him.

"I have phones I can give you to communicate with each other. I've developed a software that makes them untraceable and unhackable," Theo says, handing each of us a bulky, simple phone. It's just a rectangle with numbers and a small screen. It's like the phone my dad had when I was a kid.

"It's basic and only for phone calls. Makes it easier to make it untraceable," Theo explains.

We thank him and agree to meet again when it comes time to approach Sinclair and hope he'll help us with Eva and Patrick.

Cal and Harlow hug all of us outside of their house, promising to keep in touch. They're leaving first thing in the morning to wherever Theo sends them.

It feels like the beginning of the end.

declan

"YOU DON'T LOOK happy for a guy who's about to play in the Stanley Cup Finals," Ben says, looking up from the book he's reading on his bed. I've been sprawled out on mine and staring at the ceiling for the better part of an hour.

"I just have a lot going on at home," I explain vaguely. I want to tell him everything that's going on. Ask for his advice, but I can't. Not because I don't trust him, but because it would be dragging another person into a deadly mess. And I can't do that. I've thought about calling Finn more than once, but the distance between us and the fact that we're about to play each other for the cup hasn't helped our friendship.

"Marital troubles?" he asks, looking disappointed in me.

I frown. "No. Why are you looking at me like you're assuming it's me if there were issues?"

Ben laughs. "Because you're my friend, and I know you."

I smile. It's the first time he's acknowledged that we're friends. He sees my stupid grin and rolls his eyes.

"Don't let it go to your head." I just grin wider at that, but then sober when his expression turns sad. "You might be my best friend."

"I don't like that me being your best friend makes you sad."

Ben snorts. "It doesn't."

When it's clear he isn't going to elaborate, I change the subject.

"Since we're best friends, are you going to tell me where you got that nasty scar?" I ask, pointing to the jagged scar the runs from his right temple to the center of his forehead.

"I'll tell you if you tell me what has you so stressed out," Ben counters.

I scratch the stubble on my jaw, examining his face. His bushy beard covers the lower half of his face, which makes him hard to read sometimes, but his brown eyes are only showing sincerity.

He sighs. "I know about Jon. It was all over the news. Is that what it is?"

"Partially," I admit. There's no use denying it since he's right. It's all over the news.

"Would talking about it make you play better tonight?" he asks, the corner of his lip twitching.

I glare at him before slowly nodding. "I just don't want to drag you into it."

He shrugs. "It won't leave this room. I can't be dragged into something I don't know anything about as far as anyone else knows."

That logic works for me, and I immediately tell him what's been going on. Ezra, Jon/Patrick, how fucking terrified I am that something will happen to Willa when we're on the road. She stays with Kai and Belle when I'm gone, but not having her close leaves me in a constant state of anxiety. I even tell him about having to approach Sinclair after the season is over. There's something about Ben that makes you want to confess everything.

He takes it all in stride. His facial expressions barely change, just some slight widening of his eyes at certain points. Like when I told him James left a journal for Maverick that he's refusing to read. Or when Cal went into hiding with his family.

"Yeah, I can see why you're not excited to be here right now."

"Any advice for me?" I ask.

Ben thinks for a moment. "Is Willa safe?"

"As safe as she can be. She's flying in on Logan's private jet with Belle, Kai, and Maggie for tonight's game. She flies back out right after." She refused to just watch the game from home. We argued for days until we agreed she could come as long as she flew private and watched from a private box that I hired security for. She's not thrilled about not being able to watch with the fans, but she understands I won't be able to focus on the game if she's out in the open like that.

"I can go with you to talk to Sinclair if you want, but other than that, I don't think there's much I can offer you. You're already doing everything you can. Listening to Harlow's dad and Theo seems smart from what you've said."

I blow out a breath, my shoulders relaxing even though I

didn't realize I was tensing them. That's all I needed. Someone on the outside to tell me I was doing the right thing.

"I might take you up on the Sinclair thing because he honestly scares the shit out of me."

Ben laughs and nods in agreement. "Me too."

"So," I say, pointing to his head. "Scar."

"It's not as good of a story as yours."

"Good. I don't think I can handle more at that level," I admit.

Ben laughs. "I like to run at night. I lived in the South for a little while after college and it was too hot to run during the day. I went for a run after midnight, tripped over something, and slammed my face against a rock. It knocked me out for a while." He gestures to his scar. "I was young and embarrassed so I didn't go to the hospital for stitches like a probably should have."

I laugh. "Yeah, you definitely should have." I look at how thick the scar is. He definitely needed stitches. "We should come up with a better story, though. Make you sound like a hero."

"What?" Ben asks, laughing and shaking his head at me.

"Maybe you wrestled a guy and saved someone from being murdered and he got you with his knife," I say, making Ben laugh harder. "Oh! How about you saved a little girl from a hungry tiger that escaped from the zoo?"

We're laughing so hard as my stories get more ridiculous that my abs are hurting, and tears are running down my face. My phone rings, and I manage to get myself together enough to answer it.

"Hello love of my life," I say.

"Are you okay? You sound funny," Willa says.

"I'm fine. Ben just fought off an entire biker gang with a toothbrush and three pencils to save a Thor cosplayer."

The line is quiet as I cackle to myself.

"Ben? Can you hear me? Is Declan okay? He needs to be at the arena in thirty minutes," Willa yells, making sure Ben can hear her even though she isn't on speaker.

Ben laughs. "He's fine. We're just telling stupid stories to relieve some stress. I'll make sure he gets there on time."

Willa sighs in relief. "Thanks, Ben." She pauses. "You're good, hockey boy?"

"I'm feeling a lot better than I have in days," I tell her. "Have you landed?"

"Yeah. We're on our way to the arena. I'll be in there in forty-five minutes."

"I can't wait to see you, Princess."

She laughs. "You saw me yesterday."

"Too long."

"I love you, baby. I'll meet you by the locker rooms before your game." I can hear the smile in her voice.

"I love you too. Be safe."

"Always."

I hang up my phone just in time for a pounding on the hotel room door.

"Let's go, Dec!" Gideon calls. "We have a cup to win!"

"Fuck yeah we do!" I yell, hopping up off the bed and heading out of my room, with Ben following right behind me.

We lost. Barely. Bouchard is kicking himself for letting in the only goal of the whole game. Martinez is blaming himself for letting the puck pass him in the first place. The locker room is somber and depressing.

"We're back on home ice for the next two games. We'll have the advantage that we need to beat them," Gideon tells the team. "We fought fucking hard tonight and let them know we're going to keep fighting. This win wasn't easy for them, and they know it. We're coming for them and the cup. It's our year, boys. We're too fucking hungry for it to lose."

The guys perk up, shouting their agreement with our captain. Coach comes in right at the end of Gideon's speech. He's not happy, but he isn't as angry as I thought he would be.

"I have an announcement to make," he says, waiting until everyone quiets down to continue. "I'm retiring after this season."

The room stays silent for a moment before everyone bursts out either in congratulations or argument. Coach lifts his hands.

"It's time. No matter how this season goes, it's been an honor to coach you. But Mrs. Monroe has saved this season more than once when it shouldn't have been needed. I'm getting old and missing things that used to be obvious." He looks at me. "I'm grateful for Willa. Don't mistake my words." I nod, letting him know I understand. "That being said, I'd really like to go out with the cup."

The whole team cheers, smiles on our faces even though we just lost. Gideon nudges me. He and Ben are the only ones aware that I'm retiring at the end of the season, and I guess he thinks now is a great time to announce it.

I stand and clear my throat. Everyone stops cheering and looks at me.

"I'm retiring at the end of the season too."

"Why?" Rogers asks, looking alarmed.

"My knees can't take it anymore. I've had a really great career, and I'd like to end it on top instead of on the has-been list." I scratch the back of my neck. "Plus, Willa and I want to start a family, and I don't want my kids to have two parents who are on the road."

I can feel my face burn with all the wolf whistles filling the locker room.

"So if we can get it together to win the cup for me and Coach, I'd appreciate it."

Everyone cheers again. I smile. That smile doesn't leave my face while I change or when I shower. It just grows bigger the moment I see my wife waiting for me. Willa is leaning against the wall across from the locker room. She's wearing my jersey and a pair of ripped black jeans. Her lilac hair is down in waves around her beautiful face. She takes my breath away.

"You're sure smiling a lot for a guy that just lost," she teases me before jumping into my arms and snuggling into my neck.

I pull her away so I can kiss her. "No matter what happens with hockey, you're still my wife. Why wouldn't I be smiling?" I say against her lips. She kisses me. "I win no matter what."

I get lost in her. The softness of her lips, the noise she makes when I run my tongue along her neck, the way she pants my name. A throat clears, and I groan before looking over at Belle and Kai. They're both smirking, and Belle looks like she's a second away from bursting out in laughter.

"You guys will see each other tomorrow," Kai says. They're flying out with Willa right after they leave here. I don't leave with the team until tomorrow morning, but then I have two days off. "Plus, the next two games are home, so I think you can stop making out like teenagers now."

Willa sticks out her tongue at him and then turns to me. She kisses me too quickly and I let her wiggle out of my arms.

"I'll see you tomorrow, hockey boy."

"I love you, Princess. Be careful." I tighten my grip on her hips, and she smiles up at me.

"I love you too, baby."

I watch her walk away after one more kiss and sigh. She has Kai and Belle with her plus the security I hired.

"She's safe," Ben says. I jump and look over at him. He laughs. "I called your name, but you were so focused you didn't hear me."

"Sorry," I mutter.

He shrugs. "I get it." He claps my shoulder. "Let's get on the bus and go back to the room. You can watch her flight, and I'll order food."

"Tacos?" I ask, following him out of the arena and to the waiting bus. He lifts an eyebrow, knowing I'm not supposed to be eating unhealthy food right now. "I'll agree to chicken tacos, but I need the grease."

Ben snorts but doesn't argue.

"You're the best."

"Tacos?" Gideon asks, looking at me over his seat in front of us.

I sigh. "Get enough for him too," I tell Ben.

"Fuck, yeah," Gideon says, turning back around.

We pull away from the arena with a warmth in my chest that's been absent with how anxious I've been. I have great people around me.

FORTY-EIGHT

"WILLA, I swear if you don't stop," Belle threatens, staring at me like she's thinking about smacking me. I slowly remove my hand from the table in front of me where I've been tapping my fingers.

We're in a hotel in San Diego. Games four, five, and six of the finals are here. Game six is tonight, and Boston needs to win to tie it up and force a game seven. It's making me anxious, but that's only part of it.

Theo called this morning and said that he's still keeping an eye on Eva and her communications. She's getting desperate in her search for Ezra and even though she hasn't found even a hint of his location, he's worried she'll do something drastic to find him. Which is why Maverick and Jo are also with us on this trip. If Eva was going to do anything, it would be to Maverick.

Cal and Harlow have been checking in. It's been weird without them, but I'm glad Cora isn't near any of this.

Belle slaps my hand away from my mouth where I was trying to chew on my cuticles again. I glare at her but put my hand down. Declan is either going to speak to Sinclair tonight if they lose or three days from now after game seven. I half want it to be tonight to get it over with, but I don't want him to lose.

"You'd think for a place that charges a year's mortgage for a week's stay would have a better selection," Maverick grumbles as he looks through the mini bar.

"You're paying for security and anonymity, not snacks," Kai points out.

"We have to leave soon, anyway. You can get food at the arena," Jo points out.

"Are you planning on seeing Dec before his game?" Belle asks.

I shake my head. "I don't think seeing me this nervous is going to help him." I managed to keep it mostly together when he was here earlier, before he had to leave to get back to his hotel and team. He's not allowed to stay with me, and the team is at a different hotel a few miles from here. Kai found this hotel and insisted we stay here because of their reputation for keeping celebrity stays on the down low.

HOCKEY BOY

Where are you?

"Or not," I saw, looking at the message on my phone.

At the hotel still.

Instead of texting me back, he calls.

"What's wrong?" Declan asks the moment I answer.

"Nothing."

"Willa. . ."

I sigh. "I'm just a nervous wreck and didn't want to mess up your game."

"Princess, I'm nervous too. That's why I need to see you." There's a slight desperation in his voice that has me standing and heading for the door. I can hear Kai snort and everyone else following me.

"I'm on my way. Will there be time before warmups?" I ask, now rushing down the hall.

"Car is already outside," Jo says, keeping up with me easily. Stupid short fucking legs.

"I'll make time," Declan says.

"I'll be there as soon as I can, hockey boy." I stuff my phone back in my pocket and half run out of the hotel.

I slide into the waiting limo to find Maggie already there. She can stay in the hotel with the team since she's not high profile. I'm sure Gideon has been taking advantage of that, even though he's supposed to stay in his own room.

"Jo sent the limo for me first," Maggie explains, probably seeing the questioning look on my face.

I look over at Jo, and she just shrugs. "I knew you'd end up wanting to see him before the game."

I run through the arena the moment we get there. My security easily handles the team's since it's the third game in a row I've been here and they recognize me, anyway. They're still required to check badges, which I understand, but they'll have to wait.

"Dec!" I yell when I see him. He's standing at the entrance to the tunnel in full uniform, waiting for me. I throw myself at him, and he easily catches me like he always does, his stick clanging on the rubber floor where he drops it.

"Princess," he murmurs into my hair. "Are you okay?"

I smile. "I am now."

He searches my face and then grins when he sees I'm telling the truth. "Me too."

"Win tonight so we can go home and celebrate," I tell him.

"Yeah, and then I have to win game seven too, so that Sinclair is in a good mood," he grumbles.

"One thing at a time. Focus on this game. Don't hog the puck. Don't shoot at the left corners like Finn is expecting."

"I fucking love you," Declan says before kissing me.

"I fucking love you too. Now go win." Declan kisses me once more before releasing me and heading out onto the ice.

I make my way back to my security detail and let them lead me to the stupid box I have to watch from. I know why, and I didn't even fight Declan on it, but it would've been nice to be closer to the action.

"Willa!" I turn to see to see Ben.

"Hi Ben," I say, smiling at him. Declan told me how he dumped everything that's been happening on Ben and instead of running, he helped Dec process it. I'm so thankful he's there for Declan when I can't be.

"I'm glad I caught you. The guys want to throw Declan a surprise retirement party, and I wanted to get your input on it with. . ." he pauses and scratches his head. "With everything, I figured it would be important."

I laugh humorlessly. "I can see why you'd think that, and I appreciate it. I'll give you my number, and we can plan it." He nods and quickly types my number into his phone, sending me a text so I have his.

"I was also hoping you had or could get some pictures of

Dec playing hockey when he was young. Or if you have any. I'm going to put a slideshow together."

"Of course," I agree.

Declan had a talk with Sally and Ted about keeping their phones on them and even bought them a satellite phone before they left. They were planning to come back to watch him play in the finals, but he asked them not to. I don't know what he said to them, but they agreed. He was too nervous having them here with everything going on.

He's sacrificed so much for me. Declan doesn't see it that way, of course. I'm already planning something for when this is all over to make it up to him.

"Thanks, Willa," Ben says, waving and taking off with his camera in his hand.

"Who was that?" Maverick asks around a mouthful of popcorn, looking over my shoulder at where Ben disappeared.

"Declan's friend, Ben. He needs my help with a surprise retirement party."

Mav nods and throws his arm around my shoulders, leading me to the box to watch the game. I lean into him. Maverick has been happy recently. Or as close to happy as any of us come the closer we get to Eva's arrest. Harrison somehow got his contact to wait until the day after game seven to move in on her. I don't know what he had to promise to get that favor, and I don't think I want to know.

That also means that Declan only has one day to convince Sinclair to help us.

But Mav has convinced himself that Ezra's within reach, and Eva is already in an orange jumpsuit. We've been letting him have it since he could be right. It wasn't worth ruining his good mood over. Not yet anyway.

I'm practically hanging out of the box. Belle hasn't even bothered to stop my fidgeting. Not that she's noticed. She's just as on edge as I am. Boston and San Diego are tied with less than a minute left in the third period.

I bite down on my lip as I watch the clock run out. Both teams are exhausted. They've been fighting hard to win.

"What happens now?" Maverick asks.

"Another period, but it's sudden death," I explain.

Maverick gasps, and I look over at him to see how horrified he looks.

I snort. "It just means that they play until the first goal, not the full allotted time."

"Right. That's what I thought," he says, trying to school his expression.

Belle bursts out laughing. "You one hundred percent thought they were about to start fighting each other," she says. "Don't lie, Maverick."

"They fight each other all the time. It wasn't much of a leap," he grumbles, crossing his arms over his chest and slinking down into his seat.

"Send Dec a picture of your lady bits to motivate him," Kai says, completely serious.

"Never say lady bits ever again," Jo says, her nose turned up in disgust.

"Skating with a hard on isn't going to help him," Belle points out.

I sigh and grab my phone from where I shoved it into my boot. These stupid jeans I wore have fake pockets. What psychopath made fake pockets? Whoever they are deserves prison time.

You got this, baby.

HOCKEY BOY

I'm sure as fuck trying.

Please tell me you have some winning play in that beautiful head of yours.

I wish I did. You're both playing to borderline perfection.

I don't point out that being this far away is putting me at a serious disadvantage if he wants my observations.

I was afraid you were going to say that.

I love you, and I'll only love you a little less if you lose.

Very funny, Princess.

"Lady bits," Kai whispers out of the side of his mouth like it would make it so no one else hears him. I roll my eyes, but decide to try it, anyway.

I'll let you take my ass if you win.

Fuck.

Holy fuck, Willa. Are you serious?

Only if you win, baby.

I'm going to fucking win. I've wanted to claim your ass so bad.

I know. And you can tonight. After you win.

Fuck, Princess.

I need to get back out there. I love you.

I love you too, hockey boy.

"Yeah, that will definitely get him to score," Maverick says, laughing so hard he snorts. "He's going to score twice."

"Mav!" I scold, clutching my phone to my chest. "Don't read my texts."

"You can't score twice in overtime," Kai says.

I sigh and pinch the bridge of my nose. I watch Belle explain it to him, and his eyes widen.

"I didn't think she was going to do it!" he says, trying to defend himself.

"They're back," Jo says, getting everyone to turn their attention back to the ice.

Declan is staring right at me. He points his stick at me and even though I'm not close enough to see the look in his eyes; I know the heat that's burning there for me. I've seen it and felt it enough to have the image of how much he wants me etched into my brain.

I blow him a kiss. He pretends to catch it and holds to his chest. Then he skates off to join his team where they're gathered around Coach at the bench. I watch him lean in to listen, nod, and then skate straight to his position.

Gideon wins the face-off and passes it straight to Ivanov. I watch the predictable play unfold. It's the one they've been trying the entire game. Gideon to Ivanov. Ivanov back to

Gideon. Gideon back to Ivanov, who will shoot on Finn just to have his shot blocked.

And that's exactly what happens.

But San Diego is pulling the same plays when they win the face-off too.

"This is going to take days at this rate," I grumble, watching Bouchard stop an easy shot. Declan is on the bench, chewing on his mouth guard, eyes focused on the puck at all times. I know because the cameras keep finding him or Martinez, who looks like he's about to break his stick over his knee.

"Where's the puck blocker going?" Belle asks. I look up to see Finn skating to the bench. The cameras zoom in on his face, which is red and angry. He's yelling at his coach but ends up getting off the ice. I don't even bother correcting Belle's terminology before I'm out of my seat.

Kai quickly explains to her that they pulled their goalie so that they could have an extra guy. It's a risky strategy and one that could go either way for them. I can see the thought behind it. If they lose, they still have one more game. Or they could cinch the victory now. They really don't have anything to lose.

"I'm so nervous I might pee," Maggie says, squeezing in next to me. We're all right up front watching, so the space is a little tight.

It feels like I'm watching the puck drop in slow motion. Then time speeds back up when Gideon wins and passes to Ivanov.

"No," I grumble. Ivanov is surrounded in seconds, and I think that's the end of it, but he manages to pass to Declan, who slaps it across the ice. He doesn't get far before he's slammed into the boards, but the attention on him and Ivanov leaves Gideon open. He gets to the puck before San Diego's defense and slips the puck around the net as they chase him.

I hold my breath, watching Gideon take his shot on the empty net. The puck hits the defenseman's skate, bounces off the goal post and then skims right over the line. The lights flash and the buzzer blares.

Maggie and I are jumping and screaming in each other's arms. My friends surround us doing the same thing.

"They did it!" Maggie yells, tears falling from her eyes.

We all separate long enough for me to look down and see Declan. He smiles at me and winks. I bite my lip, knowing what that look means.

"You're going to want to get some lube," Maverick whispers in my ear, snickering when I look at him in horror.

Oh. Fuck.

declan

"BEN, I need you to cover for me if anyone comes looking."

Ben looks up from his phone with a frown. "Where are you going?"

"To Willa's hotel. I booked us a room there for the night. I swear I'll be back early so no one notices."

Ben laughs. "Go be with your wife."

"You're the best!" I yell as I run out the door.

It takes me no time to get to Willa's hotel, even with the stop I made for supplies. Checking in at the front desk took more time. Or I was possibly more impatient at that point.

My whole body hurts. I need to ice my knees and sleep for the next three days. But I need Willa so much more.

I bang on the door to her room, and it flies open like she was waiting for me. Her smile is brilliant before she leaps into my arms.

"I'll have her back before your flight tomorrow," I call into the room, hoping one of them heard me, but not waiting around to find out.

"You did it," Willa says, kissing along my jaw. If I didn't

have to see where I was walking, I would've already claimed her mouth. "You're so close to winning, baby."

I fumble with the keycard when I get to my room number. The moment the light flashes green, I turn the handle and rush inside. Willa giggles as I toss her on the bed and strip my clothes off in record time.

"Naked. Now," I growl. She laughs again but does as I ask. I kiss my way up her body. Nipping her gently just to hear the small gasps she makes. "You promised me something, Princess."

Willa stiffens beneath me, and I look up from where I was kissing along her stomach. I frown at the nervousness I see there.

"If you don't want to, that's okay," I tell her, not wanting to force her to do something she doesn't want to.

"It's not that," she says, turning her head and looking away from me.

"Look at me, Willa." She meets my eyes and bites her lip. "What is it?"

"I've never done that before," she admits, pink tinging her cheeks.

I groan, moving my hands down to grip her ass. "You're telling me no one has ever had you here before?" I slip my finger between her cheeks and gently circle her tight hole.

"No," she says, the word coming out breathy.

"Fuck," I groan before kissing her. "I'm going to fuck your sweet pussy while getting your ass ready with my fingers. Understand?"

Willa groans into my mouth.

"Words, Princess. I need to hear them." I stick my finger

into her wet heat and bring it back to her ass, slipping in to the second knuckle.

"I understand, Dec," she gasps.

I lean over, keeping my finger working inside her as I grab the small bottle of lube from the pocket of my pants. I remove my finger long enough to coat it and return it to her, making it all the way to the last knuckle this time.

"Baby," she calls, working herself on my finger.

"What do you need? Do you need my fingers? My mouth? My cock? Use your words, Princess."

"Cock. Now. I need it now, Declan," Willa shouts, trying to pull me down on top of her. She either wants hours of foreplay or none. There's no in between with her. I chuckle at her desperation and pull my finger out. The whimper she makes almost has me coming on the spot.

I love her like this.

Desperate for me.

I sit back on the bed, leaning against the headboard. "Ride me, wife."

Willa scrambles into my lap and lines herself up with my aching cock.

"Be caref —" The words aren't even out of my mouth before she slams herself down onto me, taking me all the way to the hilt. "Fuck!" I shout, my eyes rolling back in my head.

I let her take control and ride me while I go back to working on getting her ass ready for me. First one finger and then two. By the time I work her up to a third, she's panting and so close to the edge I have to grit my teeth to keep myself together.

"Come on my cock, Princess. Then I'll come in your ass."

Willa screams out her release, clenching around my cock and fingers so hard I have to name presidents, so I don't blow early and ruin this for the both of us. Once she stops squeezing me to death, I slip my fingers free and move her so her ass is hovering over my cock. I hold her tightly so I can lube up. It's probably too much and now everything is slippery, but I want to make her first time as painless as possible.

"Ready?" I ask her.

"Please, baby," she pants, reaching behind her and lining up. I gently lower her down an inch at a time. My arms are shaking from holding her up for so long, but I'd sooner let them fall off before causing her any pain.

"Relax, Princess. Let me in." She pushes out a heavy breath, and I can feel her muscles relax, allowing me to inch my way in.

"It's burns," she says once she's fully seated again.

"Don't move. Let your body adjust. I promise I'll make you feel good." I kiss her, distracting her from the burn and stretch she's feeling. The kiss turns deep and heated immediately, and soon she's moving. She moans into my mouth. "That's it. Take what you need."

"Dec," she pants. "I need more."

I reach between us, slipping two fingers inside of her pussy and using my thumb to rub her clit.

"Oh," she gasps. "Oh my god."

"There you go," I groan, hoping she's getting as close as I am. It's taking everything I have to hold back. "You're doing so good, Princess. Do you feel how full you are? Such a good girl, taking her husband's cock in her ass and his fingers in her pussy."

"Fuck, baby. Shit," she moans, moving her hips faster. I can't take it anymore. I snap, grabbing her hip with my free hand and fucking up into her. She moans even louder. I move my fingers faster and press down harder with my thumb.

"Come for me, wife. Now. Squeeze my dick with that tight little asshole."

Willa screams my name and then sobs as she comes hard. I come with her, my release shooting from me so aggressively I think I may black out.

Once we both come down from our orgasms and catch our breaths, I gently pull her off me and carry her into the bathroom. Cradling her in my arms, I run the bath. I made sure our room had a large tub when I called for the reservations, knowing we both would need to soak in some warm water after.

When the bath is ready, I sink down gently and adjust Willa so she's sitting in between my outstretched legs. She moans once she's settled.

"Don't start that, Princess. I don't think you're ready to go again so soon."

She laughs sleepily and snuggles into my arms. "I love you."

"I love you, too," I tell her. "More than anything."

"Mmm," is all she manages before she's asleep.

I sit in the water with my wife in my arms until it turns cold.

declan

THE ICE FEELS cool against the small amount of exposed skin on my wrists as I stretch. This is it. My last game. The last time I'll be on the ice as an NHL player.

I made love to Willa before the sun even came up this morning. It was slow and sweet, a complete contrast to how hard and desperate it was for most of the night.

She came to see me in front of the locker room before warm-ups. The worry shining through her eyes even with her trying to plaster a smile on her face for me. We're going together to speak to Sinclair after the game, win or lose. All our eggs are in one basket.

I go through the motions, doing the same warmup routine I've been doing for a decade now. Taking a deep breath, I turn my focus to the game, where it needs to be.

San Diego didn't take the loss lightly. I know that team, and I know their coaching staff. They're going to come out of the gate with a new strategy. Finn will have watched the tapes from every one of our playoff games and studied the shots taken on goal. It's part of what makes him as good as he is.

Unfortunately for them, we're ready to give everything to secure this win. Even if that includes both my knees. It's probably the first time in history someone's life depends on the win. It sounds dramatic even thinking that, but Theo and Harrison are both secure in their guess that Maverick would be in danger once Eva was arrested.

A warrant for her arrest was issued this morning. They didn't know what she did exactly, but it was bad enough that it forced the authorities' hands, and they had to take her in. Eva got a heads up from someone and ran. Maverick has already been questioned about her whereabouts. Luckily, his dislike for his "mother" has been well documented in both the media and within her inner circles. So, he's able to be here to watch my game and not stuck in a police station being asked questions he'll never be able to answer.

We need help, and we need it yesterday. I shouldn't have waited to ask. But Harrison said that everything he found on Sinclair was that he's a grumpy asshole and unapproachable. So waiting for a win that would put the Stanley Cup in his office for a year made sense.

But I can't help thinking about how nice he was to me when we spoke. Well, maybe not nice. Definitely approachable, though. Sort of.

I look up at the private box I bought for my family. This last game is on home ice, and I know Willa wanted to be front and center to see us win. I appreciate her not fighting me on it. I really thought she would once we got down to the last game.

My perfect wife is front and center, smiling when she

catches me looking at her. Maggie is to her right and Belle to her left. Willa drags her thumb across her throat and points to the visitor bench.

I snort while a laugh comes from next to me. I turn to see Martinez looking towards Willa.

"Your wife is the best kind of aggressive. If she wasn't so tiny, I'd suggest getting her signed and in a pair of skates."

I laugh with him. "She wouldn't even need us out here with her. She'd handle everything herself."

Martinez tilts her head as he thinks. "Do you think it's too late to add her to the roster? We're going to need her."

I shake my head. "We've got this, man."

"I like your attitude, best friend."

I roll my eyes and skate to the tunnel. Warmups are over and they need to flood the ice.

Gideon and Coach give their motivational speeches about how everything we've done has led to this moment or something. I'm not listening. My mind is on the pretty girl with the lilac hair.

"Monroe!"

I startle at the loud voice in my ear. I turn to see Gideon looking at me with concern. He has to do it through his hair, which has gotten long and is in his eyes. The helmet keeps it out of his face, thankfully. Hockey players are notorious for their superstitions. So none of us have cut our hair or shaved our faces since we made the playoffs. Ivanov usually shaves his head, so it was a shock to us all when his hair came in red. Slava's dark mane is so long he can tie it back.

"I know you're nervous, Dec, but we need you in this game with us," he says.

I swallow thickly. "Got it."

"What the hell's going on?" he asks and because he's being so loud with his concern, everyone is now looking at me.

"Nothing. I'm fine." I look around to see that not a single one of my teammates or coaches believes me.

Fuck it.

"The guy that killed my wife's tour manager the night Gideon was there is still free and could very much be after Willa and her friends," I explain plainly. "I think Sinclair can help us keep her safe, but we were hoping to win the cup to butter him up."

"Jesus fuck, Dec," Gideon says, running his hands through his hair while his eyes bug out of his head.

"Alright," Coach says, clapping his hands once. "We're going to skate tonight like Willa's life depends on it. Got it?"

"Yes, Coach," everyone says immediately.

I tear up as I look around at the team that accepted me when they didn't have to. "Thank you," I say, but it comes out as barely a whisper.

"No one touches one of ours," Martinez says, looking angrier than I've ever seen him.

"We will help you if Sinclair will not," Slava adds. I nod at him because that's all I can manage around the lump in my throat. "He is not the only one with connections." His Russian accent is suddenly thicker than usual. I don't have time to question it because Coach announces we need to get back on the ice.

I take a deep breath before following Gideon. The weight on my shoulders lifts slightly, but that's enough for me to be able to see the light at the end of this bullshit tunnel.

The first two periods have been brutal. Both teams are taking their share of time in the penalty box. No one has scored on either goalie. Finn has anticipated every shot made on his net while Bouchard has had some amazing saves.

My knees are throbbing. My shoulder took a hard hit against the boards within the first minute of the first period and has been stiff since then. Gideon has a bloody lip that keeps splitting open, and Slava's right pinky is broken and taped to hell so he can still play. Ivanov is back with the doctor after a hard hit that had him keeping weight off his left leg.

My team is broken and bleeding, and they have every intention of spilling more blood on the ice, if it means protecting my wife. I want to cry with gratitude and scream in anger simultaneously. Instead, I take a deep breath, ignoring the painful tug on my ribs from a hit last period that I've been pretending didn't hurt.

Both first lines from each team head out onto the ice to start the last period. The tension in the air is so thick you could cut it with a knife. I glance at Finn as I take my spot. His eyes meet mine. The usual intensity that's there for every game turns into a concerned frown with whatever he sees in my face. I don't have the time or desire to reassure him with a smile.

I turn my attention to the ref just in time for him to drop the puck. Every slap of my stick and pass of the puck makes me angrier. This game should be for me and my team. We should play to win because we deserve it. Not because I need the owner to do something probably shady to keep my family safe.

Is it wrong of me to think Sinclair should help no matter what? I'm a player on his team. A player who might be able to get him whatever it is Ezra knows if he helps us.

I respect Harrison, but this plan is absolute bullshit, and I'm mad at myself for waiting to speak with Sinclair. I don't even know if he'll speak with me. We could win, and he could still deny me.

Coach calls my line back, and I throw myself over the boards to take my seat next to Gideon.

"Something has to give. We can't do this for another period if it goes into OT," he says.

"Dec."

I turn to see Ben coming up behind me on Coach's bench. Coach, to his credit, just lifts his eyebrows and then turns back to the game.

"Sinclair is going to meet us after the game. He said if you're needed for press to meet him in his office immediately after."

"You're my best friend," I tell Ben, needing him to know how much he means to me. He nods and quickly gets out of the way of the players and coaches.

"I'll try not to take offense to that," Martinez says, leaning around Gideon to glare at me. I roll my eyes and focus back on the game.

Some of my anger has dissipated, knowing Sinclair agreed to the meeting without the outcome of the game having a part. I'm sure winning will still help the odds of him helping, but now I want to win more for my team. For me. For Willa and all the unwavering support she's always given me.

"Finn is a Hall of Fame level goalie. He's well on his way to being the best of all time," I say.

"Great," Gideon mutters next to me. "Maybe don't give any pep talks."

"No one has taken more shots on him than I have."

"That's really helped you," Coach says from behind me.

I sigh and chew on my mouth guard. "I've also scored on him the most."

"You have about thirty seconds before you're back out there, so make your point," Coach says.

"I'm going to fall back to defense. Martinez will take the puck. Finn won't have watched your plays because you almost never shoot on the net. Finn is as good as he is because he studies and then studies some more. You're a wild card. That's what we need." I look over at Martinez after I explain. His brows are furrowed, but he nods.

"Do it," Coach says. "Gideon, win that face-off, get the puck to Monroe. You know what to do from there."

"Yes, Coach," we all say before we're throwing ourselves over the boards and back onto the ice.

WILLA

"WHAT THE HELL IS HE DOING?" I ask, more to myself than anyone else around me.

"I think he's being a back guy instead of a front guy," Maverick says. He clearly still hasn't bothered to learn anything about hockey.

I watch as Dec skates backwards, and Martinez takes his place. Dec had passed the puck behind him to Martinez the moment it hit his stick. It's not an unusual play for them, but usually the puck is either passed back to Dec or to another forward. This time, Martinez takes off like a rocket, heading toward San Diego's blue line and knocking their team over as he goes. I'm shocked to see how fast he can skate. The man is large, built more like a wall than a man. It's part of what makes him a good defenseman.

This type of play isn't uncommon in the NHL, but Boston doesn't do much of it. They don't need to. Their offense has been the best in the league this season. I can't tell if the choice to give the opportunity to score to Martinez was out of desperation or something else.

The play feels like it's in slow motion. My eyes are glued to the screen of the jumbotron. I can't see the puck well from the box, so I have to rely on the cameraman to keep up. Thankfully, he's been doing a great job the whole game so far.

Martinez barely makes it over the blue line before he shoots. The smack of his stick against the puck is so loud I can hear it from all the up in the box. The camera can barely keep up as the puck flies. I take my eyes away from the screen and watch the ice as Finn dives for it.

And misses.

The puck sails over the top of his catcher. I'm jumping and screaming, throwing myself in Maggie's arms as she joins me in celebrating. I look up at the screen just in time to watch the replay. The change in Finn's face is obvious. He's been stone-faced and serious the entire game, not a single change in his expression. Then the moment he realizes Martinez is skating for him, his eyes go wide.

This is why they did that. Because Finn didn't know how to stop him. Declan talks about how Finn spends all his time studying his opponents and zero time having a personal life. He must not have thought about studying Martinez.

The anger on Finn's face directed at Declan says he knows who found the weakness. The latter shrugs and then looks right at me, tipping his head and tapping over his heart. The camera is still on Finn, so I see the way his brows furrow, like he's trying to work out a riddle with only a third of the information.

"There's still a lot of time left," Kai says with his signature slight upturn of his lips. Like it would be a crime to smile in public and let people know he's actually a nice guy. He's not wrong though. Eight minutes is a lot of time. Either team could score more than once in that time. Considering how tight it's been so far, that seems unlikely.

My phone vibrates in my pocket. I look around, confused. Everyone that would text me is either in this room or down on the ice. I pull it out and see it's Ben.

> BEN
>
> Hi Willa. It's Ben. I need your help. It's about Declan.

My eyes go wide and fly down to the ice. Declan is currently on the bench and seems fine.

> Sorry. This isn't an emergency.
>
> I got him a meeting with Sinclair after the game. Win or lose. I want to help. I'm going to go with him because I wasn't sure you would be able to get there in time with how security is going to be.
>
> Feel free to take my place if you're able to get through. That man scares me.

I snort.

> They're letting me out onto the ice if they win. They let all the WAGs know as we arrived. So I guess if they lose, and I have to go through the usual security, you'll have to go with him.

I'm surprisingly fine with the idea of Declan confiding in Ben. He's done nothing but be a good friend, and I'm glad

Declan has had him to lean on. Especially with how he has been so strong for the rest of us.

Right. I can do that.

I'm nervous too.

We've got this.

We've got this.

"Who is that?"

I look up from my phone to see Maverick trying to read my messages upside down.

"Ben," I say, glaring at him.

"The photographer that has a kind of hot mountain man starving artist thing going on?"

"He's Dec's best friend," I say, ignoring the kind of accurate description of Ben.

"You're lucky Cal isn't here to hear you say that," Mav says.

I roll my eyes and focus back on the game. Breathing a little easier between the goal and the reassurances from Ben that Declan won't be alone when he talks to Sinclair.

Is it too early to feel like things are finally going our way?

declan

IF I THOUGHT the first two periods were violent, they have nothing on this one. My old captain, Hank, has been going for my knees. He was out for most of the season with a shoulder injury, but he made it back in time to try to cripple me.

"What the fuck, man?" I shout at him when the whistle blows after my pathetic shot on the net that Finn easily stopped. It's hard to shoot against a guy who knows all your tricks while defending your knees from a former teammate.

"I want the fucking cup," Hank growls, skating by me, hitting my shoulder in the process.

"So do I! You don't see me going for your shoulder like a cheap asshole."

The whistle blows again, the refs way of telling us to get our asses into position.

"There's less than two minutes left, Dec. We've got this." Gideon claps my back as I skate by him to take my spot to his right.

I nod, my focus on the puck and nowhere else. It's the

only way I've been able to get through this game. If I let my focus slip back to what's at stake, I make stupid mistakes.

Gideon loses the face-off, and the puck is sent down the ice. I race after it, leaving Hank. Gagne, the asshole that replaced me, takes a shot on Bouchard. I hold my breath and let out a sigh of relief when it's caught. Coach takes the pause in play as an opportunity to call us back to the bench.

"I am going to need to meditate for several weeks after this game," Slava says next to me. Ivanov never came back so he's been the left wing on my line.

"You meditate?"

"You do not?" he asks, sounding confused.

"Uh, no. Should I start?"

"Yes."

I nod, keeping my eyes on the game. It might not be a terrible idea with the amount of stress I've been under recently.

The game clock is down to thirty seconds when Coach calls for another line change. I throw myself over the boards immediately, ready for the carnage that will be the final seconds. San Diego pulled Finn since they have nothing to lose. The sixth man could be a real issue if they did it earlier.

Gideon wins, passing it to me. I pass to Slava who passes to Martinez. He passes it to me. I watch the clock. We're letting the seconds run out. We don't need to score again. Do I want to as a middle finger to the team that refused to re-sign me? Yes. The empty goal is so tempting, but not worth the risk of leaving Bouchard vulnerable.

Just as I think about it, a clear line to the goal opens up in front of me. Slava must see it too, but he calls my name and passes the puck back to me. The moment it hits my stick, I send it flying. Time slows as my eyes flick back and forth between the clock and the puck. I'm probably the only person in the whole building holding their breath right now. The only person this particular goal is important to. The puck hits the back of the net the moment before the clock hits zero.

My teammates pile on my back, taking me down to the ice in their excitement. I laugh along with them, pushing them off so I can get back on my feet. Brushing the slush off my jersey, I look up to the owner's suite. Sinclair meets my eye and nods. The owner of the Barracudas is standing next to him, scowling down at me. I give him my best smile, wanting to flip him off, but knowing that's a bad idea. He turns around and storms off, making me laugh.

A carpet is being rolled out for the people coming on the ice for the presenting of the cup, but I see a sexy as fuck woman with lilac hair barreling her way through everyone. Quickly skating to the open door to the tunnel, I grab her the moment she gets to the ice.

"You did it, hockey boy!" Willa yells, wrapping herself around me. She pushes my helmet off my head and kisses me. I hear it slam onto the ice behind me, but I don't care. It's not like I'm going to need it ever again. "I'm so proud of you!"

"We did it, Princess. My entire career has been because you believed in me. You pushed me to be the best. I should've realized how in love I was with you a long time ago."

"I love you so much, Declan," Willa says, tears in her eyes and a bright smile on her face. I kiss her again, only stopping at the sound of a throat clearing next to me.

People really need to stop interrupting me kissing my wife.

"Coach is about to accept the cup. Quit making out," Bouchard says. I didn't even see them wheel it out here. I look around Bouchard to see Maggie in a similar position in Gideon's arms. "Married people," Bouchard mumbles under his breath. I frown.

"Where is your wife?" Willa asks him.

"With her tennis instructor in Bali," he grumbles and then skates away.

"I'm impressed," Willa says. I cock an eyebrow in question.

"His wife left him, and he somehow kept it together to have a shutout in the Stanley Cup Finals. That's pretty impressive," she explains.

I skate over to the carpet with Willa in my arms. I keep her there even when I step onto it. Sinclair gestures me over to him from where he's standing near Coach, who is giving a speech which I know will end in his retirement announcement. Mine is going to be coming tonight too.

"You can put me down, Dec," Willa says.

"Not a chance," I say, stepping up next to Sinclair.

"You're going to be wanted for press after this. I made sure you're first. Answer a few questions, announce your retirement, then get to my office."

"Yes, sir," I say immediately. The high from winning and having my wife in my arms for it comes crashing down quickly.

I watch the rest of the ceremony. Bouchard gets MVP, which was well earned. Ben gets pictures of the team and the cup. I had to put Willa down for that, and I wasn't happy about it. Not that I think she's in danger right now, but I feel better when I can feel her. I have to leave her to go to the press room too.

"I'll stay with her. I'm not needed anymore."

I look over my shoulder and see Ben walking up to us, two cameras slung over opposite shoulders.

"Thanks, man. I'm going to try to get out of there as fast as I can."

Ben nods and offers Willa his elbow. She takes it with a smile and turns to me. "It's going to be okay."

"I know, Princess."

I watch Ben lead her away in the direction of the elevator that will take them upstairs to the offices. If this doesn't work, I'm taking her straight to the airport. We'll be on a plane to whatever country she wants, but we're leaving.

Making my way to the locker room and changing as quickly as I can, I follow Gideon and Bouchard to the press room. The reporters ask their usual questions about plays and strategies. Congratulations are intermingled there. I answer robotically, my mind elsewhere and not in the mood for this.

"I'm retiring," I announce, interrupting the reporter in front that was in the middle of another stupid question. The room is silent for a few seconds before everyone speaks at once.

"Shut up and he'll explain!" Gideon yells into the mic. They listen, only the clicks of the cameras making noise.

"As everyone is well aware, I've had more than my fair share of knee injuries. Half my time off the ice has been spent in physical therapy. I've had an amazing career and winning the cup tonight was a perfect ending. I appreciate everyone in the NHL for letting me live my dream. The players and coaches on the Barracudas helped shape me into the player I became, and for that I will be forever grateful. But Anderson Sinclair took a risk signing me when no one else wanted me and to him I want to say, thank you for that belief, and I hope I didn't let you down." Reporters all start asking questions at the same time again, but I hold up my hand. "I'm not done. I wouldn't be here if it wasn't for the sacrifices my parents made to ensure I could play the sport I loved, but most importantly, I wouldn't be here if it wasn't for my wife. Willa believed in me from the moment we met as kids and has never wavered in that belief. She's the reason I signed with Boston. The reason I worked so hard to get the win tonight." I look into the news camera closest to me. "I love you, Princess. Thank you."

I stand, ignoring all the questions thrown my way. I need to get up to Sinclair's office and get this over with. Gideon and Bouchard can handle the rest. I'll have to thank them with concert tickets or something later.

The hallway to Sinclair's office is empty. Which makes sense considering everyone is either in the press room or the locker room celebrating. It's just eerie at this time of night. And of course, his office is at the very end of this hallway. I sigh and pinch the bridge of my nose. My knees hurt. My shoulder hurts. Hell, my whole damn body hurts. I'm nervous he'll tell me to fuck off and not help me.

And why wouldn't he? I'm not his player anymore. My

contract expired at the same time that buzzer went off signaling the end of the game. Then I retired. He owes me nothing.

I notice the light is on in Sinclair's office and there's no sign of Willa or Ben outside of it. She must be in there already. I hope Ben stayed with her. I pick up my pace, ignoring how stiff I'm getting. I don't know Sinclair well enough to leave my wife alone with him.

"These things are really sharp." I freeze at the voice and slowly turn around.

Jon. . . I mean, Patrick, is standing there, holding a skate in his hand and smiling at me like we're old buddies.

"What the fuck are you doing here?" My voice is practically a growl.

"Eva sent me to give you a message," he says, creepy smile still on his face.

"What message?" The question barely leaves my lips before his arm flies out. I'm too slow to stop it. I feel the burning pain of my skin splitting, my hand flying up to my throat. Hot, sticky blood coats my fingers and slides down my neck.

"Told you these things are sharp," Patrick says, laughing and tossing the skate at my feet. My knees buckle, slamming to the floor. "You should really be more careful."

My body falls to the side, too weak to do anything else. I have my hand to my throat, trying to stem the bleeding, but it won't be much use if someone doesn't find me soon. I watch Patrick's retreating form. He's still laughing.

The edges of my vision blur, and I know this is it. The last thing I hear before everything goes black is the sweet and scared voice of the most beautiful woman in the world.

FIFTY-THREE

"I APPRECIATE YOU MEETING WITH US," I tell Anderson Sinclair. He's sitting behind his large and shiny mahogany desk, fingers steepled under his chin. He's intimidating, and I wish Declan was in here with me already. Ben sitting in the chair next to me is the only reason I'm relatively calm right now.

"What is it you need from me, Mrs. Monroe?"

"I think we should wait for Declan," Ben says, nervously scratching his beard. He meets my eyes, and I frown. There's something different about him. He darts his gaze away before I can think too much about it.

Turning back to Sinclair, I smile at him. "Declan would want to be here, but the truth is, this is more of my problem than his."

He sighs and glares at me. "Let me guess. You're cheating on Declan with him," he says, gesturing to Ben with his chin. "Or is Declan the one cheating? How long do I have until it hits the press?"

My jaw drops at his assumptions, but quickly closes when Ben bursts out in laughter.

"You clearly have no idea how obsessed those two are with each other if that's what you think this is about."

Sinclair frowns, but waves his hand in front of him, a silent order to explain ourselves. I nod and quickly glance at Ben before taking a deep breath and blurting out everything that's been going on and why we need his help with Eva. More specifically, his help to protect Ezra if we call him back. To his credit, Sinclair doesn't even blink. He leans back in his dark leather chair, his eyes locked with mine like he's looking for the punch line or maybe the lie. He'll find neither.

"And you think Ezra has something I want?" Sinclair says, breaking the silence.

"He does," Ben says confidently. I smile at him. He doesn't know that. Hell, I don't even know that for certain. It's the theory we're working with that makes the most sense. But Ben promised to help Declan, and he's sitting here next to me doing just that.

"At the minimum, he has something Eva wants so desperately that she's willing to go to any lengths to get it," I amend, not wanting to make false promises to someone as dangerous as the man sitting in front of me.

"Or hide it from people that would be furious about it," Ben adds.

"That seems likely, from what I've heard about her," Sinclair says, his focus still on me. "And you're confident you can get Ezra?"

"Yes." It's the one thing I am confident about right now. I know the moment we call that number, he'll come. We may be coming up on eight years since any of us last saw Ezra, but I have a hard time believing he's changed enough to ignore a call for help.

Sinclair opens his mouth to say something but freezes when manic laughter and a large thump comes outside of his office. He flies out of his seat. I'm right behind him with Ben on my heels.

I can feel all the color drain from my face the moment I see what's in front of me. My legs are moving, a scream wrenching itself from my throat before I have time to stop it.

"Declan!" I shout, my hands automatically moving to the wound at his throat and putting pressure on it. His hot blood seeps between my fingers, and I push harder. "Help me!" I scream. Ben is suddenly next to me, checking the pulse in Declan's wrist.

"Sinclair is calling for help. His pulse is slow, but it's there."

Time moves slowly as I watch the life drain from my husband, taking mine with it. The medics sprint down the long hallway. One tries to take over for me, but I'm too afraid to move my hands.

"I need you to let me take over. I can't save him if you're in the way." The medic is speaking to me as softly as she can, but the sense of urgency in her tone has my hands lifting.

"My helicopter is on the roof. I've already alerted the hospital you'll be landing with him," Sinclair tells the medics.

I look up at him, but I can't see his expression through my tears.

Ben grabs my elbow and hauls me to my feet as the

medics get Declan on a stretcher. The one that took over for me straddles his chest, keeping her hands on his neck.

"I need to go with him," I say, trying to get Ben's grip off of me. "Ben!" I plead.

"It's a personal helicopter. They're going to barely fit in there as it is," Sinclair says.

"Come on, Willa. I'll drive you," Ben says, pulling me along with him. I slide and almost fall, the strong grip on my elbow the only thing keeping me upright. Looking down, I see it's Declan's blood that I slipped in. I rip my arm free of Ben and run to the garbage bin in the hallway, losing my dinner instantly.

"I need to stay to speak to the police, but you two should get to the hospital," Sinclair says, seeming unaffected by everything. He walks into my line of sight and gives me a kind smile that I'm almost certain I'm hallucinating. "Declan needs you."

I nod, letting Ben lead me away on my shaky legs. "Declan is going to punch me for this," Ben mutters. I frown up at him, but then my legs come out from under me, and I shriek. Ben has me cradled in his arms, and he's sprinting for the stairs.

It's on the tip of my tongue to tell him to put me down, but I hold it. He's sprinting down the stairs two at a time, trying everything he can to get me to my husband.

"What if. . ." I start, not able to finish the thought. What if he's already gone by the time we get there?

"No," Ben says, his voice stern even with how out of breath he seems. "He won't leave you." I wrap my arms tighter around his neck, letting the tears soak his shirt.

willa

THE HOSPITAL CAFETERIA IS QUIET. I guess it should be at two in the morning. Belle and Kai dragged me down here with them to grab a coffee. The black sludge that passes as coffee here is at least warm in my hands.

The doctors took Declan straight back to surgery. The good news was the blade was so sharp, and Patrick was so quick, the damage was minimal. She said it would barely even scar. He lost a lot of blood, though, and they're guessing he'll be out for at least the rest of the night. Declan had three infusions before they moved him to a room they would let me see him in. If the medics hadn't already been in the building from working the game, and Sinclair hadn't offered his helicopter, I would have lost him. The thought keeps creeping up on me like an unwanted bug, keeping me on the edge of a panic attack.

I only agreed to coffee when Ben came in and asked to sit with Dec for a while. I'm still checking my phone every few seconds in case something happens, or he wakes up looking for me.

I look at two of my best friends, their concern and love for Declan evident in the way they burst into the hospital in a panic after I called them. I knew in that moment that there was no more room for secrets between us.

"You're my best friend, Belle. Declan is too."

"Uh, that's not news," Kai says. Belle and I both turn and glare at him. "Right. I'm going to make sure the kitchen is still there." Normally, that would make me smile, but I can't. I watch Kai wander off to the other side of the cafeteria.

"I realized something recently," I start. "I realized that I'm so terrified of people leaving me that I've only ever given them parts of myself. So that when they leave, I won't be left hollow and broken."

Belle's eyes quickly tear up. "Are you mad at me for leaving too?" Kai blamed her for leaving him when she chose college over Shattered Halo. I'm not surprised that's the conclusion she jumped to.

"Not at all," I assure her. "My friendship with Declan was always long distance, so you going to college didn't bother me." Belle nods, brows furrowed, but she stays quiet, letting me get to my point. "I meant leaving in the permanent sense."

"Your parents?"

"Yeah. I didn't have any intention of keeping Declan a secret. Honestly, I probably mentioned him when we were little. I wouldn't expect you to remember if I didn't. But when my mom died, it felt like my heart split in two." Belle raises her eyebrow, having figured out where this conversation is going. She reaches across the table and holds my hand. "I gave him one half and you the other."

"You protected yourself."

"Yeah," is all I manage to say around the lump in my throat.

"But he knew all about me."

"That's the other thing I realized. I told him all about you because you're my sister, and I adore you." I lift my head so I can look her in the eyes. "But I hid him away because he was the most precious thing in my life, and I selfishly didn't want to share."

"Because you've always been in love with him," she states in a way that makes it seem like it's obvious.

"I'm so in love with him. It feels like I can't breathe." I sob, rubbing my chest. "When he's gone, I sleep on his side of the bed, just so I can feel the echo of him. So I can wrap myself in the smell of his cologne and dream of the whispers of his touch on my skin." I take in a ragged breath and squeeze Belle's hand. "I was too scared to let myself love him and as soon as I did, I hurt him."

Belle stands and throws herself around me. "You didn't do this to him. Patrick did. Eva did. You didn't hurt Declan."

"Why do I keep hurting the people I love? What's wrong with me?" I sob into her shoulder, refusing to believe her words. "I brought him into my life. I agreed to be fake married to him, knowing there was someone out there that wanted to hurt us."

"What do you mean? You fake married him?" Belle asks. I can feel her trying to pull away to look at me, but I just hold her tighter as I explain everything.

"It kind of sounds like your marriage was never fake, and you were just really slow at figuring that out."

I glare at Kai as he makes his way back to the table. He shrugs at the same time Belle sighs.

"I was wondering if that was the case when he showed up on Thanksgiving, but by Christmas, it was clear how in love with him you were, and I stopped thinking about it. I just assumed I was wrong," Belle says.

I finally pull away from her. "I understand if you're mad at me," I say quietly.

"I'm not mad, Willa. I've had months to come to terms with not being number one in your life anymore. Which I suppose is only fair." She looks lovingly at Kai when she says that. He looks back at her like she's the most precious thing in the world. I start to tear up again and rise from my seat. I need to be with the most precious thing in my world.

FIFTY-FIVE

MY HEAD IS POUNDING, and my throat is so dry I could probably cough up dust. I try to move to grab the water bottle I always keep on my nightstand, but my whole body protests. Everything hurts. Peeling my eyelids open turns out to be impossible. Turning my head makes something in my neck pull. I groan, feeling helpless and confused. What the fuck happened to me?

"Here, Dec. Small sips." A straw is pushed between my lips, and I suck down the cool water gratefully. "Slow, buddy. You're going to get sick." I take another sip, slowly.

"Ben?" I croak, finally able to peel my eyes open and place the voice with the face.

He nods. "I need to get Willa. She's going to be pissed I talked her into going to get a coffee." I watch him turn, shake Sinclair's hand, and then turn back to me with his phone in his hand.

"Glad to see you made it," Sinclair says. "I'll help you." Turning to Ben, he says, "I'll be in touch." Then he leaves.

"What the fuck is going on?" I ask.

"What do you remember?" Ben asks, typing quickly on his phone and then turning his full attention to me.

"We won the cup," I say, squinting at the wall behind Ben's head like it holds the answers. "I announced my retirement."

"Right. Do you remember what happened after you left the press room?" Ben asks.

I can't read anything on his face to give me a hint, so I close my eyes and concentrate. Then it hits me like a truck.

"That motherfucker!" I yell, or try to. My throat is still too dry, and it comes out closer to a gravelly squeak.

"Sinclair's security cameras caught the whole thing."

I look at Ben. He's looking down at his hands in his lap and fidgeting.

"What? What aren't you telling me?"

He sighs, but he doesn't have a chance to speak.

"Declan!" Willa sobs, running into the room and straight into my arms.

"Hi, Princess," I say softly into her hair. Inhaling her scent settles me in a way nothing else ever has.

"You were bleeding out between my fingers," she says, sobs shaking her body.

"I'm so sorry, Willa." Tears sting my eyes as I hold my wife tightly to me. Her words let me know she found me and must have tried to stop the bleeding. I want to strangle Patrick just for putting her through that. Never mind everything else he's done.

"No. I'm the one who's sorry. I'm the reason he was after you in the first place."

"You're not the reason, Willa," Ben says. She turns to him and frowns. I watch her eyes widen, and her mouth drop open. I look over at Ben, but he's just calmly looking at her. His blue eyes communicating something I don't understand.

Wait.

Before my sluggish brain can connect the dots, Maverick barges in my room, his arms full of vending machine snacks.

"You're awake," he says, smiling at me. I watch that smile fall along with all the food in his arms when he looks at Ben.

Ben meets his eyes but remains silent. I'm about to demand to know what's going on, but one word uttered from Maverick's stunned lips has the world crumbling around me.

"Ezra."

3 MONTHS LATER

"I'M SHOCKED to see you here," I say, watching Finn approach me. My retirement party is fairly small, consisting only of my team and a select few others, including my parents. Willa told me she invited Finn, but I didn't think he would fly all the way out here for it.

"Willa told me what winning the cup meant for you," he says without greeting. "I suspect it's much more than the explanation she gave."

I shrug and hand him a beer from the cooler by my feet.

"Why didn't you tell me?"

I look at the giant Viking of a man who is always serious and keeps his emotions locked down. He looks hurt. I've never seen him look anything other than angry or annoyed.

"It was hard with the distance. Especially because I wasn't sure anything could be said over the phone."

"You should have told me before the series," Finn says, his usual angry expression back on his face.

"Why? What were you going to do? Throw the game?" I ask, chuckling at the absurdity of it all.

Finn holds my stare, and I choke on my beer.

"I wouldn't have let you throw the game, Finn! You can't be serious!"

"You think hockey means more to me than you?" he asks, his eyes showing the fierceness there that is usually only seen when he's in the net.

I honestly thought hockey meant more to him than I did, but I don't voice that. I just swallow the emotions that became thick in my throat.

"Thank you. I'm sorry I didn't mention it."

Finn nods. "Do a better job of keeping in touch. You're unemployed. You have time."

I bark out a laugh as he walks away to mingle with the other goalies in attendance.

"He's a weird guy," Gideon says, coming to stand next to me.

"Aren't most goalies?"

He snorts. "You're not wrong."

I take a sip of my beer, trying to let my shoulders relax. Everything since the moment I woke up in the hospital has been a mixture of stressful and relaxed. It's making my head spin. On the one hand, I'm alive, my team won the cup, I have the most amazing wife, and we've been assured by Sinclair that Eva won't be a problem.

On the other hand, my best friend is a fucking liar. He lied to my face for months, even after he found out everything that was going on. And I'm honestly not convinced he didn't know at least some of it.

Willa and I are better than ever, but the moment we step

out of our bubble and interact with our friends, everything is awkward. It makes me want to squirrel her away into our house and never leave again.

She says I can't do that.

I'm going to keep trying, anyway.

"Dec. A package was just delivered for you," Willa says. "It's giant and still at the front door."

I look at Gideon like he'll have an explanation, which he obviously doesn't. He just shrugs and grabs himself another beer.

"Come on," Willa says, grabbing my hand and pulling me through our backyard and to the front of the house. "I want to know what it is."

I laugh and let her tug me behind her. Once we get to the front of the house, I see the large, rectangular box propped up against the front door.

"I didn't order anything," I say, frowning at the box. The label on it only has my name and address, no return address.

"Open it," Willa says, leaning around me to look at the label. "Maybe it's a retirement gift."

"It's heavy and awkward," I complain, carrying it into the house and laying it down on the dining room table.

"Here." Willa hands me a kitchen knife, and I quickly cut the tape on the box.

There's a note lying on top of something wrapped in bubble wrap. I pick it up and read it out loud.

Declan,

I've had this for a while, always intending on gifting it to you. I'm sorry I broke your trust. You've been nothing but a great friend to me. When you're ready, I'd like the opportunity to talk. To tell you my story.

Congratulations on the retirement.

Ben

"Why?" I ask, not sure what part I'm even questioning right now.

Willa shrugs. "Open it and see what he sent you."

I do as she asks, hearing her gasp before I process what I'm looking at.

It's a picture he took during one of my games. I don't know how he managed to get that angle, but I'm speechless.

It's a picture of Willa and me, our foreheads leaning against the glass. You can see us clearly from each side with the thick glass in the middle. It's like he had his lens right up against the glass from an open door. Our eyes are shut, and we're both smiling.

"This is the best picture I've ever seen. We have to hang it up immediately."

"Where?" I ask her, not disagreeing.

She looks around and then points to the staircase. The wall there is blank and looks like it might be the exact right size. It's already framed, so I don't have to do that first.

Slava and Rogers end up having to help me, but we get the picture hung exactly where Willa wants it.

"Fuck, man. Do you think I can get him to do that same pose with me and Maggie?" Gideon asks. No one knows about Ben. I may be angry with him, but it's not my secret to tell.

I shrug. "Maybe."

"Are you going to talk to him?" Willa asks, wrapping her arms around my waist and snuggling into my side. I put my arms around her and hold her close.

"Probably. Just not yet."

"Whenever you're ready, I'm sure he'll be there," she says, leaning up on her toes to kiss me. "Let's get back to your guests so we can keep celebrating you."

"I'd rather take you upstairs and celebrate you," I tell her, deepening the kiss.

A throat clears next to me. "That's it!" I yell. "We're going away. I don't care where. Just that we're alone!" I grab Willa and throw her over my shoulder, taking the stairs up to the bedroom and slamming the door behind me. Willa is giggling as I stalk her. She backs up until she hits the bed.

"That was Coach Jones," she says, laughing some more.

"I don't care. I'm tired of everyone interrupting me when I'm trying to kiss my damn wife."

"We're not having sex with a house full of people."

"But," I start to argue.

"They all know I belong to you. They don't need to hear me screaming your name to prove it."

"I disagree."

"Do you really want all your ex-teammates and friends knowing what your wife sounds like when she comes?" Willa asks, raising her eyebrows in challenge.

"Well. . .no."

"You know who else would hear it? Your parents."

"Motherfucker," I mutter under my breath, and take a seat next to her on the edge of the bed.

"But it sounds like my retirement gift to you might be

perfect," she says, her voice losing the teasing note it just had. She hands me a white envelope that she pulls from her back pocket. I open it and smile.

"Thank you, Princess," I say and kiss her. "When can we leave?" She rented out a cabin for two weeks at the campground where we met all those years ago.

"Tomorrow morning," she says, going in for another kiss, but I'm already up and in our closet. "What are you doing?" she calls after me.

"Packing!"

I hear her laugh and smile to myself. That sound is worth everything.

We have so much waiting for us at home. A whole mess on top of figuring out the future of our careers. Patrick is still out there somewhere. He hasn't been seen or heard from since the night he attacked me. The band isn't sure if they want to sign on for another album and tour. I haven't figured out what direction I want to go from here now that I've hung my skates.

As if sensing all the thoughts running through my head, Willa wraps her arms around me. My head is loud with all the questions and unknowns, but all the noise fades away when I'm in Willa's arms. Which is where I'll stay.

Forever.

Patrice Ashley is an author of romantic suspense. She loves writing and reading more than she likes leaving the house. If she isn't doing that, she's playing with her daughter and spending time with her husband. Patrice lives in New England and loves doing basic things like looking at the leaves change while drinking a pumpkin spice latte and wearing brown boots.

Join my readers group!

www.ingramcontent.com/pod-product-compliance
Lightning Source LLC
Chambersburg PA
CBHW070316310726
48976CB00005B/1730